An Heiress's Lot

By Tracy Edingfield

AN HEIRESS'S LOT
Copyright ©2021 by Tracy Edingfield
All rights reserved.

ISBN: 979-8-710772-64-5
Printed in the United States of America

License Notes: This eBook is licensed for your personal enjoyment only. This eBook may not be re-sold or given away to other people. If you would like to share this eBook with another person, please purchase an additional copy for each person you share it with. If you're reading this book and did not purchase it, or it was not purchased for your use only, then you should return to Smashwords.com and purchase your own copy. Thank you for respecting the hard work of this author.

Disclaimer: This is a work of fiction. Names, characters, business, events, and incidents are the products of the author's wild imagination. Any resemblance to actual persons, living or dead, or actual events is purely coincidental. In fact, it wouldn't be a stretch to admit that any resemblance to actual persons, living or dead, or actual events is purely accidental. My genius is not as great as that, Dear Reader.

An Heiress's Lot

By Tracy Edingfield

Chapter 1
February 8, 1813
Cumbria County, Northern England

Thunderstruck, Solomon, the Marquess of Lazonby read his friend's letter. The slanted words, plainly written yet incomprehensible, slowly penetrated his mind then worked their way beneath his skin. His friend, Charles Dryden, wrote of a perfidy so profound the inked markings funneled into his veins like heated coals to set his blood on fire. Boiling with rage, Solomon slammed the page onto his desktop. An eerie silence fell over the chilly room as his anger temporarily robbed him of speech.

In that stillness, his disbelief swelled from the size of a mustard seed to the dimensions of Jupiter. Not since Solomon had first discovered his father's reckless wager had he felt so enraged. He launched a stream of expletives which caused the groom, Alvin, passing outside the open window to stare slack-jawed at his lordship.

With a sweep of his arm, Solomon cleared the surface of his desk, sending everything into a chaotic spill.

"Seven years! Seven years of deprivation. Beggared by a cheat. Damn Sir John."

Pacing the length of the study, Solomon's scuffed boots struck the bare, wooden planks, ringing out doom for the wealthy baronet, Sir John Lower.

"I'll wring his neck. Squeeze the life from him until he begs for mercy," he muttered.

Sir John Lower had reduced the marquisate to poverty on a rigged wager. Damn him to hell.

If Alvin weren't such a prodigious turnip producer, his people—the staff, tenants, and villagers of Lazonby—would have starved this past winter.

Wanting a better life for his sister, Solomon had married Imogene to Ralph Phelan. Phelan was a good man, who could provide for Imogene; moreover, she detested turnips. It was better she married and moved away. Solomon missed his sister's cheerfulness, although he doubted Imogene would have been able to dispel the constant worry which nagged him these past few months.

Solomon Lord Lazonby came to an abrupt halt and stared at the blank rectangular square of wall. Its color was brighter than the surrounding area, which had faded over the years. That bare spot had been the home of a Johannes Vermeer painting.

His hawk-like gaze fixed upon a sole crystal decanter, the last of its kind, whose emptiness mocked him. The contents of the Lazonby wine cellar, once famed for its variety and plentitude, had been sold long ago. The larder was sparse, the coal cellar anemic.

As if in a trance, Solomon removed the decanter's stopper. He cradled the cool, glass sphere in his palm, idly noting it soon warmed in his grasp. Solomon pressed his fingertip to the sharpened point of the crystal stopper then slashed his palm.

A red ribbon appeared in the center of his hand, and his blood flowed. The resulting sting was grimly satisfying. A few droplets splattered onto the floor planks. Silently, he vowed to avenge his father and the marquisate. The lengthy cut brought on an epiphany.

Working quickly, Solomon jerkily removed a handkerchief from his pocket and wrapped his hand. Throughout the exercise, his signet ring flashed with his quick movements. The Lazonby herald, a winged lion, urged him to protect what was his. It was the sacred honor of every Lazonby marquess. His ancestral line was touted for being fierce and brave.

Lord Lazonby removed the ring from his finger.

"Olivia!"

At his lordship's bellow, the housekeeper, a slender, youthful woman, soon appeared in the doorway.

Olivia Rodgers asked, "What's the matter, Laz?"

Waving Charles Dryden's letter, he snapped, "This is what's the matter. I've received distressing news from Charles Dryden."

He continued to pace the floor.

Pulling her woolen shawl closer, Olivia blanched. "Is everything well with the children?"

Running his hands through his thick, black hair, Solomon answered her. "Yes. Charles and Winsome are well, as are their children, God be praised. But I must go to London on urgent business. I shall leave tomorrow."

"London? Tomorrow?"

"Yes. I don't know how long I'll remain, but I hope to return for planting season."

"So long?"

The lost look she sent him caused Solomon to check his stride. He approached her and touched her cheek, gazing into her golden eyes with a tenderness reserved for her and his sister, Imogene.

Softly, Solomon said, "Don't worry, Olivia. Willy and Alvin will remain here. They will take care of you. By the by, where is that boy? I have need of him."

Gathering her wits, the dark-haired housekeeper curtsied then murmured, "I'll send Willy to you, my lord."

"Thank you, Mrs. Rodgers," he said, returning to their usual formality.

Solomon's mind whirled with the numerous chores he needed to accomplish before setting off on this trip. Now that he'd learned the truth of his father's last, cursed gamble, Solomon was anxious to find the baronet and beat him to a bloody pulp.

A youth carrying half a pail of coal entered, mumbling, "The coal cellar's near empty, Laz. Alvin and I will visit the home woods for firewood."

"Never mind that. I need you to ride to Carlisle."

"Now?"

"Yes." Solomon bit off the word, his patience nearly unraveling. "Take King and Josephine. Tether the mare behind my saddle then sell her. You will go to the pawnbroker and hawk my signet ring—" Solomon dropped it into Willy's outstretched palm, flinching as he did so.

The boy's eyes were as wide as his mouth as he gaped at the marquess. "Are you mad, Laz?"

"Perhaps," he said. "I'm going to London to tend to urgent business. Have Olivia prepare a knapsack for you whilst I tell Alvin."

With that, Solomon pivoted on his heel and strode to the stables.

When he next saw Willy, Alvin had saddled King, and Solomon was tying the mare's lead to the saddle.

"One less mouth to feed," Solomon mumbled. "Perhaps you'll find a new home with a little girl to ride you and love you as much as Imogene did. Perhaps?"

Gently, he patted the mare's long nose. Then he whispered something that made the mare's ears twitch, but neither Willy nor Alvin would ever know exactly what his lordship told his sister's favorite mount.

The youth scuffed his toe in the dirt, outlining circles as he waited for his lordship to finish saying goodbye.

"Make haste to Carlisle," Solomon said, removing his own woolen scarf and wrapping it around the boy's neck.

He stared into the amber eyes so much like his own and gripped Willy's shoulders. "Talk to no one, tell no one what you're doing. You understand, Willy? Keep low and stay safe. You carry the last of my dreams to restore the marquisate, so take care."

"Yes, Laz."

"Godspeed." Solomon waved goodbye then returned to the house to pack his bags.

ACCEPTING THE GLASS of brandy from Charles Dryden, Solomon apologized yet again.

"Forgive me for coming unannounced. I hope my presence doesn't put Winsome out of charity with me."

"We're delighted to have you. My wife and I fully expected you to visit once my letter reached you. Besides, the children adore you, Uncle Laz," Charles teased.

Murmuring his thanks, Solomon noted how Charles's voice softened whenever he spoke of Winsome and the children. Charles's second marriage was a love match, unlike his first.

Solomon chuckled. "You know me well, don't you?"

"All those years spent at Harrow weren't wasted." With that smug pronouncement, Charles settled into the wingback chair with a sigh.

"I hope you don't mind, but I've taken the liberty of inquiring into the identity of Sir John's solicitor, a Mr. Woodson. We'll visit him tomorrow. With the groom's written confession, we have excellent odds of getting most, if not all, your funds returned."

Solomon raised his glass. "Good. This news couldn't have come at a better time. After last year's crop failure, followed by the discovery the vein of coal played out before reaching my land…"

"It's been rough for you."

"It's been rough for everyone at Lazonby. I'm down to six staff members and fewer than forty tenants. We've lived on venison, oats, and turnips for the past month."

Grimacing, Charles said, "Laz, why not let me lend you some money? I know you're good for it. When things turn about—"

Solomon shook his head. "As of right now, I don't know if things will turn about, so it's a damn risky venture."

"Then allow me to make a gift to you."

"No. We've been through this before."

"Your damnable pride."

Nodding slowly, Solomon agreed. "It's the only thing Father left me."

Silence reigned as the men drank their brandy.

Quietly, as if fearing to broach the topic, Charles inquired, "Do you intend to call him out?"

It was a testament to their long-standing friendship that Solomon's mind had been traveling the same path. Solomon had never felt he understood anyone half as well as he understood Charles Dryden. He was the best of fellows, and his stalwart friendship had been an anchor for Solomon.

"No." He polished off his drink and set the glass on the small side table with a decisive *clink*. "No, the man would taint a field of honor."

"That surprises me. I'd have wagered anything you'd seek revenge."

"Oh, you'd have won that bet!" Solomon barked out a laugh. "Truth be told, that *was* my first impulse—to strangle the man with my own hands. Having the past two days to reflect on that matter, though, I think that's too good for him. I'd prefer to draw out the man's suffering."

"For seven years, at least?"

Solomon smiled briefly then leaned forward. "Tell me again what his man said."

Charles sipped his drink before answering. "Sir John's head groom came to my front door, presented the baronet's card. Told Dobson he had a message for me to deliver to the late marquess's son."

"What was his name again?

"Grimes. Jordan Grimes. He admitted he worked for Sir John and that he'd tampered with Diablo. That was the last Newmarket race your father attended."

"It ruined him."

Nodding, Charles replenished their brandy glasses before he continued, "There was also a side bet Sir John made with two others that he could fleece an aristocrat. By the end of that day, Sir John had made a fortune."

"What I don't understand is why the Grimes fellow came forward after so long."

Charles shrugged. "He said he was leaving for the colonies, wanted to make a clean breast of things."

"And you believed him?"

"Laz." His friend looked at him over the top of his glass. "I'm no Johnny Raw recruit."

Laughing in protest, Solomon raised his glass to the former army captain of the 48th Foot. "Beg your pardon, Charles."

"No, I told him I'd personally reward him if he'd sign the confession. He was very eager to do so."

"Probably thanked his lucky stars you were such a light touch, for I suspect you wrote out everything in his admission truly, faithfully, and without embellishment."

"Of course it was."

"I'll repay you Grimes's purse. Did Winnie write the confession?" He nodded toward Charles's mauled hand, which had been injured during the heavy fighting at Bussaco.

"She typically handles my correspondence, but she did not work on this delicate matter. Dobson did."

"Your butler?"

"Yes."

"So, Winsome doesn't know."

"Of course she knows. The woman's not an idiot. Nothing happens in this house that escapes her notice."

"Winsome is a worthy wife, something I shall never have."

Charles gave his friend a long, thoughtful stare, after which he said, "These past years have hardened you. The army did that to me as well."

Solomon waved that away.

Flashing a boyish grin, Charles continued, "I met Grimes at the docks, paid him for his troubles—"

"How much?"

"Ten pounds."

Feigning shock, Solomon exclaimed, "Ten pounds? You are a light touch."

His eyes glinting with humor, Charles made a rude gesture.

Solomon snickered. "And then?"

"Then I watched him board the ship and set sail to Virginia. Or was it Philadelphia?" Charles shrugged. "It cannot possibly matter."

"No."

"What do you plan?"

Solomon shrugged. "If I thought Sir John were capable of feeling shame, I'd print Grimes's confession on the front page of *The Times* and let the world know he's a cheat."

The two gentlemen bent their heads together, discussing various strategies for reprisals. The often-ribald conversation withered when Winsome entered the room.

"I thought Arianna would never fall asleep." Winsome leaned against the door she'd closed behind her. She wiped her brow, pretending to be exhausted, a façade that crumbled upon her sudden grin. "She's excited to have Uncle Laz play horsey with her."

Solomon's laughter rang out. "I can't believe how much she's grown, and Nicholas, too."

"Yes," Charles murmured. He agreed with Solomon, but his gaze remained on his wife, who stole a sip of her husband's brandy.

"Thank you, dear." She handed back his glass then settled on the arm of his chair.

Charles quickly put his arm around his wife and demanded to know if that was all the thanks she had for France's best brandy.

Rolling her eyes, Winsome kissed his cheek. "There. Better?"

"Hardly."

Solomon was quite sure that, if not for his presence, the kiss would have led to a number of other things. Feeling *de trop*, he stood and asked, "What time is breakfast?"

"Oh, no, my lord, I didn't mean to chase you off," Winsome said, rising from Charles's chair. "Please don't retire so soon."

Charles gave a half-hearted protest, but Solomon had glimpsed the heat in his friend's eye.

"Really, Winsome, I'm tired and long for my bed."

"Nonsense." She inched toward the doorway. "I'll leave you two to visit. I had no intention of cutting your talk short."

"Darling, if our guest is weary after traveling non-stop from Penrith, let him rest. By the by, Laz and I are going into the city tomorrow on business."

Her eyes narrowed. Suspiciously, she asked, "Does your business have anything to do with that nasty Grimes fellow?"

"Dobs tell you about that?" her husband asked.

"Naturally." She patted smooth the nap of her gown, answering without guile.

Charles's gaze was filled with exasperation.

Solomon sent up a whoop of laughter. "Just as you predicted."

His hostess folded her hands, patiently waiting for the men's hilarity to subside before asking, "Predicted what precisely?"

"Charles said nothing occurs in this house without you knowing it."

"High praise, indeed," she said dryly, setting off another bout of masculine chuckles.

"Charles has stumbled across a possibility, which may allow me to recoup the loss we sustained at the hands of Sir John Lower."

"Good."

Solomon nodded. "Naturally, I must pursue the matter."

"Naturally," she agreed. "My own father bankrupted our estate. Disregarded the marriage settlements and wasted my dowry. If Lady Northampton hadn't hired me as a governess, I don't know what would have become of me."

"You advise me to become a governess?" Solomon teased.

She smiled, appreciating his joke then returned to her husband's side.

It had been a very long time since Solomon had found anything amusing. If nothing else came of this visit to London, he was glad he'd rediscovered his sense of humor.

"What I am trying—rather awkwardly—to say is that I was in a similar situation, and I understand your feelings, Laz." She faced her husband. "Do you know I once asked St. Peter to scold my father before opening the pearly gates to him?"

Charles patted the back of her hand then entwined his fingers through hers.

Solomon understood with perfect clarity how his friend had become so thoroughly ensnared in his wife's charms. After bidding the couple goodnight, he wandered up the carpeted stairs to his well-appointed room. A welcoming fire greeted him, as did a whisky decanter and bowl of sweets on his nightstand. These small luxuries reminded Solomon of the stark differences between his standard of living and his friend's.

Charles was indeed lucky to have married Winsome Montgomery. She was the polar opposite of his first wife, the faithless Vivian.

As he undressed with the assistance of Charles's valet, Spec, Solomon realized this trip to his friend's had awakened more than his dormant sense of humor. He'd experience guilt and envy, as well.

The guilt stemmed from enjoying a seven-course meal served by his hosts. Those he'd left at Lazonby Manor would sleep with their bellies half-full of turnips and oats. The envy came as he observed the closeness Charles shared with his wife. He did not covet his friend's spouse, but Solomon hadn't realized how empty his life had been without a helpmate of his own. It was damned lonely in his drafty manor in northern England, particularly since Imogene had moved away.

"Will you require my services to shave in the morning, my lord?" Spec asked.

How long had it been since he'd been shaved? Far too long, for he'd nearly forgotten the luxuries of his former lifestyle. Before his father had been bamboozled by the baronet.

"Would you mind?"

"Not at all, my lord. It would be my pleasure."

The valet appeared delighted by the prospect, which instantly terrified the marquess. "Why are you so damned happy at the prospect of holding a blade to my neck?"

Spec chuckled. "Because Mr. Dryden prefers to shave himself—"

"With his wounded hand?"

"Yes. Now you understand the source of my mortuary. I'll see you in the morning, my lord."

Mortuary?

Shaking his head, Solomon concluded he must have misheard the valet, for surely he'd meant to say 'mortification' instead. The valet was a master of malapropism.

Solomon thanked Spec. "Glad to have your assistance in removing the boots, Spec. Difficult to do by oneself."

"I would imagine so, my lord," the valet said, bowing before leaving the room.

Alone, Solomon poured himself a nightcap. This trip to London couldn't have come at a better time, for Solomon was near despair. Briefly last autumn, he'd hoped to mine his lands for coal, but those aspirations were smashed when an apologetic surveyor informed him the coal stream ended ten miles short of marquisate lands.

So, Solomon and his remaining male tenants returned to digging ditches. He could not afford to have another crop flooded. He must protect the only income he had.

Tomorrow, he'd find Sir John and begin the process of righting the wrong done to his family. Solomon would learn everything he could about the baronet, discover his weak points, then exploit them, just as Sir John had done to his father.

At his father's knee, Solomon had learned stories of Lazonbys' courage and the meaning behind their family crest. A winged lion would fiercely protect what belonged to him with cunning and bold, decisive action. He would plot down to the last detail then strike at Sir John Lower.

Before his London trip concluded, the winged lion of Lazonby would have a sniveling weasel in its jaws, its puny corpse ripped to shreds. Upon that thought, Solomon finally tumbled into bed.

Chapter 2

"Heavens, Mena!" Nancy flung the door open, reached for her mistress's hand, and hastily pulled her from the smoking shed.

Coughing as she emerged, Philomena thumped her chest as her eyes watered.

The companion pushed her mistress's arms over her head. "Breathe in. That's it, that's a good girl."

Still coughing, Philomena worked her lungs to expel the bad air and take in the good. When she recovered her breath, she used her fists to rub her eyes. "Ooh, they hurt."

Nancy led Philomena across the yard to a pail of water then guided her hands to the bucket's rim.

Philomena cupped her hands together then splashed her eyes with the cool, soothing water. The pain lessened but didn't disappear, so Philomena doused her eyes again and again.

"My poor dear girl."

Breathing heavily, Philomena rested her forearms on the bucket's rim. "The door wouldn't open."

"Latch jammed." Nancy's lips flattened and nearly disappeared. "Heavens! If I hadn't heard your screams…"

Unable to finish the thought, Nancy sat on the ground and dug out a handkerchief.

Philomena reached for it, but Nancy was oblivious to the gesture and instead dabbed her eyes then blew her nose.

Philomena dropped her hand.

"Well, no harm done in the end." The companion pocketed the handkerchief, her usual optimism resurfacing.

Biting her bottom lip, Philomena mumbled, "A case of bad luck. Maybe Papa and Clarissa are right."

"You're not bad luck," Nancy said firmly.

Philomena wouldn't argue with the woman who'd tended her since her mother died, but neither was she convinced.

Nancy grumbled, "Of all the disservices your father and his wife performed, labeling you as bad luck was the worst amongst them."

"Hmm."

"You aren't, Mena."

They walked across the courtyard through the back garden and into the house. As soon as they stepped over the threshold, they heard shouts of a loud disagreement from the drawing room.

Philomena raised her palm to silence Nancy.

They stood, listening to the raised voices.

Nancy grimaced. "Holden and Clarissa."

"Going at it again," Philomena agreed, shaking her head as they climbed the stairs.

Her seventeen-year-old stepbrother had been sent down from school. Holden didn't wish to attend; he desired to join the navy. For the past several weeks, Holden had done everything he could to wheedle and cajole his usually indulgent mother to allow it. Matters had deteriorated rapidly when Clarissa refused, and now the household was subjected to daily shouting matches between the pair.

They entered Philomena's chambers.

Nancy touched her eyebrow. "I've had it up to here with the pair of them. Glad we're leaving tomorrow."

"Yes." Philomena might have exaggerated her shudder, but she shared Nancy's distaste for the constant squabbling between her stepmother and stepbrother. In truth, Holden wasn't a bad seed when he wasn't plaguing his parent, but Philomena had never enjoyed Clarissa's company. Her father, not a kind man, had chosen a mirror-image of himself for his second wife, forever turning his back on Philomena's mother's attempts to improve him.

"That was a real stroke of genius, telling Clarissa you wanted to buy a new wardrobe."

Nodding, Philomena said, "I've only three weeks before my birthday. This London trip will allow me to meet my trustee and dissolve the trust. It was considerate of Clarissa to send a letter to Mr. Peck, requesting he speak with me."

Nancy harrumphed.

Chuckling, Philomena said, "Well, it was nice of Clarissa to exert herself on my behalf."

"And surprising," Nancy said. "First time she's done anything to help you."

"True. I'm glad she's decided to remain here. You wouldn't want her to join us in London, would you?"

Shaking her head in quick, short movements, Nancy rejected that idea.

Philomena's chuckle mellowed as Nancy continued to speak.

"It won't hurt for you to finally meet Mr. Peck. I still say he should have visited you at your father's funeral."

"I was in no state, unfortunately."

Nancy nodded. "Clarissa and I met him then, of course, but I cannot understand why he's not visited you in this past year."

"Or at least sent the trust agreement, as I requested," Philomena added.

Nancy opened the windows. "Take off that gown, and I'll air it for you."

"I smell like the chimney, don't I?" Philomena wrinkled her nose as she pulled the front of her gown away from her.

Briefly and matter-of-factly, Nancy assured her she'd smelled worse.

Philomena bit her bottom lip, trying not to laugh at her companion's unintentional humor.

Later, Philomena sank into a warm hip bath, bringing her long legs to her chest to fit into the tub.

"Perhaps we should stay in London on a prolonged visit. Until Holden returns to Harrow and Clarissa leaves for her Marylebone residence."

Nancy harrumphed. "Surrender the Chelmsford house to that pair?"

"A strategic, temporary retreat. Besides, I don't think either one of us fancies being subjected to more of their arguments."

Nancy shrugged then poured a pitcher of water over Philomena's hair. "Your father was a wretch, but for all his sins, bringing that woman into our home was the worst."

Philomena lathered her arms then rested her calf on the tub's rim to soap her slender leg. She smiled because Nancy seemed to have forgotten that, as the owner of the residence, Sir John could bring whomever he pleased into his own house.

Nancy was as protective of her as a mother hen her chicks, and Philomena would have it no other way. Nancy had been her nanny then served her father while Philomena attended finishing school. Now Nancy was her companion, a post she'd held for the past seven years. She'd embodied home throughout Philomena's mad childhood as the baronet frequently moved his household from place to place.

"While I'm at dinner, Nancy, please finish packing."

"When do you want to leave tomorrow?"

"At first light. I'll say my goodbyes to Clarissa and Holden tonight."

Philomena sniffed, still smelling of smoke despite her ablutions. She went down for dinner, hoping her father's second family could be cordial for the next few hours.

This was her house, inherited from her father, Sir John Lower. Philomena was content living in Chelmsford, having shunned the social life in London, unlike her stepmother. Since the baronet's death, Clarissa primarily stayed at her

Marylebone residence, visiting Chelmsford during Holden's school holidays.

Coming late to the table, Philomena murmured her apologies, but neither Clarissa nor Holden noticed her arrival.

They were still bickering.

Lady Lower's blonde hair was tucked beneath a purple silken turban, embellished with a diamond pendant. In stentorian tones, the widow pronounced that her son was not going to be a common sailor, and that was absolutely the last she would hear of the matter.

"But Mother—"

"Not another word, young man. You may not have been born a gentleman, but you weren't born a yeoman, either, sirrah! I've already made plans to secure your future. You must put these schemes from your mind."

The silence stretched to an uncomfortable length, which only ended when Lady Lower made a loud, exaggerated sniff. "What *is* that awful smell? Is that *you*, Philomena?"

"I don't mind how Mena smells," Holden offered.

Darting a glance toward the youth, Philomena smiled at him, and he returned it in full measure.

The party ate in continued silence until Holden blurted out, "I want to join the navy, Mother."

Clarissa's fist crashed onto the tabletop. "No! Absolutely not! You will finish Harrow then attend Oxford or Cambridge, where you'll meet other distinguished persons."

"I don't want to continue schooling. It's boring. I want to join the navy. Think how grand it would be for me to meet heroes like Lord Admiral Nelson."

It wasn't the first time Holden had expressed a hankering for life on the high seas, but after listening to him rhapsodize about various ships of the line, the number of their guns, Philomena couldn't question his sincerity. The boy was navy mad. Harrow might not have educated

Holden about Latin, Greek mythology, or mathematics, but it had fanned the flames for his nautical passion.

Did Holden possess the necessary mettle to sacrifice himself for either country or fellow man? Could one predict how untried boys would fare in battle? The truth would out; before Holden participated in any nautical warfare, Philomena thought it far more likely his captain would flog him. If the decision to send Holden to sea were hers, Philomena would allow him to go. Removing him from beneath his mother's thumb could prove the making of him.

Suddenly, Philomena itched to leave Chelmsford. One didn't need to have a crystal ball to predict her household would be very unhappy this spring and summer. Holden would be cross at being denied his chance for glory, and even under the best of circumstances, Clarissa's temper was peevish.

Turning the conversation from their squabble, Philomena said, "Nancy and I plan to leave at daybreak. Shall I send word once we arrive in London?"

"Please do so and inform me when you'll return home." Clarissa curled her upper lip.

On the surface, her stepmother's words seemed to reflect concern for her wellbeing, yet Philomena remained certain Clarissa did not care one jot for her. To Philomena's mind, there always seemed to be a hint of derision in her stepmother's interactions with her. Philomena didn't understand why.

Choosing to confront the woman, Philomena asked, "Have I said something stupid?"

Holden glanced at his mother then his stepsister before lowering his gaze to his plate.

"No, you've not said anything stupid." She mumbled before taking a drink, but Philomena heard Clarissa say, "At least, no more than usual."

Philomena made a sound of impatience.

Clarissa cast a wide-eyed look of innocence, which confirmed Philomena's suspicions.

"Would you prefer if Nancy and I didn't stay at your Marylebone residence? I can make other arrangements."

Releasing a tinkling laugh that grated on Philomena's nerves, Clarissa demurred, insisting she and Nancy make use of her home.

"While you're in town, Philomena, you should find a competent dresser."

Calmly, Philomena said, "Nancy suits me very well."

"At the very least, hire a hair stylist to do something with that ridiculous mop of yours."

"I like Mena's hair," Holden said. "The color, the curls—very pleasing."

Philomena gave a tepid 'thank you,' not certain if Holden was sincere or simply trying to annoy his mother.

"Do be quiet," Clarissa snapped.

"No, Mother. I told you I want to enlist, and it's time you paid attention to me. I'm a man now."

"You're too young to know your own mind, Holden," his mother said.

Philomena slipped away as the two began a royal battle. She didn't bother to say goodbye, because they wouldn't have heard her anyway. Privately, Philomena was rather impressed with her stepbrother, giving him points for sheer doggedness.

When she returned to her room, Nancy whisked Philomena's dress off and slipped her nightgown over her head. "You must sleep now, Mena, so that you'll be well rested on the trip."

"London isn't that far," she protested. "Besides, I don't feel the least bit sleepy."

"Aye, but we'll be leaving in just a few short hours."

Philomena tried to oblige her long-suffering servant but found it difficult to sleep. She kept coming awake, afraid she'd oversleep and miss her chance to leave. She didn't sleep soundly enough to dream, but nevertheless, a pressing sense of urgency nipped at the edge of her consciousness.

At three o'clock in the morning, she gave up the pretense. Quietly, Philomena dressed before waking Nancy. The two women decided not to use a footman in the house, carrying their trunk to the carriage in an inelegant fashion.

The first thing she'd do when they arrived in London would be to meet her trustee. Clarissa had vaguely assured her at her father's funeral that the trust ended when Philomena turned twenty-five, but Philomena would have preferred to have had a copy of the trust to read for herself. She had done very well managing her finances, and it irked that this was unknown to her.

As the sun peeped over the eastern horizon, Philomena and Nancy sat, side by side, in her crane-neck phaeton drawn by a pair of grays.

"At least we'll arrive in London in style." Nancy indicated the gray velvet upholstered bench.

"Yes." Philomena chuckled. "I've always loved this equipage."

"At least the baronet was a good judge of horseflesh and phaetons."

They had traveled little more than a mile before they saw the solitary figure of a youth walking alongside the road, carrying a valise.

Identifying the stout figure, Nancy groaned, "We're dished."

The youth glanced over his shoulder, his eyes alight with devilry.

As she was not a hard-hearted person, it was out of the question that Philomena would drive past her stepbrother. Obviously, Holden was running away. Because that was essentially what Philomena was doing herself, she couldn't fault him.

Reining in the grays, she asked politely, "Running away to join the navy, Holden?"

"Mena! I'm so glad to see you!" He tipped his hat to both females. "You, too, Nancy, dear."

"Holden." The companion acknowledged him with a nod but didn't move from her place on the seat.

Sensing he needed to earn his place on the phaeton, Holden clasped his hands together. "Please take me, Mena. I've no money to take the stage."

Philomena expelled a sigh. "You do realize life on the seas is one of hardship?"

"I'm not as soft as you think."

"You've neatly engineered this situation so that I'd have to take you up, haven't you?"

"It's not a trick," he protested.

Nancy piped up. "It is."

Holden narrowed his eyes on the older woman, but he turned to Philomena and said, quite reasonably, "Look, we can discuss this on the way to London, rather than in the middle of the lane."

Clarissa wouldn't appreciate Philomena facilitating Holden's joining the navy, but she resented Philomena anyway, so Philomena thought she might as well be hung for a sheep as a lamb. Holden might make a fine naval officer, given proper training and time. He certainly wouldn't amount to much if he remained in Chelmsford.

Sighing, she said, "Fine. Climb aboard."

He gave an excited whoop as he strapped in his valise then motioned for Nancy to make room for him on the bench seat. After climbing aboard, he squirmed before settling into his spot.

It was a mid-size perch with ample room for three to ride abreast, but Holden chose to spread his knees apart, taking up space. Using the butt of her driving whip, she pressed his knees shut, telling him not to be vulgar or selfish.

"What a tartar you are, Mena! Only think how tiresome you'll become when you grow really old."

"Yes," she drawled. "At nearly twenty-five, I'm an ancient."

"Mind what you say, or we'll set you back down," Nancy warned.

Holden's lips thinned, then he gestured as if he were turning a key in a lock.

Trying not to laugh, Philomena focused her attention on the team.

Miraculously, Holden managed to maintain his silence for roughly a quarter mile. After that, he entered into a lively conversation with Nancy about naval battles. Philomena could have sworn no pages had been cut on any of his textbooks, but if there was the remotest possibility that the words 'ship' or 'navy' would appear in it, Holden had read it and committed it to memory.

"Did you tell your mother where you were going?" she asked, glancing over her shoulder as if Lady Lower were chasing them in her landau.

"I left a note."

Holden was seventeen, an age not known for long-range planning.

"She'll be very unhappy."

He shrugged. "Most likely."

Philomena and Nancy exchanged amused looks.

"I want to find the first outgoing navy vessel and sign up for duty."

"I think you should enquire into the captain's character before you entrust yourself into his care," Philomena advised after careful consideration. "Many are good men, but some are not. No need to serve a merciless master if it can be avoided."

Holden's tongue rested while he pondered this advice. Finally, he admitted that was a good point. "I'll stay at the Marylebone residence until I sail out."

"You really wish for a naval career?" Nancy's skepticism rang in her voice.

In irritation, he slapped the tops of his knees. "What else am I supposed to do? I'm no scholar. Have no interest in the church. Can't make a living out of gambling."

Her stepbrother had never evinced a desire to work in Sir John's button factory, but it would be profitable, and safer than going into the navy. She offered, "You could work for Father's company. I'm sure they'd find a place for you."

"And do what? Make buttons?" He burst into laughter. "Don't be daft."

She bristled. "Father's button factory has provided well for us during his lifetime and beyond."

His eyes goggled. "You don't know? You really don't know."

"Know what?" From the corner of her eye, she watched Nancy pinch Holden in his side.

"Ow!"

"Hush now," Nancy hissed.

Holden glared at her but subsided into a sullen silence.

"Shamed you, I see," Philomena observed with a nod of approval.

He appeared on the verge of protesting, but Nancy glared him into silence.

Morning had broken. A new day was beginning, and optimism welled within her. Away from Clarissa's unpleasantness, Philomena was determined she and Nancy would enjoy their brief sojourn to the city. Perhaps her knack for finding bad luck would be left in Chelmsford, as well as Clarissa's taunts about her height and grace.

After a mile, she slowed the team's pace, noticing the reddened cheeks of her fellow travelers.

"Sorry," she said sheepishly. "It's exhilarating, though, isn't it?"

Holden laughed. "So, do you plan to cut a dash through the great city of London? Is that why you want a new wardrobe?"

Unwilling to admit her sudden desire to update her wardrobe was a ruse to leave his mother's company, Philomena scoffed.

"Don't be ridiculous. Those are the foolish wishes of a young girl, and we've already established I'm ancient."

He chuckled. "But you'll be hailed as a Toast! All heiresses are."

"Naturally," she agreed pertly. "In my youth, I had an abbreviated season. My bevy of admirers were mostly impoverished aristocrats. The lords weren't particularly enthralled by my freakish height or curly hair, but they thought my fortune was lovely."

Strange how she could talk about that painful episode now with wry amusement. At the time, it devastated her. Oh, Philomena would not wish to be seventeen and so green again.

Holden frowned. "They said that to you?"

"I overheard." She shrugged. "A particular peer expressed his reluctance to align himself with me due to the stench."

"Stench? What stench?"

"From the smell of the shop, the odor of being in commerce, among the riffraff."

"But your father was a baronet."

Shaking her head, Nancy answered, "Whose father purchased his rank from the fortune he acquired through commerce. Sir John Lower ran through his inheritance within a few years. You knew Sir John after he amassed his fortune, but in the *ton*, Sir John will always be considered common."

Philomena pulled the reins, studying the signposts. "Gallows Corner. Dismal name. Still, we'll continue on the London Road. Shall I take you to the Horse Guards?"

"Were you going that direction?"

She twitched her nose and parried, "Were you going to join the navy?"

"Absolutely."

"Horse Guards it is."

"Drop me off at St. James Park."

They stopped to break their fast and allowed the team to rest. Clarissa was never one to rise before noon, so the threesome was quite content to take the meal in a leisurely fashion. By the time they trotted out of the inn's yard, the day was well begun.

In a conversational lull, Holden asked, "Why didn't you finish the season?"

"Beg your pardon?" Philomena asked, baffled.

"You said you had an abbreviated season," he prompted. "Why didn't you stay for the remainder of the season?"

She struggled to explain. "As a person, I was invisible. The only thing people noticed about me was my fortune. They admired or despised me because of it without seeing the real me. Money tends to blind people."

After a long, pregnant silence when she'd thought that topic of conversation had dropped, Holden spoke up. "Better to be hated for being an heiress than for being a disreputable scoundrel."

Nancy pinched him again, and he squealed.

Her companion's short temper with her stepbrother amused Philomena. Nancy had never been one to suffer fools gladly.

Pointing to the building set along the Thames, Holden exclaimed, "Ah! Whitehall!"

Philomena turned the crane-neck phaeton onto Horse Guards Road, appreciating the idyllic scenery of St. James Park on the opposite side.

Once the carriage halted alongside the curb, Holden jumped down and chatted as he removed his valise from the boot. The vein of his leave taking was inquisitive, friendly—and shady. Holden's chatter made her suspect something was amiss. Why was he taking so long to unstrap his valise and secure her own?

He offered a glib goodbye. "Take care of yourself, Mena. Good day, Nancy."

"Holden!" Philomena called out, rising from the bench to her great height. "Stop this instant!"

"What?"

She extended an outstretched palm. "Hand it over, you lout."

Heaving a sigh, he retrieved her bag of money from his pocket, flushing.

"Shame on you, Holden," Nancy scolded, her lips primed in a disapproving pucker.

Shame-faced, Holden placed the leather pouch into Philomena's hand. "Don't be angry, Mena. I've only three pounds, six shillings."

"Running away with a near-empty purse is poor planning on your part."

He nodded before lifting his face with a hopeful glint in his eyes. "Will you loan me some money, Mena?"

"You'd never repay a loan."

"I will," he insisted.

"You won't."

"I will, too."

Holden wasn't a blood relation, but she was fond of her stepbrother. Disliking that she was caving into his 'puppy dog eyes' appeal, she took four guineas from her purse then held them out of reach.

"You promise to join the navy?"

"Yes."

"And defend England?"

"Yes." He smiled, buoyed by the thought.

"To never bring shame on the family?"

He swallowed hard, smothering laughter, she suspected, as he choked out her name in admonishing tones.

"I wish you the best of luck, Holden." Philomena gave him the money.

"Likewise, Mena." He saluted her then tucked the guineas into his waistcoat pocket.

"Farewell."

"Goodbye." With a careless wave, Holden picked up his valise then trotted toward Whitehall.

She and Nancy watched him disappear into the throng.

"He's a rascal," Nancy pronounced. "Will probably be tossed overboard by the crew in the first month."

"It's a distinct possibility," Philomena agreed. "However, I think being raised by a heartless mother may actually serve him well aboard ship. Holden wouldn't dream of expecting leniency or rationality."

Before she pulled into traffic, Philomena took a moment to collect herself. Slowly, she scanned the area, startled as her gaze lit upon a black-haired man who stood nearby in the grassy park. His jacket hung on his loose-limbed frame. The material itself was high quality, Bath superfine, but woefully outdated.

He stood, watching her closely. Throughout her long-ago season, no man had ever stared at Philomena so, as if the back of his eyes burned into her flesh. His golden gaze weighed upon her, like a physical touch.

Her heart beat faster, and she caught her breath.

Then he did the most extraordinary thing. He lifted two fingers to the brim of his hat, giving Philomena a brief salute.

Inexplicably pleased by that show of support, she gave a cordial nod to him and the fashionable woman who accompanied him.

Driving past, she glanced at the handsome stranger, hoping for another, closer look.

Unfortunately, at the crucial moment, a girl shrieked, "Uncle Laz! Uncle Laz!" Her thin arms outstretched, she begged to be picked up. His attention veered from Philomena to the child.

The opportunity for a second look vanished.

As Philomena Lower drove her phaeton up the street, she relished the warmth of that all-too-brief encounter.

Chapter 3

"Extraordinary, Laz," Winsome Dryden giggled, lightly smacking Solomon's sleeve. "Somehow you've managed to simultaneously fix two females' interests onto you."

He chuckled, before tossing Arianna into the air.

The girl squealed in delight.

"Nay, I just admired her clever ruse in thwarting that would-be thief."

Winsome stared at the disappearing carriage. "I wonder who she is. I've never seen her before, and she's not easily overlooked. So regal."

Solomon set Arianna on the ground. "So tall, you mean?"

Privately, he agreed with his hostess. The woman had been regal. Possibly even taller than him, and Solomon topped six feet.

"She must have eyes in the back of her head to have known he'd pinched the purse," Winsome said with a chuckle.

The woman put him in mind of the tales he'd read of the Amazon women, known to be fierce warriors. What would it be like to bed such a woman? To have those long, lean thighs wrapped around his waist?

Arianna called to him, dispelling those delightful, lascivious wanderings.

"Come on, poppet." He stretched out a hand to the girl. "Time to head home. Your papa and I are to go to the city on business."

"Charles has an appointment tomorrow with his tailor. Have you heard of them? Schweitzer and Davidson of Cork Street? You know, I do not think your tenants will begrudge a new jacket for their marquess. Let us make it a gift for you."

"I'd rather not," he said, uncomfortable with accepting charity. "I've already imposed upon your household more than I ought."

"Would you rather I staked you for a card game?" Winsome Dryden's face went so entirely, so carefully blank, she appeared to be a stranger to connivance.

That had been precisely how he'd thought to make some money.

He growled, demanding to know, "How do you do that?"

"Do what?"

He pointed at her cherubic expression. "Act and sound so innocent while delivering a mighty blow to one's ego."

She tossed her head back and laughed. "I do not!"

Arianna laughed, too, taking Solomon's hand and cheerfully replying, "You're right. Papa complains about it all the time."

The way she stretched out the words 'all the time' made Solomon laugh so hard his stomach ached.

"Arianna." Her mother reprimanded the girl in that stern governess's voice, but to no avail.

Solomon and Arianna's shared laughter only increased.

They arrived from the short romp in the park, still chuckling, at the Dryden townhouse to find Charles finishing his breakfast. Quickly, Winsome explained the little joke to her husband.

"It's true," Charles agreed. "You use that blasted innocent look to unfair advantage."

"Piffle," she scoffed but with a hint of a smile that showed she was rather proud of having cultivated the trick.

Soon, Solomon and Charles had taken tearful goodbyes of Nicholas, the nearly two-year-old, with the promise to bring him a sweet from the shop. Then they had to soothe Arianna, who demanded a sweet, too.

"Dear, you shouldn't even have brought up the idea if you wished to avoid the cacophony," Winsome told her husband as she bussed his cheek. "Now, go. It'll be up to me and Miss Swinson to distract our little darlings, so the sooner you're both out of sight, the better."

"How very tactful, my dear," Charles said dryly as he kissed his wife's cheek.

Winsome rolled her eyes.

"You've been outgunned, my friend." Solomon clapped his friend's shoulder, while Charles closed the front door on his domestic tableau.

Grumbling about living under the cat's paw, Charles protested but only half-heartedly.

Clearly, his friend was content with his life, and why shouldn't he be? Charles had done his duty to his family and country and now reaped the rewards.

Within an hour, they arrived at the solicitor's office. Mr. Woodson was rotund with a bald, gleaming head and somberly dressed. He crossed the room and signaled the peers to have a seat. After the formalities were observed, Solomon presented him with Jordan Grimes's written confession.

"This is signed by Sir John Lower's former groom. He admits to rigging the horse race so that the baronet would win my father's fortune. Although I should very much like Sir John's head on a pike, I am willing to accept immediate restitution for the full amount of the initial wager."

The man scowled, reading through the letter more than once. "Where is Mr. Grimes?"

"Sailing across the Atlantic," Charles drawled.

Smoothing his shiny pate, the solicitor said, quite firmly, "This cannot be paid."

Solomon sneered. He'd come to this meeting with the full expectation that Sir John, a reprobate of the highest order, would hire a solicitor who was his moral twin. The marquess was already prepared to strangle the baronet. Throttling a solicitor would be excellent practice for the ultimate revenge Solomon intended for the baronet.

"If he finds it difficult to raise the wind, I'll accept a stake in his financial holdings."

"No, my lord. You misunderstand me." His countenance was troubled.

Solomon's unease grew, while Charles shifted in his chair.

The grip on his dreams of restoring the marquisate was beginning to loosen. He spoke sharply. "What do you mean?"

"Yes, man," Charles Dryden urged. "Say what you will without roundaboutness."

Returning to his seat, the man weighed his words before he flailed his palms in a helpless gesture.

Solomon's heart sank. Those dreams were slipping from his grasp, and he could feel it. The suspicion solidified into a greasy ball pitted in his belly with a sickening weight.

"Sir John Lower shuffled off his mortal coil well over a year ago. As a potential creditor of his estate, that is, any claims you had against him should have been brought within six months of his death. That time has expired. You're too late."

The solicitor drew breath then continued, "Morcover, wagers are not legally enforceable, so even if you *had* presented it within minutes of Sir John's passing, I could not have paid it without the heirs' consent. Lastly, if you wish to recover your monies on the grounds that the wager was fraudulent, you must bring the matter before the Chancery Courts with a live witness, that is to say, with Mr. Jordan Grimes to provide testimony. You cannot do that, can you?"

"I'll fetch him from Virginia myself," growled Solomon.

"Then you should have fetched him five years after the fraud was committed, before the statute of limitations expired," he explained gently.

"It's a debt of *honor*," Solomon hissed, emphasizing the last word.

"Which is treated with priority amongst gentlemen during the course of their lifetimes, but I have found after many years in practice that females don't regard such debts of honor." The solicitor shrugged, as if the response mystified him. "I have yet to convince a woman who had no part in making a wager to acknowledge it. Wholly incomprehensible, but so it is."

That heavy, greasy ball in Solomon's belly grew heavier then rolled back and forth, squashing his hopes for redeeming his estate. In a throwback to the day the surveyor told him he'd found no stream of coal on Lazonby lands, Solomon fought the impulse to cast up his accounts, so sickened was he by this news.

Charles gave him a concerned look, which Solomon ignored. Heavily, Solomon said, "Then we're dished."

The words sounded hollow to his ear, but Solomon couldn't help it. Once more, his aspirations had been ground beneath the sharp heel of a merciless giant.

Charles persisted, "No recovery from the baronet then. What about the heirs? Did he leave a wife? Children?"

"Both, actually. His wife inherited only the widow's allotment. It seems theirs was not the happiest of unions. Sir John settled the lion's share of his fortune upon his adult daughter."

"The lion's share of my family's fortune," Solomon growled.

With forced patience, Charles asked the solicitor, "There's nothing to prevent us from applying to the women that this particular debt be paid, correct?"

"No." The solicitor stretched the word out, injecting a long syllable of skepticism into it.

"Then if the women agreed to pay the debt, in whole or in part, we would right a situation that never should have occurred, had Sir John Lower conducted himself honorably," Charles summarized.

"You are free to try, Mr. Dryden, but Sir John's widow, Lady Clarissa Lower, terminated my services immediately after the funeral. Mr. Peck is the trustee for the daughter."

"Where can we find Lady Lower?"

He shrugged. "She spends her time between Marylebone and Chelmsford."

"And the daughter?"

"Lives in Chelmsford. I've never met her."

"What? Not even at the reading of the will?"

"No. I believe Mr. Peck performed that service," he said.

Charles stood and placed a few guineas on the man's desktop. "For your time."

Noting another expense he'd have to repay his friend, Solomon murmured goodbye and donned his hat.

"Good luck, Lord Lazonby."

As he stood, Solomon said, "This trustee… Peck? Where can we find him?"

"If rumor is believed, you'll find him in Lady Lower's company."

"Interesting." Toying with the brim of his hat, Solomon bid him good day.

Wordlessly, he and Charles returned to the curricle. They took their seats, and Solomon stared sightlessly at the scenery. The rocking of the wheels passing over cobblestone streets loosened his tongue, and he eventually spoke.

"That was a leveler, straight to the gut. A few days ago, I had fire in my belly, and now…" He shrugged. "I feel ill."

Charles nodded but remained silent.

"Why did Father—?" Giving himself an admonishing shake, Solomon stoppered the plaguy question. "Doesn't matter. I must let it go."

"Can you?" Charles asked, eyeing his friend.

Curling his upper lip, Solomon bitterly acknowledged the impossibility of that task. "I don't know, Charles. I've lived with this anger for so long… I just don't know."

"Anger is only one letter away from danger."

Solomon scowled at him. "Don't quote embroidered samplers to me, Dryden."

Charles grinned then gave a nod of apology. "Something my wife's fond of saying."

Solomon made a vexed sound. "Accustoming one's self to poverty is difficult. My hopes died with the baronet. I fear I might go mad, Charles."

"You're won't," Charles assured him.

Staring at the passersby, Solomon wondered if any of them felt their own lives were so fragile. His existence seemed to hang by a slender thread.

Briskly, Charles said, "So, shall we visit Lady Lower in Marylebone?"

"Might as well. I'm at a standstill. Still, it's demeaning."

Bracingly, Charles said, "If you don't ask, you'll never know, and once you return home, you'll kick yourself if you left any stone unturned."

Rounding the team around the corner, Charles proceeded to Cavendish Square. Then he asked philosophically, "How bad can the widow be, anyway?"

The pair mounted the front steps of the Marylebone residence, only to be told by an elderly butler that the lady was not in London.

"Visiting her family's country estate, my lord," he said, taking their calling cards.

"When do you expect her to return?" Solomon asked.

"Cannot say, my lord. She never notifies us of her plans in advance."

Charles asked, "Can you provide us with her direction so that we may write to her?"

Solomon chafed at another delay, his irritation mounting. He promised himself that if there were still daylight by the time he returned to Bruton Street, he would go to Gentleman Jackson's. Perhaps he could vent his frustration in a sparring match with the famed boxer.

"Do you wish to meet with Mr. Withers, her son, Lord Lazonby?"

"Yes, thank you."

"I will inquire if Mr. Withers is available," he said, ushering the two gentlemen into a salon, outfitted in luxurious splendor. Yards of silk draped the long windows, while gilded picture frames filled with masterworks adorned the walls. The rugs were made of thick wool, having been imported from the Far East.

Viewing the ostentatious display of wealth caused Solomon's hackles to rise. "Damn Sir John's blackened soul."

He and Charles settled onto a sumptuous sofa and overheard the butler's measured tones speaking with a louder, more immature voice.

"Who's Lord Lazonby? And isn't Charles Dryden the brother of an earl? Is this your idea of some kind of joke?"

"Lord Lazonby is a marquess, Master Holden." The butler maintained his dignity, but Solomon heard a trace of humor in the man's voice.

"Good God."

Solomon and Charles exchanged amused looks. Mr. Withers was not accustomed to being in the presence of British peers, apparently.

His suspicions were confirmed directly. Holden Withers entered the salon with a cowed expression, mincing his steps. Nervously, he brushed a hank of blond hair from his eyes and cleared his throat.

Solomon would place the boy at either sixteen or seventeen years of age. Nearly the same age as Willy. Solomon's raven-colored hair was already streaked with grey at the temples, but this boy made him feel ancient.

"I beg your pardon for intruding upon your solitude," Solomon said, rising from the sofa to perform an exquisite bow. "I am Lazonby."

"My lord," the young Mr. Withers said with a courtly bow.

The butler reappeared and lifted a pair of bushy brows. His young charge stared blankly at the servant.

"Perhaps the gentlemen would care for tea, Master Holden?"

Facing them, Holden repeated, "Would you care for tea?"

Solomon smiled. "Yes, please."

The butler removed himself from the drawing room, his expression unreadable.

"You are Lady Lower's son?" Charles asked.

"Yes."

"My friend, Lord Lazonby, had business with your stepfather, Sir John."

Mr. Withers motioned to them to resume their seats then gathered his coattails and took a chair adjacent to Charles.

"My stepfather," he drawled, as if the words tasted strange on his tongue.

Solomon wished they had not come. Damn himself for falling in with Charles's suggestion. What was he to do next? Tussle with a toddler for his fortune?

"Shouldn't you be in school?" Solomon asked.

The lad shrugged. "I was sent down from Harrow, but it's of no consequence. I wish to join the navy and shall do so before week's end."

"Fancy a life at sea, do you?" Charles asked.

Solomon's gaze slewed to his friend, as he found humor in this interview. "We're Harrow men, as well."

"Were you?" Holden Withers' smile faltered as the elderly butler ushered in the tea tray. "I say, Jameson, don't you think Harrow men should be entertained with brandy or wine? Not tea."

The man straightened from setting down the tray and turned a gimlet eye onto Mr. Withers.

Solomon coughed into his fist to cover his laugh at the boy's audacity.

"No, no. I'm parched," Charles said smoothly, robbing the lad of a chance to imbibe spirits.

Solomon agreed. "Tea's exactly what I need. Are those macaroons? My favorite."

Crestfallen, Holden Withers signaled the butler to pour tea as he served the biscuits.

Once the servant withdrew, Solomon plunged in with his first question. "I don't wish to be indelicate, but how much did you know of Sir John's business?"

The boy scratched a little dimple in his cheek. "Why do you ask?"

"A particular transaction has come to light," Charles said. "It occurred seven years ago and involved the prior Marquess of Lazonby and a rigged horse race at Newmarket."

"Your father, my lord?"

"Yes."

The youth grimaced. "How much did he lose?"

"Twenty-five thousand pounds."

The boy whistled.

"Yes," Solomon drawled, chafing at the pup's insolence.

"So, what brings you here? Hoping to recoup?"

Solomon was taken aback by Mr. Withers' bluntness. "I had hoped his widow might wish to make amends, reimburse…"

The youth was already shaking his head. "Mother would regard that request as foolhardy. You're free to ask, but—"

"What about the baronet's daughter? We understand she inherited the bulk of her father's fortune. Would she, in your mind, be amenable to righting the wrong done by her father?"

"I don't know. I'd certainly counsel Mena not to, though, if she were to seek my opinion, which she won't."

Solomon stood. "She resides in Chelmsford?"

"Until yesterday."

In clipped tones of exaggerated patience, Charles asked the lad, "Will you tell us where we could find her?"

"I don't know." Mr. Withers also rose to his feet. "I'm not being deliberately obstreperous, gentlemen, but I will say this: my sister deserved better from her family than she ever got. Even if I knew her whereabouts, which I don't, I wouldn't give them to you. Stealing back the fortune my stepfather stole from your father is madness. At some point, you must let bygones be bygones."

"It's not stealing!"

With a cavalier shrug, Mr. Withers conveyed the belief that semantics weren't important. He ushered them to the door and bid them goodbye.

"Impudent pup!" Solomon snapped, donning his hat again and stepping into Charles's curricle.

"What a pragmatist," Charles murmured. "Still, he may be in the right of it. Without the law being on our side, is going after the widow and daughter the morally right thing to do? Frankly, I hadn't considered it before."

"The original sin lies entirely at the baronet's feet," Solomon gritted out. "Why should his family profit from thievery?"

"There is that, of course."

Scowling, Solomon sat in silence. "Something about that fellow… something's familiar about him."

Chapter 4

"Mena, slow down. You're frightening people," Nancy panted, struggling to match Philomena's long, angry strides along London's pavements.

"Good. They should stay out of my way."

"I'd think Napoleon's Imperial Guard would stay out of your way."

Whirling on Nancy, Philomena declared, "I have the right to be furious."

Having stabled the horses and phaeton at the Harlow Mews, Philomena and Nancy stalked down Bruton Street, making their way toward the Bristol Hotel.

"What a stupid trustee I have! Criminally stupid, I should say. How could he have kept this from me for the past year? Why would Father make such an asinine condition?"

"I cannot fathom," Nancy said, jogging.

Slamming her fist into her palm, Philomena said, "Peck is nothing more than a cheat, liar, and bamboozler! What good is three weeks' notice? This is impossible! He never meant to tell me. Peck never meant for me to know."

"Please slow down, Mena."

Perhaps it was the plaintive wail that finally reached Philomena's ears, but she stopped and promptly apologized.

"I know." Nancy patted Philomena's arm.

"I'd love to see Peck swing from Tyburn's tree."

"Mena!"

She ignored the stricture. "If I weren't a female, I'd already have my hands on Father's money."

The companion reminded her, "If you had a husband, you'd have your hands on the money."

"If *I* had a husband, *he'd* have his hands on my money."

"Touché," Nancy acknowledged, rubbing her side.

Philomena noted the gesture and immediately grew contrite. "Do you have a pain in your side from walking so fast? I'm sorry, Nancy."

"It'll pass shortly."

"Shall we gaze into the shop windows on Bond Street? I promise not to rush you."

Having agreed on that plan, Philomena and Nancy turned the corner and admired the work in a milliner's display case.

"You must marry."

"I suppose," Philomena agreed without enthusiasm. "When I was younger, I wanted to marry someone I loved. Then I thought I could marry a man I admired. Now I may have to marry someone I can't even tolerate. I detest being married for my money."

"Ah, but you're looking at this from the wrong end of the spyglass," Nancy chided. "In order to gain your inheritance, you must marry before your twenty-fifth birthday, so *you'll* be the one marrying for money, not necessarily your spouse."

Philomena stared at her companion for a long, quiet minute before turning wordlessly away. Putting aside Nancy's absurd notions, she slowly admitted, "I can't think of a single person to marry. Even the vicar and blacksmith are married already, so I must marry a stranger. In three weeks."

Nancy raised her forefinger skyward, cheerfully pointing out, "You'll be liberating your money in three weeks."

Paying no attention to Nancy's rosy outlook, Philomena pressed her gloved hand against the milliner's windowpane. Sightlessly, she stared at the display of bonnets, struggling to hide her devastation.

On the other side of the glass, re-arranging the display, a salesclerk nervously smiled at the two women.

Distracted, Philomena only faintly smiled then pressed her forehead against the chilly pane of glass. Its cool surface soothed her. Groaning, she asked, "Why didn't Mr. Peck inform me of the marriage requirement? My whole future is determined by that vital clause, and he stood mum."

"Thank your lucky stars his clerk let us read your father's trust. Mr. Peck might never have mentioned it. As it is, it's good we came to London and met his clerk. Now we have three weeks to plan a wedding."

"Ensnare a groom, more like."

Nancy remained quiet.

The clerk, seeing the women's scowls, removed one bonnet from its stand and hastily replaced it with another. She cocked her brow, and Philomena raised her hand in acknowledgment.

"If I'm not married in three weeks, the fortune goes to Clarissa. I'd have an annual stipend of three hundred pounds."

"And the Chelmsford house."

Philomena didn't have to struggle long to understand why Mr. Peck had been so woefully negligent. "Clarissa got to him. That's why she was so vague about the trust, why she fired Mr. Woodson, father's solicitor."

"She told you it ended when you became twenty-five?"

"Yes," Philomena said dryly. "To be fair, Clarissa didn't specify how it ended."

"Do you think she always planned to steal your fortune?"

Philomena scowled.

Looking bewildered, the salesclerk cast another bonnet aside and called for more headgear.

"It's the only explanation. She must have promised Mr. Peck a percentage of my inheritance. Otherwise, I can think of no earthly reason he kept the truth from me."

"Nonsense!" Nancy denied then wavered. "Isn't it?"

The salesgirl threw her hands into the air and stomped away.

Philomena hastily stepped back from the window and collided with the solid form of a gentleman.

"I do beg your—"

The stranger gripped her by the shoulders to steady them both, but during the jostling, his hat fell. Philomena stooped to pick it up precisely at the moment he decided to do the same thing. Their foreheads crashed together with a loud crack.

"Ouch!"

"Ow."

"Mena!" Nancy cried.

With one hand, the gentleman held Philomena at arm's length, while his other hand rubbed his forehead. A hank of his raven-dark hair dipped over his fingers, giving him a boyish appearance. His eyes were tawny-colored, a strange mixture of gold and brown. He was taller than Philomena by a few scant inches.

The beat of her heart quickened, and she blurted, "You're the gentleman from the park—the one who saluted me."

"Hello again," he said, dropping his hands to his sides. His low, husky voice held a marvelous timbre that sounded rich to her ear.

He smelled of soap and starch, simple and clean, and more pleasing than the bay scent some men used.

"Are you all right, ma'am?"

Turning to the gentleman's friend, Philomena marveled how she could have failed to notice him. With his chestnut hair and broad shoulders, he was a fine figure of a man and held himself with military correctness. He'd tipped his hat to her in a mannerly fashion. She met his gaze, comforted by the kindness behind his brown eyes.

"Yes, thank you. That was foolish of me," Philomena said, rubbing the bump on her forehead.

Her attention returned to the first gentleman, whose golden gaze roamed her figure, lit with appreciation and warming her insides.

During her long-ago season, Philomena had met her share of handsome aristocrats. This man might be in that league. Horrified by the thought, she glanced at his hands. No signet ring. No wedding ring. She heaved a sigh of relief. His hands were calloused, proclaiming he toiled for his living. He was not a dandy, a useless fribble. Philomena's liking grew stronger.

She sensed the feeling was mutual.

He folded his arms and leaned against the building. "Well, I greatly admired how efficiently you routed your would-be thief."

His crooked smile caused her heart to flutter, hammering at a more rapid pace. Her insides warmed, and a sense of well-being came over her.

"It felt very gratifying, I assure you." Then she giggled. Giggled! And at her age, where she might well be leading apes in hell.

Wonder of wonders! Before her stood a handsome, eligible man who seemed to appreciate her. The Fates had literally cast this bachelor into her path, just as she'd discovered a most desperate need for one.

Spurred by a sense of destiny, she blurted, "I hope you don't think me too forward, but I must ask—what is your name?"

He blinked, and Philomena could have kicked herself for committing the *faux pas*. It was rag-mannered for a woman to introduce herself to a stranger. If he were interested in making her acquaintance, he would find someone to introduce them. If he didn't wish to further their connection, she should fade away. That's what was expected of powerless females.

"Never mind," she mumbled, chastising herself for foolishly building marriage fantasies with this stranger.

Clarissa and her father's criticisms echoed in her head. She slumped her shoulders, recalling she was too tall, her hair unruly, and her manners unpolished. Hadn't she just proven that?

He stooped, as if willing her to look at him.

"Solomon."

Her lashes flew open, and she found herself staring into that mesmerizing pair of tawny eyes. Despite her ragged manners, he'd given her his name! The edges of her mouth turned upward, hesitant in the beginning then broadening.

"Oh."

Heat flooded into her cheeks, but she stuck out her gloved hand, determined to conclude the meeting in a pleasant fashion.

"I'm pleased to meet you, Mr. Solomon."

Slowly, he took her hand and shook it. He had a firm grip, a sign of reliability.

He appeared on the verge of saying something. Suspecting that he might give her a set-down, Philomena spoke hurriedly, "I thank you for your earlier salute. It came just when I needed cheering."

She turned to her companion. "Nancy, if you're ready?"

Nodding in the gentlemen's direction, Nancy murmured, "Yes, Miss Lower. Good day, gentlemen."

Philomena noted how Mr. Solomon started even as his friend gaped at her.

Mortified by her cork-brained behavior, Philomena put her long legs to good use and quickly strode from the scene. In an unusual twist, Nancy didn't complain of being rushed. The pair scurried down Bond Street, making toward the safety of the Bristol Hotel.

"YOU DON'T THINK... I mean, is it possible... Just how many Miss Lowers can there be in the City of London?" Charles asked, confounded.

His voice came to Solomon as if it traveled across a great distance. Indeed, as Solomon stared after the women who swiftly progressed down Bond Street, his mind traveled hundreds of miles away. He remained like that, his hands thrust in his pockets, his mood contemplative.

"Her maid called her Mena. I didn't mark it at the time..." Solomon began before his thoughts veered into another direction. "That was him."

Confused by the non-sequitur, Charles frowned. "What do you mean?"

"Her would-be thief," Solomon said abruptly, describing the events of the previous morning in St. James Park. "Recall that I said Holden Withers looked familiar?"

Frowning, Charles asked, "Do you mean to say the youth we met earlier is Miss Lower's would-be thief?"

"And stepbrother," Solomon said, snapping his jaw shut in annoyance.

Stroking his chin, Charles gazed along Bond Street. "So, that's Sir John's daughter."

Taking his friend by the elbow, Solomon pointed their steps toward Bruton Street. His next words were delivered through a clenched jaw. "The heiress who received the lion's share of her father's fortune, most of which he stole from my father."

Charles whistled. "Damned rotten luck."

"It's Providence. I sought a means of avenging the wrong done to my father and literally stumbled across it."

The anger, never far from the surface these days, welled within him. Granted, it had mutated slightly. Instead of weaving air dreams of strangling Sir John with his bare hands, Solomon now had a distinct desire to place Miss Philomena Lower over his knee and administer her a good paddling.

"Philomena Lower as good as offered herself to me."

"Offered herself? I don't think so," Charles said skeptically.

Solomon faced his friend and demanded, "Did you not see her bold stare? How she flirted with me, a complete stranger?"

The grin Charles Dryden made was unholy and unrepentant. "Slow down, Laz. I was there, remember? *You* flirted with *her*. She merely asked your name."

Solomon snorted. "The baronet's daughter is as bold as brass."

"Hardly," Charles politely disagreed.

Struck by the sudden thought that he'd allowed that woman to slip from him, he muffled a curse.

"What's wrong, Laz? You look as if you've seen a ghost."

"How will I ever find her again? I can't lose her!"

Solomon tore down Bond Street, side-stepping or shoving aside passersby as he mumbled his apologies. "Beg your pardon. Sorry 'bout that. Oops."

"Laz!" Charles called out. "For God's sake, man, let it go."

Solomon ignored his friend's advice. Charles had no idea how desperate things were at home. He would find Philomena Lower, talk to her, and convince her to give back his fortune.

Damn.

He stood, winded, at the spot where Vigo Street crossed Bond. Scanning both streets, he could not see her anywhere.

Damn.

There were dozens of ladies strolling away from him, all wearing either bonnets or caps, and Solomon hadn't taken note of hers. Instead, he'd been transfixed by soft brown curls framing woodsy-green eyes and a smattering of freckles across the bridge of a pertly upturned nose.

Damn.

He felt, rather than saw, Charles's presence at his elbow. Without sparing his friend a look, he barked, "Do you see her? Did you see where she went?"

"No."

Solomon turned his head toward his friend, something in Charles's tone sounding definite and unfriendly.

"You aren't even looking for her!" Solomon accused.

"No, I'm not. Nor should you. There's a reason I told you to let it go."

"There's a reason I ignored that crackbrained advice," Solomon said bitterly.

Charles lifted his brows.

Solomon punched Charles's shoulder, lamenting, "I wish you'd strip and spar with me at Jackson's."

"With you in such a fury? Not a chance, thank you very much." Charles clapped Solomon's shoulder and steered him up Bond Street.

"Why should I let this pass?"

"Because I'm not sure you don't mean to harm our Miss Philomena Lower."

Briefly, the image flashed through Solomon's mind of spanking the hoyden. It wasn't what Charles meant, of course. He referred to punishment, but the image titillated Solomon. He'd wager Philomena Lower had a nice, rounded derriere. Probably smooth, too.

"I merely wish to lay the facts before her and urge her to correct the wrong her father committed against mine."

Charles snorted. "Why do I not believe you?"

"It's true."

Charles pulled up short to give him a penetrating stare. "Shall we take stock for a moment of what we've uncovered in just a day's work?"

"Fine."

His friend nodded as he began the inventory. "We've discovered the woman is an only child. That she inherited a large sum of money in the past year. That for some inexplicable reason she chooses to reside in Chelmsford, of all places."

"What's wrong with Chelmsford?" Solomon asked testily.

Rolling his eyes, Charles didn't deem that worthy of a response.

"We've discovered she drove a new phaeton through St. James Park yesterday. That her stepbrother tried to steal from her, then informed us Miss Lower had been treated unkindly by her family. Her father wasn't happily married to her stepmother, which leads me to surmise that woman would be no happier with said husband's child."

"What's your point?"

Glancing at Charles's tightened lips, Solomon knew he'd pushed the former army captain past his patience.

Sounding very much like a stern father, Charles lectured, "The woman is probably alone in the world, save for her abigail. It's delusional to expect a woman so vulnerable to part with her fortune. I don't believe you'll be able to convince her to do so, nor do I think you should try. More and more, I think less of our proposed solution."

He paused, letting his words sink in before continuing in a gentler tone, "Let me make you a loan. We can find another solution, perhaps retrenching and leasing the estate? No? Then how about I stake you at White's, and you can repay me from your winnings. If you lose the stakes, then you needn't repay me."

Shaking his head, Solomon said, "It's kind of you, Charles, but you don't understand."

"I understand you're on a collision course."

"She has no right to that fortune."

Charles threw his head back and closed his eyes, as if praying for assistance from heaven. "You won't let this go, will you?"

Tightly, Solomon said, "I cannot. I made an oath."

Shaking his head, Charles said, "Pity. I thought she was rather gallant."

"Gallant?"

The word held a healthy helping of horror.

"Yes," Charles said firmly. "She impulsively asked for your name so that she could thank you, not because she's some light-skirt. Or did you miss her blush?"

"Hah! That's what you observed, is it?"

"Not only that, I also saw your response to her."

Solomon wiped his forehead, wishing he could have quelled his reactions. Both times their paths had crossed, he'd wondered what it would be like to bed her. That was not his typical response to every woman he encountered, and it frustrated the hell out of him. To be attracted to Sir John's daughter? He might as well have stabbed his father in the heart, it felt like such a betrayal.

"Yes, dammit."

"A person would have to be blind not to see those eddies of attraction that circled you both. Why not simply follow up on that? Let the chips fall where they may." Charles unlocked the door to his townhome then ushered them both inside.

The butler, Dobson, shuffled forward to relieve them of their coats and hats.

"Thank you, Dobs," Charles said, his usual cheerful manner returning.

"I will not betray my father." Solomon raised his hand, showing Charles the pink cut, freshly healed, where he'd taken his blood oath.

"Mark me, Charles. I won't be duped like my father was."

Chapter 5

Solomon hadn't rested well the previous evening, tossing in his comfortable bed most of the night. He blamed his friend for his restlessness. Well, Charles and Miss Lower, he amended. Because damn if the tall, curly-headed female didn't stir him. Blast Charles's hide for confirming his attraction had been reciprocated. That knowledge led him into the dangerous territory of erotic dreams that kept him awake.

He had another reason for being irritated with Charles. His friend's observations about Miss Lower's personal life annoyed him. He didn't wish to think of Philomena Lower as someone who was lonely and vulnerable. She wasn't the one who deserved pity, by George. She benefitted from her father's chicanery.

It was mid-morning before he and Charles arrived at the tailors on Cork Street, having spent time in the nursery trying to coax a coherent sentence out of Nicholas.

He spent an agreeable hour with Mr. Schweitzer while Charles was tended to by Mr. Davidson. They parted ways at the shop, as Charles had other business matters to attend. Solomon lingered, purchasing a new shirt and hose with the money remaining from the sale of Josephine, his sister's horse.

He emerged from Schweitzer and Davidson hungry. He intended to take his luncheon at the Bristol then go to Hoby for a new pair of Hessians. Spec, Charles's valet, had done an excellent job polishing his old boots, but they would not last until summer, he feared.

The Bristol Hotel hosted a restaurant which offered simple fare to Solomon's liking. He'd just finished his mutton, potatoes, and tankard of ale when he spotted the tall figure of Miss Lower passing through the lobby. The regal lift of her chin and her lengthy strides confirmed her identity even before he noted the shorter companion who traipsed alongside her.

A slow smile curved his lips; he was pleased to see the baronet's daughter again. God was smiling upon him today.

Bolting out of his chair, he tossed some coins on the table and hurried from the dining room.

"Miss Lower!" He raised his voice, disregarding the polite rules of niceties. Too much was at stake to be concerned with proper behavior. His gamble paid off, for the curly-haired woman stopped then turned on her heel.

Solomon closed the distance between them, smiling as he hurried to her.

Wide-eyed, she faintly exclaimed, "Mr. Solomon! What are you doing here?"

She greeted him with such enthusiasm that Solomon forgot to correct his name. Joy washed over him, an emotion so long dormant that it took him aback. What an amazing day this was turning out to be.

"I thought I'd never find you again," he said.

Her smile grew brighter. His chest tightened upon seeing how brilliantly her eyes sparkled. He had a flash of insight. It was no wonder God made Miss Lower so tall—all that radiance couldn't fit in a smaller package. She was dazzling when happy.

Her head tilted sideways, and he thought a fairy had sprinkled golden dust over the bridge of her nose. When had he become so fanciful? Solomon had been so pressed with the effort of ensuring his people's survival he hadn't had the luxury of being whimsical. This was very unlike him.

"I'm happy to see you this afternoon, Mr. Solomon."

"As to that, there's been some confusion. I provided my Christian name to you, Solomon."

She touched her cheek in dismay. "Now I understand why you stressed the need for formal introductions," she said in an aside to her grinning companion.

"Had I behaved less like a hoyden yesterday, I wouldn't have placed you in such an awkward position. Forgive me."

"Nothing to forgive."

"What is your surname? I can't very well call you by your first name."

Here he hesitated. Solomon didn't wish to lie outright, but on the other hand, he couldn't risk giving her his rank in case she knew her father's victims. He had to tread lightly and slowly build up her confidence in him.

He struck a happy medium, giving his surname without mentioning the title. "Braxton, but I'd be pleased if you called me Solomon. I would very much like us to be friends."

They stood, staring at one another, in the lobby of the Bristol Hotel. Pedestrians jostled them, calling him back to his surroundings.

"I am Philomena Lower. Mena to my friends."

"Are you going out?" Then he inwardly moaned. It was obvious they were going out.

"Yes. Nancy and I were going to shop for hair ribbons."

"Ah. I would happily accompany you, should you wish." He lifted a dark brow.

"To shop for hair ribbons?"

Her companion nudged her in the ribcage, and Philomena shook her head.

"I mean... naturally, Nancy and I would be honored to have your escort."

He winged out his elbow and she placed her hand on top of his sleeve. As she did so, he noted her white cotton gloves edged in lace set near his worn cuff.

The stark contrast between her wealth and his impoverishment made him cringe. Anger flared in his breast. Anger and resentment, and perhaps a hint of embarrassment, too. Solomon refused to brood on the feelings at the moment. It had been his intention to soften Philomena Lower for his request, and he chose charm as his weapon of choice for the task.

With her maid walking discreetly behind, they left the hotel.

"Have you enjoyed your stay in London?"

She hesitated then carefully replied, "London has its advantages. The theatres and museums are wonderful. Tonight, Nancy and I are to attend the opera."

"What a coincidence. So am I," he said, resolving on the spot to attend.

Tightening his fist so he felt the sting of the cut in his palm, he brought his oath to mind. He'd befriend her then discuss addressing the wrong her father had done.

"The Italian opera at the Pantheon?" He wished to clarify which opera she'd be attending this evening. He would make certain he attended the same theatre, foregoing his evening plans to gamble at White's.

"Italian, although I don't know how much I'll be able to comprehend," Philomena said demurely. "My language lessons are far behind me."

"As are mine, but that's what the playbills are for, is it not?"

They exchange sidelong glances and smiles. Philomena Lower appeared to be an amiable person. He did not wish to believe she would exploit her father's crimes once they were made known to her. He would befriend her, set the reckoning straight, then regain his father's lost fortune. His first duty was to his dependents, and he pictured the bare coal cellar at Lazonby.

However, Solomon's conscience wondered if she weren't the baronet's daughter? To assuage that concern, Solomon promised any gains on the lost wager would belong to Miss

Lower, and he intended to have a pleasant association with her. Their friendship need not end once he achieved his objective. He would heed Charles's caution to do this woman no harm.

"It's strange how we keep inadvertently meeting, isn't it?" she said.

"I prefer to think of it as destiny."

"Destiny? As if the Fates placed you into my path at the park, the milliner's, and the lobby of the Bristol?"

He chuckled. "Well, put like that, it does seem a strong argument, doesn't it? I so despaired having lost you yesterday that I chased you."

"Did you?" She shook her head. "That's foolish beyond permission. Someone might have mistaken you for a footpad."

He nearly choked trying to quell his laughter. Never would he imagine that the Marquess of Lazonby could be mistaken for a common thief.

Unlike her father, who had been a thief.

His laughter halted.

In the awkward silence that followed, she eventually asked if they could visit her grays at the Harlow Mews.

"If you wish." He gritted his teeth, recalling the splendid team she'd driven a few days before. They were prime goers, purchased with her father's ill-gotten gains. Stolen from his family. They'd eaten turnips and oats, while she'd been able to afford a pair of matched grays.

"We don't have to, if you'd rather not." She looked uncertain, as if sensing his resentment. Her shoulders turned inward.

If he were going to be her friend, he should at least act friendly, he chided himself.

"Why do you do that?"

"Do what?"

He pointed to her shoulders. "Curl inward like that. Are you trying to disappear?"

From her stunned look, he sensed he'd caught her off guard, so he pressed. "You have the bearing of a queen, but when you hunch your shoulders, it quite dispels the image."

Her companion chuckled so that Solomon received the impression Nancy had scolded her mistress in the same vein.

They entered the Mews where the smells of hay, horse, and leather replaced the odors of the street. An improvement to Solomon's thinking, although he preferred Miss Lower's rose scent above all others. It suited her, somehow.

"You're to be congratulated on your grays. Tell me, was it by design that your horses matched the phaeton?"

"Yes. I'm glad you noticed."

She approached the horses, removing her dainty gloves as she did so. She stroked the gelding's neck, and the mare nosed her way into its share of the affection. Speaking softly, but in a gentle tone, she communicated her ease with the grays as she smiled upon them.

Philomena Lower had an ordinary face, yet Winsome had been entirely correct. She was regal. Partly that impression was due to her height and the intelligence which lit her eyes, but her smile was transformative. Solomon couldn't recall any woman whose face became so luminous when she smiled.

She was quite a taking thing.

Solomon ran his hand down one gray's nose.

"You're quite the beauty, aren't you?" Still petting the horse, he said, "I had to sell my sister's horse, Josephine. Imogene recently married and moved to Ireland."

"Both of those things make you sad."

He nodded, wondering why on earth he'd even made the pensive statement.

"I understand. I lost my father last year, and although we were never close, I miss him."

"You weren't close to your father?"

She shook her head. "No, and do you know something strange? With his death, I know that we will never be close, and I think that idea makes me sadder than actually missing him."

"Few people leave this world unlamented," he said dryly. "Your sorrow is proof either of your sterling character or that even *your* father wasn't entirely worthless."

As soon as he said the words, Solomon wished he had not. He had wanted his friendship with Philomena to exist outside his disgruntlement with her father, yet he dragged it back into the mix as if some unseen force compelled him. He had shown the daughter how cheaply he regarded the baronet. It was not well done of him.

The companion, Nancy, clucked her tongue and shook her head.

Miss Lower's countenance closed, and she lowered her arms to her sides. An awkward stiffness crept into her lithe body. She lifted her chin, as if she were trying to balance a penny on the end of her nose.

"Even *my* father?"

"Forgive me." He removed his beaver hat and rifled through his black hair.

Solomon cleared his throat and donned his hat again. Damn his unwieldy tongue. These past few years stuck in Cumbria had caused his social skills to deteriorate.

"I meant no offense, Miss Lower."

She shifted from one foot to the other, evidencing a clear desire to escape. Her gaze darted over his shoulder and down the alleyway, as if she planned to take to her heels and leave him stranded at the mews.

It was a novel experience for the Marquess of Lazonby to have anyone, especially a pretty, unmarried female, wish to be shed of his company.

He did not care for it.

He found it more frustrating than irritating, though. How was he ever going to convince her to part with her fortune if she felt he'd insulted her?

This situation was rapidly devolving to a point of no return. He needed to retreat and regroup. Solomon should change his strategy, develop another campaign to worm his way into her good books. He must confer with his good friend and military man, Charles Dryden, about how best to proceed.

Stepping back, Solomon waved an expansive arm. "Shall I return you to the Bristol now, Miss Lower?"

Her eyes narrowed, she said, "Yes, please."

The companion heaved a sigh and continued shaking her head in that slow manner of a person sorely tried.

Solomon felt thoroughly chastised.

Little was spoken during the short walk to the hotel. Philomena had withdrawn into an invisible, ironclad shell, which Solomon had no way of penetrating.

His steps were heavy, filled with regret for having ruined the natural, perfect accord between them. Solomon had hoped to befriend Philomena, but there was no chance of that now. He missed her luminous smile.

They parted on the pavement of the hotel before the doorway, with Philomena hastily bringing their time to an end. She gave a jerky nod and tangled her slender fingers together.

"G—good day, Mr. Braxton."

By George, she couldn't wait to get rid of him.

Solomon didn't mention the opera. She wouldn't be there, not if she thought there was a chance she'd encounter him again.

His gaze skimmed her pale face then dropped to her mouth. He wished he'd had kissed her, had felt those soft lips part beneath his own. That lost pleasure stung more than the cut on the palm of his hand.

Solomon watched her trim figure depart through the Bristol's door with the faint hope his leave-taking had been proper. It was impossible to recall if he'd thanked her for their outing or wished her a pleasant evening or even returned her goodbye.

Gloomily, he reminded himself that all cuts heal, and so would this sense of loss.

Clasping his hands behind his back, he walked through Green Park. He didn't wish to return to the Dryden household just yet. Solomon shied from joining the idyllic domiciliary when his mood was at low tide. He couldn't rid himself of the solid belief he'd squandered a fantastic opportunity this afternoon.

Chapter 6

"Made a mull of it, didn't he?" Nancy said, trudging up the stairs. "More's the pity."

"Do you know, I think he envied my horses?"

"Does that matter?"

Philomena tossed her head, shaking off the unfortunate afternoon with Mr. Braxton. Not even to herself would Philomena use his first name. She would put him from her mind. Slopping thinking led to sloppy decisions, and she must keep her head during this London foray. The Fates had not tossed down a bachelor for her; she must continue searching for a marriage partner.

Philomena had foolishly believed she might be on the precipice of a making a match, thereby solving her problems.

He had seemed happy to see her, but that hadn't lasted. She'd seen how his jaw tightened when she suggested visiting the Mews. She only suggested it because she thought the man would rather visit horses than Bond Street shops.

Did he think she was bragging about owning such a fine team? Inwardly, she grimaced at that. For herself, Philomena considered displays of wealth to be vulgar.

But he had resented her horses, she'd not been wrong about that. Mr. Braxton apparently fell into the second category of London gentlemen—those who despised an heiress for her wealth.

She wondered if Mr. Braxton realized her father's fortune had been recently acquired. He'd only enjoyed it a handful of years before he passed away. During her childhood, they lived hand-to-mouth as her father worked his business schemes.

After gaining entrance to her hotel room, Nancy removed Philomena's pelisse. She eyed her for a moment then shrugged in defeat. "Then he's dished. Pity. He had the loveliest head of hair, Mena."

The older woman fluttered her lashes, pressed a hand to her bosom, and sighed.

Philomena rolled her eyes.

"Do you still wish to attend the opera tonight?" asked Nancy, chuckling.

"I must." She sighed. "If I've less than three weeks to find an eligible man to marry, I can't waste an evening at home."

Her companion eyed her for a long beat of silence before she briskly rubbed her palms together. "Let's go husband hunting then!"

Nancy pulled a scrap of paper from her bodice. "Now, earlier this morning I talked to some of the footmen here—quite discreet, if you please—and got a list of eligible bachelors."

"How industrious of you," Philomena murmured.

Nancy ignored the sally. "I told them they didn't need to be lookers, but on no account should they be poor."

Philomena pouted. "I should have liked to have a handsome husband."

"Mena." Nancy wagged her finger, and Philomena chuckled.

"Very well." Her mind wandered to the image of thick, black hair with a curl hanging over the forehead. How would it have felt to run her fingers through that mane? She mentally shook herself. "No fortune hunters. What have you come up with?"

"Willoughby Kirkwood. Fifty-five years old, never been married."

"So, ancient?"

Nancy gave an exasperated sigh. "The older he is, the sooner you can be rid of him."

"Point taken," Philomena said demurely, having to bite her bottom lip to keep from laughing.

"Niles James," Nancy read from the list, lowering it to give her a slanted look. "He's a forty-year-old viscount."

Philomena shook her head. "No lords, thank you very much."

"You've an unreasonable prejudice! I'm certain there are some very respectable peers."

"Then you'd be wrong. I learned during my Season never to trust an aristocrat. Read on."

"I fail to see why you're such a stickler with aristocrats. Heavens knows, Randall Scott wasn't a lord, but he managed to be thoroughly disreputable."

"Randal Scott was an unconscionable rake, and I was too stupid to recognize that, much to my regret."

"You were naïve, not stupid."

"I was deflowered," Philomena said abruptly before turning away. After all these years, the shame still burned from her first liaison.

Nancy grumbled, scanned the paper for her place, then said, "Henry Blythe. Owns coal mines."

Smiling in appreciation for Nancy's change of conversation, Philomena asked, "How old is he?"

"Thirty."

"Possibility."

Nancy ventured, "He uses children in his mines."

Philomena winced. "Put an asterisk by his name. We may have to come back to him."

"Mena!"

She snapped, "I've neither the time nor luxury for principles."

"Here, then," Nancy huffed, offering up the list. "Read it yourself."

"Thank you." She took it, her gaze roving down the list as she mumbled gentlemen's names. "Caldwell Effington? Sounds like a prig. Ah, I see he's nearing seventy! How marvelous. Our marriage could last as long as a fly's lifespan. Heinrich Schuler—German? We might rub along nicely, if I'm unable to understand every third word he speaks."

Nancy shuddered. "The Germans always spray when they speak. All that '*auch und nacht.*'" She made a phlegmy sound.

"True."

"Richard Tennett. A solicitor who made his fortune on the Exchange." Philomena squealed. "He's eight-and-twenty—and widowed."

"His last wife fell down a flight of stairs," Nancy said, clasping her hands together.

Philomena lowered the list and gasped. "That's dreadful!"

"Rumor says he pushed her."

Shocked, Philomena stared at her companion. "Then why would you put him on this list?"

"I wasn't sure how picky you'd be."

"Why would I marry someone to gain my fortune only to have him kill me to collect it?"

Her companion's mouth twisted.

Slapping the page against her thigh, Philomena asked, "Do you mean to tell me in this whole great city there are only—" quickly, she counted the names, "six eligible bachelors?"

"That I discovered this morning," Nancy patiently explained. "We can always inquire for more tomorrow."

"Discreetly? I wouldn't think so. Good Lord, I may as well put an advertisement in *The Times*!"

"There's an idea!"

"Or hire a Bow Street runner," Philomena said, straight-faced, adding another heap of absurdity to the dunghill.

"Nonsense." Nancy took the stub of a pencil from beneath her mobcap to scratch a name off the list. "You might be wed to a burglar, peagoose."

Philomena stayed Nancy's hand as she placed the pencil to paper. "Wait."

A heartbeat pounded before Philomena said, "Put an asterisk by Tennett's name instead."

"The one who shoved his wife down the stairs?"

Grimly, Philomena observed, "Yes. You're right. This is no time to be picky."

"Still, Mena…"

"Well, you keep reassuring me that I'm not bad luck. May as well put it to the test." Philomena lifted one shoulder in a fatalistic shrug.

"YOU'RE STARING, LAZ, and I shouldn't wonder if everyone in the auditorium doesn't take note of it," Winsome Dryden hissed. "If you're so entranced by Miss Lower, go to her box and converse with her like a normal person."

"Leave the man alone. Can't you see he's posing as the anguished, romantic poet, Lord Byron?" With his elbow, Charles nudged Solomon. "What, no glare? No rude hand gesture or vile suggestions of anatomical impossibilities? Just who is this fellow and what has he done with my good friend, the Marquess of Lazonby?"

Winsome's mouth twitched then she smacked her husband's forearm with her fan. "Ooh, she's looking this way! Hush, Charles!"

Solomon glanced at her box, but Philomena had already turned her gaze elsewhere. "Do you think she saw me?"

"Yes," said Winnie.

"Good God," scoffed Charles.

"I can't believe she's come," he said, ignoring his friend's exasperation.

Philomena was dressed in a low-cut silk evening gown that shimmered, but he couldn't describe its color. Maybe silvery grey? All Solomon knew was the effect was… spectacular. Stunned, he repeated for the second time, "I would have sworn she'd stay home this evening."

"I wish we'd stayed home," Charles grumbled.

"Charles," his wife rebuked.

"Winsome's right, Laz. Go talk to the woman."

Glumly, he replied, "She doesn't want to talk to me."

Spreading her hands across her lap, Winsome advised, "Fix the conversational topic upon her. Pay her a compliment, ask whether she enjoys the opera."

"Offer to fetch her some coffee," Charles said.

When Solomon paid no attention to this sage counseling, Charles snapped, "For the sake of upholding the dignity of six generations of ancestors, stop making calf eyes across a crowded theatre."

His gaze riveted to Philomena's private box for the third time in as many minutes. On this occasion, though, their eyes met and held. He could have sworn the atmosphere in the Pantheon crackled with anticipation.

Abruptly, he came to a decision. "By God, I'll do it."

Pinching the bridge of his nose, Charles muttered, "It's not a battlefield, Laz, just the opera."

He ignored that remark and Winsome's smothered giggle.

Winding his way from their seats to Philomena's box, Solomon felt self-conscious. His palms were sweating, so he surreptitiously wiped them on his evening clothes, or rather, Charles's evening clothes.

For the first time in a long time, Solomon was dressed like a marquess. He missed his signet ring, as if the chunk of metal somehow anchored his identity. Without it, Solomon felt lost.

He'd never been terrified of speaking to a woman before, but then again, he'd never offended anyone as badly as he had today. The time had arrived to prove whether he was a mouse or a marquess.

He pulled back the velvet drapes marking the entryway of the heiress's box and peered inside, irritated by what he saw.

"Good evening, ladies and gentlemen," Solomon said as pleasantly as he could.

What was the ninny thinking to keep company with Richard Tennett? It was widely suspected he'd murdered his wife. Caldwell Effington was there, he noted, marveling at his connection to Philomena. He did not know the other gentleman so lifted his brow.

Philomena snapped her fan shut then bared her teeth in a travesty of a welcome.

"Good evening, sir. We're pleased to have your company."

Liar.

She waved toward her companions. "This is Mr. Tennett, Mr. Effington, and Herr Schuler. Gentlemen, this is—"

"Laz, old boy! How are you?" Caldwell boomed, vigorously pumping Solomon's hand. "Sorry to hear about your father. Shame, that. He was a fine gentleman."

"Yes, he was. Thank you." Solomon regained his hand and flexed it so that the blood flow would return. He then bowed to Nancy, who had cast off her mobcap and usual black dress and wore a lavender-colored gown trimmed in flounces.

"You look most becoming this evening, Miss Nancy," he said.

She tittered, fluttering her eyelashes in a coquettish manner.

He smiled for the first time since the Harlow Mews incident. Feeling emboldened, he winged out his elbow, practically daring Philomena to snub him.

"Shall we take a walk, Miss Lower?"

Although the English appreciated Italian operas, hardly any bothered to learn the language well enough to follow along, so his country's love for the medium became a distant second to the more immediate enjoyment of socializing. The Pantheon provided a coffee shop where the strains of the music could still be heard, theoretically. Often the hub of conversation surpassed the musicians' efforts.

Her eyes flashed, which warned him she was still in high dudgeon, but she slipped her hand onto his coat sleeve.

"As you wish."

He ushered her from the box, and when they were out of earshot of the others, he said, "I have a problem and need your advice."

Her startled gaze collided with his, driving his rehearsed phrases out of his mind. Those moss-green eyes opened wide with surprise. That pair of soft, plump lips slightly parted by a gasp. This is how Philomena Lower would appear when she made love. She would take her pleasure and return it tenfold, Solomon was certain of that, sensing the woman wouldn't deal in half-measures.

God, he wanted to be the man who saw that countenance, who created it.

Words poured from his mouth, low and husky. "Someday I'm going to count the number of freckles sprinkled across your nose."

She whipped her hand up to touch her face then laughed and lowered it.

"You're teasing me," she said, her eyes still lit with humor. "I cannot stay angry with you if you make me laugh, and that's very ungentlemanly of you."

Solomon smiled, feeling the tightness ease from his chest. "I'm not teasing but am serious. I wish to know all your secrets, Miss Philomena Lower."

Her cheeks pinkened, which pleased him. She wasn't as impervious to him as she might like to believe.

Perhaps Charles had the right of it. Perhaps he could pursue this mutual attraction, explore the possibility of a London flirtation with Miss Lower. It would be a pleasant way to pass time and provide him with fond reminisces once he returned home.

Home. A place ruined by this girl's father. Damn, would he never find peace from the consequences of his father's reckless wager?

He coughed into his hand then said, "For now, however, I'll settle for learning how you take your coffee."

Philomena studied him, as if he were a puzzle she were trying to solve, but then she moved, preceding him in the throng of the theatregoers.

He wracked his brain for a conversational gambit then recalled Winsome's advice.

"Are you enjoying the opera?"

She lifted her brows then waved her hand to encompass the coffee shop. "How can I say?"

Smiling at her sarcasm, he pressed on. "You do look well tonight, Philomena. Quite lovely."

"Thank you," she said primly.

And just like that, his patience snapped. Thrusting his hands into his pockets, he spoke sharply, "Would you drop this prickly act if I promise never to disparage your father again?"

"Sir John may have been a poor father—" She paused to correct herself. "He was a poor father, but that is for me to say, not you."

"Agreed."

His sudden agreement set her back on her heels. She pressed her hand against her décolletage, her expression baffled.

"What is it?"

"You confuse me, Mr. Braxton. As an heiress, I understand some will seek my company, fawn over me because of my wealth—"

"I never fawned over you."

She stilled, tilting her head as she considered his words, then finally nodded. "Some despise me because of my wealth, but if we're to be friends, I must feel confident that it's because you enjoy me simply for myself."

"I do like you—very much so, despite your being an heiress."

"You view my wealth as a drawback?"

"Yes," he snarled and threw a hand in the air. "Would that you never had the blasted fortune."

As soon as the words were spoken, Solomon knew they were true. Initially, he wanted to strike up a friendship with Philomena to gain her confidence, butter her up for his big request. Somewhere along the way, that had changed. Now he wished to know her better simply because he found her company enjoyable. Yes, he wanted her friendship, but he was damned attracted to her and wouldn't mind bedding her, as well.

A brief silence reigned before she managed to say, "Well."

"Yes. Well, here we are."

Philomena quietly absorbed this new information. "You don't care for heiresses?"

"How can I say?" He mimicked her earlier words.

Briefly, she smiled at the irony before admitting, "Earlier today, Nancy accused me of being prejudiced. I admit I loathe aristocrats, but I see no harm in furthering an acquaintance with you, Mr. Braxton."

That set him back. "You loathe aristocrats?"

"Why, I suppose that's overly broad." A little notch appeared in her fine forehead as she considered the matter further. "I suppose it's gentlemen with empty pockets and empty flattery that repel me. During my season, I encountered a great number of impoverished aristocrats who were fortune hunters."

He didn't know quite what to say to that, only he agreed, yet he couldn't bring himself to condemn his fellow peers. Estates were damnably expensive, and Solomon sat squarely in that category of empty-pocketed aristocrats.

He ushered her through the crowd and up the carpeted stairs to her private box. "You're terribly exacting, Miss Lower. I wonder if my ego will survive our acquaintance."

Flashing him a grin, she quipped, "Well, how about this then? I couldn't help but notice how many attractive women have tried to catch your eye this evening and have envied me my escort. It's daunting to be in the company of the most handsome man in the theatre. Now is your ego restored, good sir?"

Solomon laughed, and Philomena joined him. As they grinned at one another, he marveled at how easily their perfect accord had returned.

Chapter 7

Once this visit to London ended, Philomena would remember how Solomon Braxton's presence at the opera imbued the evening with a special quality. Tomorrow was soon enough to begin her hunt for a husband. Tonight, she had made a friend. He didn't despise her for her fortune; he felt it burdensome. That was a novelty, and so for now she would enjoy a laugh and cup of coffee with the gentleman who'd taken her breath away.

Before the opera had begun, Philomena had the oddest sensation of being stared at and scanned the crowd, trying to find the source. Amid the gentlemen dressed in black evening attire and the women gowned in colorful, expensive silks, she spotted Solomon Braxton. Sitting in the third row of seats on the main floor, he stared at her intently, as if his gaze traveled the distance between them to touch her.

Her breath caught.

Garbed entirely in black, save for his ivory silk cravat, there was only one word she could conjure to best describe Solomon: striking.

Philomena forced herself to concentrate on something Herr Schuler was saying. Unfortunately, at that precise moment, he made a guttural sound, which reminded Philomena of Nancy's complaint. Her companion had been right about that—his speech sounded phlegmy.

She wiped her forehead, hoping to smooth her frown. From the corner of her eye, she tracked Solomon's movements, drat the man. He left his seat, and the Pantheon lost its bright gaiety.

Philomena was cross with herself for noticing his departure and feeling this unaccountable wave of depression.

Then Solomon appeared in the doorway of her box, setting the cat among the pigeons and her heart aflutter.

For a short minute, he'd conversed with members of her party. His height and dynamic personality dominated the small space. Over the course of the first act, Philomena's conversation with Herr Schuler had limped along in fits and starts. Herr Schuler was a dear man, only slightly shorter than herself. Next to Solomon, though, the German not only was dwarfed by Mr. Braxton, but he had a receding hairline to boot.

Against Caldwell Effington, Solomon appeared strong, athletic, and a man in his prime; whereas poor Mr. Effington seemed like a man who was trying too hard. Such vigorous handshaking! Philomena suspected Effington was compensating for other shortcomings. She didn't wish to consider what those might be.

As far as looks were regarded, Richard Tennett's were on par with Solomon's, but the kindling glint in Mr. Tennett's eye discomforted Philomena. She half-believed he had murdered his wife in a jealous rage.

Without a by-your-leave, Solomon Braxton whisked her out of the box. Within a twinkling of her leaving her guests, he'd made her laugh, forgive him, and compliment him.

What a startling turn of events.

Dazed by the inroads he'd made through her outer guard, she decided to enjoy herself.

After coffee, Solomon asked if she wished to meet his friends, Charles and Winsome Montgomery. Shyly, she agreed. The young married couple were very nice to her, greeting her with gracious smiles. When Mrs. Dryden invited her to their home for a private dinner on Thursday, Philomena accepted.

From his expression, it was clear the invitation pleased Solomon, as well. That knowledge warmed her.

Philomena and Mrs. Dryden were of the same age, but Mrs. Dryden was far more beautiful. She had silvery-blonde hair and the most unusual eye color—light topaz. It didn't escape Philomena's attention that Mrs. Dryden also had a very attentive husband who frequently touched her. Clearly, this was a woman adored.

After bidding the Drydens *adieu*, Solomon returned Philomena to her private box.

Eagerly, he asked, "There's a balloon ascension day after tomorrow in Richmond. Would you care to accompany me?"

"Yes," she answered without thinking. His enthusiasm ignited her own. Then she frowned. She had twenty days in which to find a husband, and she mustn't allow herself to become sidetracked.

"You're wondering how we'll get there, I suppose, but fear not. Charles will lend me his curricle."

Philomena slightly shook her head. "That sounds perfectly fine, but that wasn't why I frowned."

"You're terrible for my ego," he sighed, placing a hand over his heart as if she'd wounded him.

"And you've monopolized me this evening, which means I've treated my guests poorly."

"Then you should return to your hostess duties." He waved her through the velvet curtains of her box.

"Thank you, Mr. Braxton."

He frowned again, appearing uncertain. In an atypical fashion, he hovered on the threshold before mumbling something then departing.

She watched him walk away, feeling the rest of her evening would be anti-climactic. Sighing, she returned to her guests.

The next day, she and Nancy browsed through London's newspapers, searching for bachelors' names. They came up with a few more prospects—a wealthy gentleman visiting relatives near Cavendish Square and a middle-aged bank manager. Nancy combed through the obituaries, thinking a nice widower would do for her mistress.

"But their wives haven't been dead a fortnight! Why would they re-marry so quickly?"

"You'd be surprised how helpless a man can become without a wife," Nancy said.

Philomena speculated about how she could arrange meetings with any of the men. "Without formal introductions, it will be difficult. They might think me some sort of adventuress."

"I can't be expected to think of everything now, can I?" Nancy complained.

Out of sorts, Philomena bit her tongue. She did not care for the dire position in which her trustee had placed her. Wedding a stranger appealed even less.

Fortunately, in a balm to her frayed nerves, Herr Schuler had sent a posy, and Mr. Tennett delivered a box of chocolates to express his appreciation for sharing her opera box. She delivered notes via the penny post to both gentlemen, thanking them for their gifts, but she didn't invite either to call upon her.

Instead, she very much looked forward to seeing Mr. Braxton again. She and Nancy spent an inordinate time selecting her day gown and performing her toilette for the outing. It was ridiculous. She felt as young as a schoolgirl and was a basket of nerves. For the past two nights, though, Philomena had dreamed of Solomon Braxton; his image came to mind throughout the day, too.

For the third time in her life, Philomena Lower was smitten. Her first *tendre* had been for the butcher's son, then there'd been Randall, the man who'd ruined her for other men. Philomena had never been suspicious until Clarissa made her feel as if she were bad luck, but she hoped the third time was the charm.

The next day brought the long-awaited outing in Richmond. The novelty of a balloon ascension filled the spectators with thrills. The canopy was filled with heated gas, allowing the silk to expand to the shape of a teardrop. Two men, dressed in suits and leather goggles, stood in the basket gondola, waving to the crowd while the ground crew tended the ropes and sandbags.

"I never realized silk could be so strong," Nancy said.

Mr. Braxton agreed. "It's deceptive in appearance, certainly."

Nancy leveled a long look upon the man then murmured, "Some things are like that, I suppose."

He gave Philomena's companion a long look, but Nancy maintained a bland countenance. Silently, Philomena chuckled to herself. Her friend had always been protective of her; Nancy wasn't about to stop the long-standing habit this week.

On this sunny day with a light, teasing breeze, Philomena pushed her worries from her mind. She had eighteen days to find a spouse, so if she squandered this day with Mr. Braxton, that left her with seventeen days. The difference was so small it hardly mattered.

The wind lifted Mr. Braxton's beaver hat just enough to reveal a glimpse of his raven-colored hair. Grinning, he quickly caught it and yanked the brim firmly around his ears.

Philomena laughed out loud.

Mr. Braxton caught her hand and kissed the back of it.

Pleasant, tingly sensations spread through her, and she resisted the desire to bring her hand to her lips.

Once Nancy cleared her throat, Philomena recalled herself and reluctantly removed her hand from his loose grasp.

After they watched the balloon ascend, Mr. Braxton took the curricle to a more secluded spot in the park and pulled out a picnic hamper. Nancy spread a blanket on the ground and waved them to sit.

Philomena wondered how she would maintain her dignity as she lowered herself to the blanket in a muslin dress. Its skirt formed a loose-fitting sheath, but she did not know if the seams would hold once she squatted.

His dark brows lifted. "Have you never sat on the ground?"

She frowned. "If I have, I don't remember it."

Nancy's chuckle swiftly turned into a muffled cough. "I'll just—" she pointed to a spot beneath a tree, "sit over there."

Solomon removed plates from the hamper and dished out the cold chicken, along with some pickles, cheese, and a bottle of wine. He handed Philomena her plate, made another for Nancy, then took it to her before heaping food upon his own.

Philomena appreciated his kindness toward her companion.

Trying to be discreet, Philomena watched his hands perform the tasks. His movements were quick and deft. She admired how his leg muscles flexed when he stood then sat back down on the blanket. A picture of strength, grace, and competence.

Oh, yes. She was smitten.

It was easy to forgive his disparaging comment about her father. Sir John hadn't been well liked, and Solomon had a right to his opinion. They had decided to disagree on that issue, which was perfectly acceptable. Philomena enjoyed the ease with which they'd put that behind them.

Soon she would be married to a man she did not know and might not like, one with whom their differences might not so easily be resolved. A chill ran down her spine, as if a cloud had passed over the sun. She pushed those fears aside, determined to enjoy Solomon's company on this sunny day.

Before that thought evaporated, another grew in its place. Could Solomon be her future husband? Was it possible the Fates truly had tossed down a bachelor when she most had need of one?

Wrinkling her nose, she tried an experiment. She closed her eyes and imagined being married to Solomon Braxton. The picture was fuzzy, out of focus. In the interest of science, she expanded the experiment and visualized being married to Herr Schuler. Nothing.

"Am I boring you, Philomena?" he asked.

Her lashes flew open. "I beg your pardon, Solomon. Of course you don't bore me. I was just remembering… some tedious chore I have waiting for me at the Bristol. I hope you don't mind? I promise not to woolgather anymore."

Cocking his head to the side, as if he debated whether he should accept her explanation, he then nodded and changed the subject.

"Did you grow up in the country or town?" he asked.

"In towns. We've lived in several cities throughout my lifetime."

"Name them."

"Well," Philomena twitched her nose, trying to call the towns to mind. "I was born in Leicester. Mama died in Dublin, we spent a long stretch in London, a few months in Dusseldorf then Brussels. I hardly remember living in Edinburgh, although that's where I first fell in love—"

"How old were you?"

She chuckled. "Twelve."

"Twelve?"

"Oh, yes. It strains credulity, but I was bowled head over heels by the butcher's son. He had the loveliest hair." Her tone softened as she clasped her hands to her heart.

"What a handful you must have been," he mumbled.

"Most twelve-year-old girls are handfuls."

"Do you recall the name of that boy?"

Philomena gasped, aghast that that particular detail completely escaped her memory. She touched her cheek in dismay. "And I pledged to love him forever and ever. Oh, I am fickle and faint-hearted."

He laughed.

Grinning, she nodded before continuing, "We lived a few months in Manchester before Father married Clarissa, then we moved to Chelmsford."

The grooves in his forehead deepened. "So many places?"

She laughed. "I take it you've always lived in the country?"

"Except for my years at Harrow," he admitted.

"Ah, then naturally you are familiar with picnicking."

"Naturally, Philomena. Country boys learn how to eat outdoors sooner than they learn to ride."

He licked the tips of his fingers and his thumb as Philomena watched from beneath her lashes. She fought the temptation to openly stare at his hands, but she did marvel at their shape. Long, tapered fingers with callouses. They were strong, yes, but they could also be gentle.

She already knew that, recalling in a flash of insight how he'd lifted the Drydens' little girl the first time she'd glimpsed him in St. James Park.

"You once mentioned a sister. Do you have any other siblings?" she asked.

"No. My mother passed away in childbirth after delivering Imogene," he said.

Her lashes fluttered open. "Oh. I am sorry."

Solomon waved off her condolences. "It's a harsh life in Cumbria, my home."

"In the north?"

"Yes. Our weather tends to be chilly and—hullo? What's this?"

From the shrubbery, a fur ball of a kitten stepped forward.

Philomena reached out a finger and made a welcoming noise. The kitten was curious but leery, yet Philomena remained patient and finally coaxed the kitten into her lap.

She glanced at Solomon, her cheeks pleasantly flushed with embarrassment. "I've a fondness for cats."

He made a smile of gentle amusement as Philomena dribbled water droplets into the kitten's mouth. When he tore a piece of chicken for it, Philomena knew the man was also partial to animals. Another point in his favor? Perhaps the Fates knew what they were doing?

"Pity you can't keep it," he said. "You enjoy the rascal, don't you?"

Her merry eyes lit with a sly, scandalous suggestion. "Who says I can't?"

"I'm sure the Bristol…"

She shook her head. "The hotel will let an heiress do anything she wants."

"If she's willing to pay for it," he warned.

She lifted the kitten, bringing it nose to nose. "I am. I love animals of all kinds."

"What will you name it?"

"It's too soon to name it. I shall have to get to know her better."

"It's a she?"

"Naturally."

For the rest of the afternoon, their topics weren't so personal, but by the end of the day, when he brought her, Nancy, and the kitten to the Bristol Hotel, Philomena reviewed all that she'd learned about Solomon Braxton. It was simultaneously a great deal and far too little, she thought as she climbed the stairs to her room.

She looked forward to dining at the Drydens' home that evening. When Solomon introduced them at the opera earlier in the week, Philomena had liked them.

Absurdly, Philomena looked forward to accompanying Solomon to the Royal Academy's lecture tomorrow. It's not that she held any interest in the Peloponnesian War, but she truly enjoyed being in his company. When she was with him, her body felt as if she'd awakened from a too-long slumber, her flesh tingled.

"Aha! So, there you are, Philomena!"

The greeting startled her, and not in a good way. Lady Lower stood in the hotel lobby.

Heart sinking, Philomena's gaze encompassed her stepmother, Clarissa. She wore a red cloak with a tall collar made of black velvet. Lace cuffs peeped from the sleeves. The shoulders had heavily gilded frogging, giving it a military air. Her headgear resembled a shako, and on anyone else, Philomena would have thought the ensemble ridiculous. The baronet's widow, however, commanded the attention of everyone in the hotel, she was such a compelling figure. Lady Lower was a stunner. Little wonder her father had thrown good sense to the winds and married her.

"Dished," Nancy muttered *sotto voce*.

"Clarissa," Philomena said with a noticeable lack of enthusiasm. She handed the kitten over to Nancy. "Take her to the kitchens for milk, won't you?"

Nancy curtsied to Lady Lower before leaving.

"I've come to invite you to dinner," Lady Lower said with a thin smile.

Frowning, Philomena wracked her brains for an explanation of how Clarissa had tracked them to the Bristol. It couldn't have been through Holden; she had dropped him off at the Horse Guards before checking into the hotel.

"Mr. Peck's clerk told you where to find me," Philomena guessed.

"Yes."

Hoping to throw her off-scent, Philomena said, "Odd that he would be so cooperative with you. He was not so with me."

"Is that right?"

"Yes. Mr. Peck was out of the office when I called, but his clerk wouldn't tell me when he was expected to return." Philomena deliberately refrained from telling her relative she'd finally read her father's trust.

"What a shame."

She clenched her fists, hating Clarissa's phony sympathy.

"So, you and Holden haven't eloped?" Lady Lower asked.

"Eloped?"

Her voice squeaked on the ridiculousness of that suggestion. For several moments, Philomena stared at her stepmother before laughing.

"You're quizzing me. How stupid of me not to realize it sooner."

Philomena's mirth turned awkward as it dawned on her that Clarissa hadn't been joking. Shuffling from one foot to the other, she wasn't sure what to say.

"Well, when you both disappeared at the same time…" Clarissa trailed off as the corners of her mouth twitched.

"Coincidence, I assure you."

"If you think of it, marriage to Holden wouldn't be so terrible, would it? Your father would have wanted the alliance, rest his soul." Clarissa dabbed the corner of her dry eye with the edge of her lace sleeve.

Stiffly, Philomena responded, "This really isn't the time or place to have such a discussion."

"You're right, of course, which is why you must come to dinner tonight. Holden will be there, too."

"Holden is much too young to marry."

"Not if I give permission."

Wary, Philomena tried to extricate herself from this uncomfortable conversation. "We'll discuss this later. I'm afraid right now I have a crashing headache."

"Where were you, by the by?"

"Shopping," she lied.

Clarissa's brows lifted. "You didn't purchase anything. The only package I saw you carrying was that scrawny kitten."

More smoothly than she could have believed, Philomena said, "I ordered some dresses, which won't be ready until week's end. Finding the kitty put my other errands out of mind."

"I know you and Nancy are inseparable, but there's no need to bring your companion tonight. Give your servant an evening's respite."

Philomena's hackles rose, and she demurred. "If my headache goes away, I shall dine with you to—"

"Fine. Tonight at seven." Clarissa failed to turn away quickly enough to hide her smirk.

Having spied that evil grin, Philomena was glad she was already promised to the Drydens. She would not join Clarissa and Holden for dinner. Nothing good could possibly come from it, and Philomena didn't wish to embarrass Holden with the silly idea that they would marry.

Fretting, she entered her room. Before she closed the door, Nancy demanded, "What did she want?"

Touching her wrinkled brow, Philomena admitted, "She wants me to marry Holden."

Eyes as round as saucers, the companion gasped, "What?"

Philomena nodded. "Clarissa invited me to dine, alone, with her and Holden this evening."

"She'll have your inheritance either way."

"Yes," Philomena said, picking up the kitten and stroking its fur to calm herself. "If I were to marry Holden, he could go to sea and name his mother as his Power of Attorney. For all practical purposes, she'd control my fortune."

"She's very determined. And greedy," Nancy finished grimly.

"We must pack."

"And leave?"

"Yes. I don't feel safe with Clarissa knowing my whereabouts."

Nancy folded her arms, demanding, "And go where?"

Vaguely, Philomena gestured, indicating elsewhere. "Outside London."

Even as she uttered the words, it felt as if a tiny arrow stabbed her heart. She would miss Solomon.

"It must be done," she said aloud, as if to quiet her misgivings.

"May I remind you that you've less than three weeks to marry or become a pensioner?"

"I'm well aware!"

"Then why run into the country where eligible bachelors are so scarce?"

"It's not as if they're thick on the ground in London," Philomena noted.

Nancy sliced her hand through the air. "You have a pair of decent prospects, so pick one now. Once you marry, the bull's-eye will be removed from your back."

It was difficult to argue with Nancy's assessment, but for some reason, Philomena found herself dangerously dawdling.

"Who's it to be—Mr. Braxton or Herr Schuler?"

Philomena cast a sidelong glance at her irritated companion. "I hardly know either one of them. I haven't spoken German since I lived in Dusseldorf, and that was fifteen years ago."

"The sooner you marry, the better."

Philomena lay on the bed and groaned. "I can hardly approach the gentlemen and propose to them, can I?"

"Why not?" Nancy shrugged.

Propping herself up on her elbows, Philomena gawked. "Propose—myself?"

"What I'm suggesting is that you take your future into your own hands. Why wait? Get married, move so far away that you'll be out of Clarissa's reach."

Sitting up, Philomena said tentatively, "Herr Schuler was a nice gentleman."

"True. Very nice."

"He's already wealthy, so I don't believe he'd squawk if I were to ask to keep part of my fortune for myself."

Her companion agreed, removing an evening gown from the wardrobe then spreading it out on the bed. "I should think he'd be a generous husband."

"Living as far away as Germany would certainly keep me safe."

"Absolutely." Nancy motioned for her mistress to rise so that she could unbutton her muslin day gown.

"I don't love him," Philomena tapped the kitten on its nose. "There's no 'zest' between us, but I don't suppose we'd have to live together. We could have a marriage in name only."

Rolling her eyes, Nancy cooed, "And if you later had another man's baby, Herr Schuler would, by law, still be considered its father, and he would not shame a child."

Alarmed by the thought she could so far forget herself and cuckold her husband, Philomena wrung her hands together. Forbidden fruit was alleged to taste sweeter, and how much sweeter would it be to make love to a man tall enough to look her in the eye? These were worldly considerations, indeed.

She whispered, "Don't think poorly of me, Nancy, but I suspect I need that zest."

Nancy nudged Philomena to step out of her gown and chuckled. "Course you do. Will you propose to Mr. Braxton before dinner or afterward?"

Chapter 8

"Shall we play whist?" Winsome suggested, rising from the dinner table after a long meal. "Miss Lower, would you care for that?"

Winsome was being thoughtful, trying to entertain his guest, and Solomon had never been more grateful for her gracious nature because his temper was on edge.

Solomon had been delighted when Winsome invited Philomena to dinner, and since their balloon outing, he'd anticipated tonight's entertainment. He'd truly enjoyed Philomena's company. Hell, he'd even found pleasure in petting her expensive horses her father purchased with blood money, and didn't that mark him as a traitorous son?

So, where had his charming companion gone?

Philomena Lower had been as stiff as lumber as soon as she'd arrived with her companion, Nancy. Her demeanor grew rigid when the children appeared with their governess before the meal, and the color drained from her cheeks.

Arianna had performed a perfect curtsy, dimpling in the process. She really was the very image of her mother, Vivian, Charles's first wife. Nicholas had delivered a rather sticky salute, being an exact replica of Charles.

Rather than being delighted at Arianna's antics and Nicholas's adorableness, Philomena had looked as if she were sickening with the ague. Her countenance was bleak, as if she'd been sentenced to be hanged like a common criminal, rather than being entertained by the Dryden children.

She'd been tense throughout dinner, often dabbing a small gathering of beaded perspiration that clung to her upper lip. Solomon kept count of nearly every occasion she'd done this because he'd been closely watching her mouth, wondering what it would be like to kiss her. As the meal progressed, though, his desire waned. Had he offended her again? If so, she over-reacted, particularly for an offense so slight he couldn't bring it to mind.

Philomena Lower's mercurial moods were becoming tedious.

He ran his hand through his hair, wondering if a friendship between them was viable. Could she have discovered their fathers' connection? Is that why she appeared so inanimate this evening?

"I apologize for losing the thread of conversation," Philomena said, having the grace to look shamefaced when prodded by Winsome.

Charles gave Solomon a quizzical, sideways glance, which he shook off. Solomon was just as baffled by Philomena's distracted air as his host.

This fiasco of a dinner couldn't end soon enough.

"I asked if you'd care to play cards," Winsome repeated.

"Yes!" Her enthusiastic response was disproportionate to the treat, and Philomena realized it belatedly. She blushed.

Chattering now, she assured Winsome, "Yes, Mrs. Dryden, I enjoy cards. My father taught me to play whist."

Philomena gracefully rose from the table, missing his jaw tightening at the mention of her father.

A marvelous idea came to him. If he couldn't convince Miss Lower to do right by his marquisate, then he'd give her a taste of her own medicine. He'd beat her at whist, and to rub it in, he'd cheat.

It wouldn't be anything that would ruin the heiress, just enough to make it sting so she'd understand his circumstances. If he combined Philomena's mite to his winnings from last night, he'd have enough money to buy coal and perhaps a new plow.

"While you finish your port," said Winsome, "I'll ask the footman to set up the card table." She then took Philomena by the arm, and they left the dining room.

Charles held his finger aloft and shushed Solomon, waiting for the women's footsteps to become fainter. Once the drawing room door snapped shut, he faced Solomon and demanded, "What did you do?"

"What did *I* do?"

"Clearly, she's angry about something." Charles's wave encompassed Solomon's person. "That something must be you. Did you ask her to return the fortune?"

"Not yet."

Charles placed his chin in his palm and drew his brows together. "Are you sure you haven't offended her?"

Solomon shrugged.

Charles said, "I can't imagine why she'd behaved so rudely to such a high-ranking peer. You'd think a commoner would see the folly—"

Reluctantly, Solomon lifted his gaze to meet his friend's accusing one.

"What *have* you done?"

Tugging his cravat, Solomon admitted, "She doesn't know I'm a marquess. She thinks I'm a commoner, too."

"Good God."

"I told her my name was Solomon Braxton."

Charles pinched the bridge of his nose, a gesture Solomon interpreted as him restraining his desire to strangle someone.

"Although it's technically correct, it won't matter," the married man flatly told the bachelor. "Why in God's name would you mislead the woman? Your chances for restoring the marquisate rely upon her."

"I didn't want to reveal my identity in case she knew her father cheated mine out of a fortune."

"My God. Winsome!" Charles scooted his chair back so quickly it scratched the floor.

Solomon flinched.

Striding away, Charles said over his shoulder, "You'd better pray Winsome hasn't mentioned anything about you being a marquess."

They entered the drawing room, apprehensive and nearly on tiptoe, as if they'd been summoned to the headmaster for canings.

Once they'd gained the drawing room, Charles smoothly inquired if things were all right.

His wife's lips curved, and her eyes glowed warmly, indicating matters were better than the gentlemen had any right to expect.

Solomon cleared his throat then sat at the card table. The four played whist for more than an hour, Philomena having finally cast off the pall that had held her in its grip, and Solomon not cheating.

A perceptible loosening occurred in Solomon's chest. He hadn't realized just how much of Philomena's tension had transferred to him.

When the game finished, Philomena spied the ormolu clock on the mantel. "It's already eleven? I had no idea it was so late. Thank you for the lovely dinner, Mr. and Mrs. Dryden, and your children are charming."

"It was wonderful to have you, Miss Lower. I hope you'll visit again," Winsome said in a friendly manner.

Charles echoed his wife's sentiments.

Philomena glanced at him, and he bowed.

"Shall I fetch your cloak, ma'am? And send for your companion?"

"Oh." She touched her cheek, dismayed. "I… I had rather hoped… hoped for a word with you, Mr. Braxton?"

"Mr. Braxton?" Winsome's gaze darted toward Solomon, and he was saved as Charles swooped in and said, "By all means. Dobson, would you send the tea tray into the drawing room?"

"Thank you," Philomena murmured, biting her lip.

"Dobson, please fetch Miss Nancy. I feel certain she will wish for tea," Solomon instructed.

Even if Philomena didn't have a care for her reputation, he did. It was highly improper to seek out a private conversation with a man. Philomena must know this. It would explain her present awkwardness.

"Goodnight, Miss Lower. Laz," his hostess said with a glint in her eye.

Solomon understood he'd have some explaining to do for Winsome tomorrow. She would not let this mix-up of titles and names stand. Women, he'd noticed, were very protective of other women, and he sensed that Philomena and Winsome were fast becoming friends, which would make her defense fierce.

Taking his wife's elbow, Charles said, "Goodnight. Come, Winsome, let's ensure the children are tucked into bed."

As prescribed by societal rules, Solomon left the door to the drawing room ajar as they awaited Nancy's arrival.

Philomena wiped her forehead.

She was uncomfortable. Solomon waved her to the sofa.

What possible reason could Philomena have to request a private meeting with him? Something which mattered more to her than the conventional rules regulating male/female relations, but he remained mystified. And more than a little leery.

"Oh, dear." She frowned. "You have a rather mulish look on your face."

If she were intent upon embarrassing herself in front of his friends, Solomon had every right to be as uncooperative as he liked. His expression did not change.

She stared at him then blinked several times before glancing away.

His gaze traveled over her brown curls. In certain lights he glimpsed reddish tones, hints of tiny flames. Her eyes reminded him of the woodlands near his home, and those freckles were flesh-colored stars twinkling from a clear Cumbrian night sky. A picture of innocence, intelligence, and something else he couldn't quite define.

Her cheeks became blotchy, staining her satiny skin then creeping down to the sides of her neck. Lacking her usual fluidity, Philomena jerked upright to pace the length of the room. Her color remained high, and her fingers entangled themselves.

"Would you care for a sherry?"

"Yes!" The word burst from her mouth like the shot from a canon. "Please," she said, more demurely.

He lifted his brow, and her shoulders curled inward, as if she were cringing at her gaucheness.

He reached for the decanter of sherry, but she stayed him by clearing her throat.

"Do you know I don't care for the taste of sherry? May I have whisky instead?"

His eyebrows shot up, but he silently poured whisky for her.

Taking the glass, she smiled nervously then drank the contents in a single swallow.

"Miss Lower," he tried to warn.

She sputtered and thumped her chest.

Patiently, he waited for her to catch her breath.

"Strong." She smiled ruefully. With a shake of her head, she murmured, "I never dreamed this could be so difficult."

"Drinking whisky?"

"No." She pressed her gloved finger against her upper lip, dabbing at the perspiration. Frustrated, she yanked the gloves off and held them in her hand.

"Are you all right?" he asked.

"Yes," Philomena said the word slowly, uncertainly. Then she placed her whisky glass upside-down on the sideboard. With a snap of her gloves, she patted the bottom of the whisky glass. "Yes, I am. Thank you for asking."

Philomena raised her gaze, staring straight at him. Her mouth opened, but no words fell out. She frowned at the phenomenon, squared her shoulders, and tried again.

The hairs rose on the back of his neck.

"I need to marry. Immediately. Straightaway."

His knees almost buckled.

There were a thousand things he thought Philomena might say, but never would he have guessed this. No wonder she thought nothing of her improper request to be alone with him! Philomena Lower was a highly improper young lady, her innocent look notwithstanding.

Taking a deep breath, he stepped backward to create some distance between them. His temper flared, and he angrily shoved his hands into his pockets so that he wouldn't shake her until her teeth rattled.

"What is the meaning of this?" he asked in a harsh voice.

Her eyes took on an owlish look. "I have to marry. I must be married."

Why the hell had he given her whisky? That couldn't be healthy for the baby. His gaze dropped to her belly then meandered upward, lingering on a well-rounded bosom. Her décolletage was splotchy, a blush covering her exposed skin, but Solomon couldn't say if those blushes were shades of embarrassment or shame.

His hands shook with fury as he poured himself a whisky then tossed it off in short order. Balefully, he stared into the glass, wishing he could horsewhip her lover who'd left her in such an untenable predicament. Solomon carefully placed his glass on the sideboard, far from hers.

He glanced at the door, hoping Nancy would soon arrive and escort Philomena home. He would bid her farewell and never see Philomena Lower again.

To hell with recouping his father's swindled fortune. He'd do as Charles suggested, vacate the manor house and lease the premises. Solomon and Willy could live in one of the estate cottages. He'd make other arrangements for Olivia.

Losing the marquisate through chicanery galled him. The father/daughter team didn't have one shred of integrity, which disgusted him, but the majority of Solomon's anger was saved for himself. Just as his father had been bamboozled by the baronet, he had been duped by the daughter.

"Miss Lower? My presence is requested?" Nancy asked. She hovered on the threshold, wearing a concerned expression.

Solomon remembered Nancy's comment about deceptive appearances at the balloon ascension. The old girl must have been sly to her mistress and tried to warn him. Too bad he'd been so slow on the uptake.

Solomon gestured sharply toward Philomena. "Your mistress requires your assistance in returning to the Bristol. I hope you have both enjoyed your evening."

Stalking out of the room without a backward glance, Solomon underscored the end of their acquaintance with a terse goodbye.

Philomena gaped. "I'm not to receive even the courtesy of a reply?"

"No!" Solomon roared, spinning toward her, which was a critical error.

Philomena's pale face crumpled asymmetrically. Something cautioned him that Philomena Lower would be an ugly crier. She'd be the kind of woman whose sobs would tear at a man's conscience and heart. At least, that's how he felt now.

She brushed a few tears from her eyes and blubbered, "I'm so sorry! I honestly thought we might suit. I didn't mean to offend you—it never occurred to me…"

"It never occurred to you?" His voice splintered like shards of ice. "Did you think I'd welcome your cuckoo into my nest?"

"Cuckoo?" Nancy gasped, clutching her chest. She sat heavily in a nearby chair.

Hunching her shoulders, Philomena wrapped her arms around her waist and rocked, back and forth, on her heels.

Alarmed, he roughly asked, "Are you going to be sick?"

She swayed faster but remained silent, save for a couple of despairing sniffles, which nearly drove him to his knees to beg her pardon. He'd never seen such a pathetic sight, and it moved him.

Solomon didn't know how much longer he could hold out against Philomena. He forced himself to remember his father's humiliation, his oath, his tenants' destitution.

"Well?" he prodded.

She lifted her face, revealing a pair of glistening tear tracks on smooth, colorless cheeks.

An angry glow crept into her eyes as she thrust out her chin and came to where he stood. Challenging him, she asked, "You think I'm pregnant? That I'd foist my child onto you?"

Solomon could never recall what exactly set off his temper again. Whether it was Philomena's defiance in standing toe-to-toe with him or the phrase 'my child,' but he snapped, not caring whether he sounded belligerent.

"Aren't you? Clearly, some lucky bastard planted his seed within—"

The remainder was never spoken as Philomena slapped his cheek so hard his head whipped to the side.

Instinctively, he touched the stinging surface of his face then slowly balled his hand into a fist.

Philomena stared at her reddening palm, shocked.

A veil of silence fell upon the drawing room, muffling all noise save the ticking of the clock, which sounded as loud as thunder.

Slowly, Philomena's gaze met his, and he saw her pain laid bare in her tear-filled eyes.

He felt an utter cad.

With her skirts whipping around her long legs, she darted from the room and slammed the front door.

Nancy flinched.

He stood, pressing his fist against his forehead as the flesh of his cheek burned. With his icy rejection and heated insults, Solomon couldn't believe he'd been so cruel to her.

Quietly, her companion explained, "Mena's not with child, my lord."

He noticed she referred to him as a lord, but that matter didn't concern him at the moment.

"Why?" he asked, unable to be more coherent.

Drawing a deep breath, the companion explained, "Mena turns twenty-five at the end of the month. On Monday, she learned there's a stipulation on her inheritance—she must be married before that birthday."

"She didn't know this until Monday? Of this week?"

"Yes, my lord." Nancy quickly walked to the foyer, donned her wrap, and took Philomena's cloak from Dobson with a mumbled thanks.

"Wait." Solomon stayed Nancy as she stepped into the night air. "Dobson, bring my coat, please. I'll walk the ladies home."

They departed without speaking, shocked by the nasty discovery that Philomena had not waited on the pavement.

"Foolish woman," he cursed. "Walking alone in London."

Nancy cast him a look full of antipathy. "Well, we both know the reason for that, don't we?"

Meekly, he nodded. A sense of crushing failure lent his feet urgency.

Chapter 9

Tugging on her gloves for warmth, Philomena bit her bottom lip to keep from crying. Her hand still stung from the slap she'd administered, but that would fade in time, she consoled herself. She was appalled she'd slapped another person. Never had she dreamed she'd be capable of such violence, but when Solomon—in that hate-filled, harsh voice she didn't recognize—made that vulgar remark... Well, Philomena reacted without thought.

How dare he impugn her honor? How dare he dismiss her so contemptuously, without the courtesy of a reply?

She'd been so nervous about proposing, too. She gave a bark of mirthless laughter and tugged her gloves again. Chiding herself for leaving the Drydens without her cloak, she lengthened her strides.

Considering the nightmarish quality of the past half hour, Philomena marveled how stupid she'd been to think she and Solomon would suit.

Dashing tears away, she was grateful for the chilly night air to cool her hot cheeks. She turned the corner, glimpsed the Bristol Hotel ahead, and quickened her pace.

Out of the corner of her eye, she spied someone coming from the shadows. The person lunged at her, ramming her and knocking her off her feet. Robbed of her breath, disoriented, she rose to her hands and knees, but her assailant was quicker. Despite her feeble attempt to scramble away, his strong hands gripped her waist in a punishing hold. Next, he flung her over his shoulder, again knocking the wind from her. Seeing spots in her vision, she balled her hands into fists and pounded his back, terrified she was being kidnapped.

As she was on the verge of screaming for help, he turned sharply and smacked her face against the pole of a streetlamp. The impact jarred her. This heathen would be merciless toward her.

So be it.

Blindly, she twisted her torso then bit deep down on his earlobe, sinking her teeth into the fleshy part with a savageness she found strangely satisfying. He howled and danced around a bit, jouncing her, but she chewed on that tender skin.

He cursed and swung wildly, forcing her to grip the sides of his head. As her hands touched him, she raked her nails down his cheeks until the scrapings from his skin curdled beneath her fingertips. She clawed, hunting for his eyes.

The curses grew louder and nastier.

He tossed her to the pavement where she landed hard on her bottom and an elbow. Her head bounced, and in that instant, she felt utter terror in her soul.

"You'll pay for that, bitch!"

Clamping his hand over his ear, he swore as blood ran down his neck. Clad entirely in black, she could not identify him even as he drew nearer with his fist raised.

She screamed and threw an arm over her head as she tried to crawl away.

A blurred fist shot forth from the shadows, crashing into the side of her assailant's face. With a loud, ferocious battle cry, Solomon Braxton struck the man twice in rapid succession.

They wrestled. Their grunts and groans carried on the night air, accompanied by the crunching of bones breaking as Solomon delivered another blow, hitting her assailant directly on his nose.

Blood arced like a fountain. The stranger's knees wobbled, but only for a second before his legs folded and he collapsed on the pavement.

Stretched flat onto the pavement, her would-be abductor lost consciousness. A part of his ear dangled, loosened from its mooring.

Bile rose in her stomach, forcing Philomena to look away from his wrecked visage.

Solomon hardly looked better. Spittle formed on his lower lip. Blood splatters dotted his crisp, linen shirt and cravat, but it was the frenetic gleam in his golden eyes that alarmed Philomena.

"Good heavens! Is that Mr. Peck?" Nancy squinted in the gloom.

Solomon's head jerked. "You know this man?"

Gasping, Nancy pointed a shaky finger to the prostrate form. "'Tis Mena's trustee, Mr. Peck."

The news jolted Philomena. Bizarrely, she thought it was a hell of a way to meet her trustee.

"Why, that scaly bastard!" Solomon's temper rekindled, and two gentlemen had to restrain him from pummeling the fellow into the pavement.

"Don't murder him, Solomon!" shrieked Nancy.

"Easy there!" cried one of the men.

"Enough!" shouted the other.

Struggling mightily, Solomon hollered for release.

"Call the watch!"

The stranger's words acted like a bucket of cold water thrown into Solomon's face. He drew a deep breath, straightened and brought his arms to his side.

They stared at him warily until he snapped, "I'm fine. You have my word. Someone call for a physician to tend to Miss Lower."

One man lifted a brow, wordlessly asking his friend if he trusted Solomon to behave. With a short nod, his friend answered, and the first man dodged inside the Bristol.

The other man stepped between Mr. Peck and Solomon, pressing his hand against Solomon's chest, as if that might hold him at bay.

Solomon no longer seemed interested in grinding the trustee into a powder. Standing with his hand outstretched, he helped Philomena rise. "Philomena."

Cradling her throbbing cheek, Philomena felt a fresh wetness there. She'd been unaware she'd been crying. Uncertain if she could stand, she allowed him to assist her.

A footman from the Bristol, clad in the recognizable blue uniform, went to check on her assailant while Solomon wrapped his arm around her shoulders, and spun her from the sight.

"Oh, my poor dear."

Despite the throbbing in her head and the thumping of her heart, Philomena heard the anguish in Solomon's voice.

Philomena's gaze flitted to a parked hackney cab, which remained conspicuously still by the curbside. While she watched, the cab pulled away. As it turned the corner, its interior was briefly illuminated by a gas streetlamp.

Inside the hackney, a blonde female drew down the shade.

With a sinking heart, Philomena identified her stepmother. The stinging betrayal drove her to burrow deeper into Solomon's body, which was still vibrating with rage.

His hand ran down her back, bringing comfort and warmth.

"Th-thank you," she said as her teeth chattered. "I... I th-thought he was going to kill me."

"There, there, my love. Everything's fine," Nancy murmured, draping Philomena's cloak around her shoulders. "Let's get you out of the cold, shall we?"

"If I may, Miss Lower?" Solomon asked, pulling out of their embrace.

Philomena stared at him dumbly, having no idea his purpose.

Gently, Solomon lifted her in his arms while Nancy tucked her cloak about her.

"Keep him until I return," Solomon barked.

"Yes, sir."

Once he carried her into the lobby, Nancy asked the staff to send a bath, some ice, and a tea tray to Room Nineteen.

"And have a doctor brought, as well," Solomon tersely ordered.

"Yes. Of course," Nancy added, placing her hand on Philomena as if she needed the touch to anchor her own unsettled feelings.

"I-I-I c-can walk." Despite having her cloak and Solomon's warmth, Philomena felt horribly chilled.

"Allow me this," he said softly, adjusting her weight in his arms. "I'm sorry you were scared, Philomena."

Her throat tightened, preventing her from speaking, although she had no idea what she would have said, anyway.

"I've never been so close to murdering a man. When he slammed you into that pole…"

Astonished to hear the disgust in Solomon's voice, Philomena wondered if he cared for her. No, of course not. He'd cruelly rejected her proposal, hadn't he? He was probably disgusted in himself for displaying such medieval instincts.

Gently, he gazed upon her, and Philomena was heartened to see the feral light had left his golden eyes. Perhaps he retained a hint of the gallant from the medieval knights.

Nancy darted around Solomon, dangling the key from her hand. She unlocked the door then waved Solomon into the sitting room, signaling him to place Philomena on the sofa.

"She needs to lie down," he said, discarding the unspoken suggestion.

Nancy sped to the bed and turned the covers down. Smoothing the sheets, she announced, "Here, you are, pet."

Solomon placed her on the bed, and Nancy unlaced her boots.

Philomena sat, propping herself against a stack of pillows while Solomon sat on the edge of the mattress.

A knock at the door signaled the arrival of a maid.

"Excuse me, ma'am?"

Nancy motioned to the chambermaid to set the tea tray on the table in the sitting room.

"Bring me the ice," Solomon told her.

He brushed a curl off Philomena's brow with such tenderness, her eyes welled with tears. It was quite unfortunate he'd been insulted by her proposal. Remembering what he'd said…

"You're safe now. Don't cry, Philomena."

Nancy brought him the bowl of ice.

He broke off a chunk, removed his handkerchief, then snapped it open. Wrapping the ice in it, he gingerly applied the cold pack to her cheek.

"Is that better, my dear?"

Philomena nodded, unable to trust herself to speak.

Solomon dropped a kiss on her forehead, adding to her bafflement. Why did he have a care for her now when he'd been so cruel in the Drydens' drawing room? The reason escaped her, and she felt lost.

"You'll do," he said, patting her ankle before he rose. "Right. Now, Nancy, you see to it that Philomena bathes while I chat with this Mr. Peck. I'll return as soon as I can. Will that be all right?"

"Yes, my lord," Nancy said.

Again, Philomena experienced that hint that something eluded her. Oh, how she wished her head would cease its pounding. It was enough to drive a person mad.

"Make certain the doctor applies balm to her bruises and gives her laudanum. Is that clear, Nancy?"

Nancy agreed and ushered Solomon from the outer door.

Leaning her heavy head against the pillows, Philomena beckoned her rescue kitten. It sniffed as it approached her then curled onto her lap.

Stroking its fur, Philomena gingerly pressed the ice to her cheek and closed her eyes.

Once the servants brought the pitchers of water, Philomena relied upon Nancy to help her to the hip bath. She winced as she lathered soap over her body, finding the sore spots from Mr. Peck's drubbing. The ritual had the added benefit of cleansing her thinking.

By the time she emerged, pink and warm, several foggy spots had cleared. Her earlier suspicions of Clarissa colluding with Mr. Peck were confirmed. Had the abduction succeeded, Philomena would have been tucked away for a fortnight while her birthday—and fortune—passed.

The scheme had a fatal flaw, and it was that which unnerved Philomena the most. Any kidnapping would be short-term. At some point, she'd either escape or be released. Once freed, Philomena would go to the authorities. To prevent that, to keep the fortune and save her own neck, Clarissa would have had Philomena killed.

Chills traveled down Philomena's spine.

Seeing them, Nancy helped her mistress don a flannel nightgown then hastened her back to her bed.

"I'll be covered in bruises tomorrow," she moaned, easing between the crisp sheets.

"You'll need an unguent for those. If the doctor doesn't have one, I'll go to the apothecary tomorrow and buy the ingredients."

"Thank you."

Philomena determined her first order of business on the morrow would be to confront Clarissa. Just as swiftly as it came, she dismissed the thought. Her stepmother would deny knowledge of the dastardly plot, and Philomena had no evidence against her.

It was perfectly legal to ride in hackney cabs while assaults happened nearby. Even if Mr. Peck implicated Clarissa, there were no guarantees it would rebound onto Clarissa. Who would take the word of a disgraced fiduciary?

"What troubles you most, Mena?"

Slowly, Philomena said, "If he lives, Mr. Peck will be sent to the Roundhouse then possibly Newgate."

"Yes."

"I'm quite certain Clarissa was his co-conspirator. As long as she remains free, how can I feel safe?"

"Mr. Braxton just saw to your safety."

"Rather handy with his fives, wasn't he?"

"He was magnificent."

"Like an avenging angel bent on smiting the unrepentant sinner," Philomena said. Recalling his earlier insult that she was *enceinte,* she added, "But I do not believe I can rely upon him rescuing me again."

Nancy frowned, and the moment was lost upon the doctor's arrival.

The older gentleman conducted a thorough examination, dosed her with laudanum, but didn't prepare an unguent. Instead, he suggested a bleeding.

"Whatever for?" Nancy asked, pouring Philomena a glass of water to drink after the sour medicine.

"For the patient's health," Dr. Harsborough said shortly.

"Nancy knows I don't care for leeches," Philomena explained, wishing he hadn't taken offense. She wanted nothing more than to sleep and hope her soreness faded overnight.

"Nevertheless, I am the physician and know best..." Dr. Harsborough brought forward a box of leeches.

Philomena inched away from the white-headed doctor, repulsed.

Nancy stepped in front of Philomena, using her body to shield her from the doctor. "There's no call for a bleeding."

He wagged his finger at her companion. "You are not to question my authority."

Batting his hand away, Nancy said nothing, but she didn't yield, either. Instead, she remained with her arms outstretched, preventing him from reaching Philomena.

Where this showdown would have ended, Philomena had no idea, but she was grateful another knock sounded at the door.

"Come in!" Nancy hollered, not yielding an inch.

Solomon Braxton cracked open the door and peered into the sitting room.

"Come help!" Nancy shouted.

Philomena's head dropped; she was too exhausted to do more than cringe at the loud bickering between Nancy and the doctor. The poppy syrup began to take hold of her, and Philomena rested her eyes.

Solomon came to the door of her bed chambers and asked calmly, "Is something wrong?"

The doctor jerked his snow-colored head toward Philomena. "This woman won't cooperate. I need to bleed Miss Lower."

"She doesn't need a bleeding," argued Nancy. "She needs an unguent, and this old goat won't provide her with that."

"I say!" The doctor adjusted his glasses, his eyes wide with astonishment. "There's no need to be rude."

"There's every need," Nancy corrected the good doctor. "You're too arrogant to listen."

The beleaguered doctor turned to Solomon, his palms lifted as if he were seeking help.

Raising his dark brow, Solomon peered past the two and asked Philomena, "What do you wish?"

"No leeches," she said, barely able to squeeze out the words. Lassitude crept over her body.

Solomon nodded. "Then you shall not be bled. Can you provide Miss Lower with an unguent?"

"In the morning," the doctor said.

"Don't bother," Nancy snapped.

Solomon sent her companion a silencing glare, which, strangely enough, worked.

"Then we thank you for your services."

The doctor pointed to the bottle of laudanum. "For the patient. You may give her teaspoon in the morning."

"Very good, sir." Solomon escorted him from the room.

When he returned after dispatching the doctor, Solomon quietly asked, "Why didn't you want to be bled?"

"I don't like leeches."

He gave a short laugh. "You're exhausted, and I wish this would keep until tomorrow, but..."

Aware her cheeks were flooding with heat, Philomena grew wretchedly self-conscious, recalling his insinuation she must be impregnated to have proposed. Gowned in nothing but a flannel nightdress, Philomena brought the covers to her chin.

"Would you please stand behind the screen while we converse?"

"Beg your pardon?" Those dark brows slashed across his forehead.

"You. Screen." Philomena pointed, wishing there were parts of her body that didn't ache.

He shook his head slightly, as if it were a mad suggestion, but moved behind the screen.

It annoyed her. Solomon must truly consider her a light-skirt to behave so casually in her bedchamber. Particularly when she was made groggy by the laudanum.

"How is Mr. Peck?" Philomena patted the still-unnamed kitten, glad for the distraction.

"He's conscious, has a broken nose, and lacks the tip of one ear," Solomon said.

"He will live?"

"Definitely."

Nuzzling up to the kitten, Philomena said nothing.

"The watchman has taken him to the Roundhouse, and he'll be brought before a magistrate in the morning."

"What did he intend to do with Mena?" Nancy demanded.

Philomena heard the slight hesitation in Solomon's voice. "To abduct you and keep you under lock and key until your birthday."

So, that *had* been their plan. Philomena shivered.

His voice gentled as he said, "I am sorry, Philomena."

Philomena stumbled onto a rather nasty discovery of herself: she'd rather Solomon Braxton thought her a fallen woman than pity her. Her eyes stung, and she buried her nose in the kitten's fur to hide her emotions.

"Did he implicate Lady Lower?" asked Nancy.

"No."

Eager for her sleep, Philomena told Nancy, "I'm too vulnerable here. Tomorrow we'll remove from this hotel."

"But Peck's been arrested," Solomon said, scowling as he poked his head around the screen.

"Nevertheless…" Philomena gestured for him to remain behind the panel. "Thank you, Mr. Braxton, for rescuing me. I shall always be in your debt."

"Nancy explained why you need to marry so quickly."

Philomena gave her companion a sideways glare, which made Nancy grimace in apology.

Her mortification growing by leaps and bounds, Philomena struggled to stay awake so she could reassure him. "Don't worry about me. I will propose to another candidate by the end of the week. I've already someone in mind, and he's a fine man. Thank you again. Nancy and I agreed you are handy with your fives."

She heaved a sigh and closed her eyes, snuggling deeper under the blankets. "I am tired, so I bid you goodnight and farewell."

"We shall marry tomorrow by special license."

Had the man suffered a blow to his head?

She lifted her lashes to find him now standing resolutely at the foot of her bed.

"We will not," she said firmly.

A glint appeared in his eyes as he moved from the foot to her side.

She yawned then said, "Excuse me. I already proposed, you declined, so the matter ends there. Nothing changes that. Goodnight and thank you, Mr. Braxton."

"That's another thing—" Solomon frowned, rubbing the back of his neck.

If he only knew how appealing that gesture was, he'd dare not do it in her presence. Feeling overwhelmed, Philomena cast an imploring look at Nancy. If she couldn't remove Solomon soon, Philomena would become a watering pot with noisy wails and sobs. She'd rather regain her dented dignity than have Solomon observe that loss of composure.

"Enough. Mena needs her rest. You may discuss everything else in the morning."

Hesitating, Solomon finally nodded. He stroked the kitten in Philomena's lap. "She needs a name."

Philomena caressed the kitten's back, aware of a profound sadness settling in. "Yes."

"Are you afraid of me, Philomena?"

Startled by the question, she answered without thinking. "No."

"Good. I'm sorry I acted like a Philistine this evening—"

"I'm glad you did."

"Then we will marry. By the by, you should always wear your hair down." Before she knew what he was about, he kissed her.

And then he left.

Philomena stared at the closed door, uncertain if the events of the last few minutes were real.

"That's all and well," Nancy said with a satisfied smile. "Now go to sleep. Tomorrow will be a busy day."

Blankly, she looked at her lifelong friend and argued, "He didn't mean it."

"I think he did."

"It wasn't a proposal," she pointed out. "More like an order."

Mena shrugged, as if the manner of Mr. Braxton's proposal didn't make the slightest difference.

Philomena frowned, knowing without trust or affection, marriage to Solomon would be vastly different than what she'd originally thought they could have.

Chapter 10

From the time his feet landed on the floor the next morning, Solomon's pace was frenetic. After dressing, he met Charles for breakfast and announced his decision to marry Philomena Lower that same day. While his friend gaped, Solomon briefly described the trustee's attempted abduction and the hidden trust condition requiring her to marry. Charles's jaw dropped even lower upon hearing that tale.

"Are you certain, Laz? Granted, she seemed nice enough, but... well, are you certain you could have a lasting marriage?"

Solomon grinned. "She's attractive."

"Marriage is more than that. You must be able to be companions, as well as lovers. Do you have any common interests?"

Charles stopped, his face drawn as a sudden thought occurred to him. "Does she know her father fleeced your father? Because it wouldn't do at all for her to think you married her for revenge."

"Marrying well is the best way to replenish my coffers, and living well is the best revenge, so I've heard."

"But you need not have married this particular heiress to accomplish those objectives," Charles argued.

"No, and I haven't," he agreed. "Understand this, Charles, when I saw that man slam Philomena's head against the lamp pole, I was ready to kill him. Money didn't matter. Revenge didn't matter. Neither of those even came to mind."

Charles gave him a steady look before extending his hand. "Congratulations. I wish you both very happy. How may I be of assistance?"

"As to that... I need a loan to pay for a special license."
"Done."
"And can I get a ride to Doctors' Commons?"

Charles laughed then ordered Dobson to call for his curricle.

They swiftly finished their meal before driving to Doctors' Commons for the license, which they took to the archbishop for signing. The trip to Addington Palace necessitated another delay, and once they arrived, the house ran amuck with children, predominantly girls. Loud, shrieking girls.

That dear fellow begged them to come into his private study, delighted to speak with patrons.

"It's quiet in my study. It's my favorite room in Addington," said the archbishop.

Amid a cacophony of shrill screams, Solomon did not doubt it.

He gave them vigorous handshakes, declaiming them, "Good fellows!" Then he apologized profusely for being forgetful, but he was unclear on a point of the Battle of Trafalgar and could they refresh his memory of which wound proved fatal to the late, great Admiral Nelson?

"He lost an eye and an arm," Solomon supplied, cudgeling his memory.

"Oh, Laz," Charles said at his woefully skinny answer then pulled up a chair to discuss military strategy.

"Of course. That was long before the battle, though," the archbishop gently replied then called for tea.

The Archbishop of Canterbury is outranked only by the royal family; despite this, Charles Manners-Sutton wasn't the type of person to stand on ceremony. Solomon rather thought the dozen children archbishop had sired proved him against such vanities, but it wouldn't do to offend the man, so Solomon suppressed his sighs and sat.

Charles, being a former army captain, plunged into a protracted discussion of the naval battle, which veered into possibilities for containing the French upstart, Bonaparte Napoleon, on land.

Normally, Solomon lived in solitude without benefit of stimulating conversation and would have enjoyed this masculine talk. It was no hardship to spend an afternoon with the archbishop, who was an amiable man and generous host. However, Solomon was aware someone had hurt Philomena last night and might try to do so again today. Only by exerting the sheerest willpower did he keep his impatience leashed. While she was out of his sight, Solomon worried for her. He had to see her, make certain she was safe. She would ache today, after last night's assault. Would she be able to rise from her bed? Was Nancy capable of helping Philomena? Did she need him?

After several cups of tea with the archbishop, Charles and Solomon returned to Hanover Square to speak with the reverend of St. George's Church. Reverend Hodgson, a distant relative of the queen, kept them cooling their heels for more than an hour. However, when it was made known that the Marquess of Lazonby wished to be married in his parish that same afternoon, he was as amenable as anyone could wish, so long as one didn't wish to marry that day.

"St. George's is very busy," the reverend informed Solomon. "We have three ceremonies already scheduled for today, if you'd believe that."

Eyeing the empty nave, Solomon gritted his teeth and said, "No. I wouldn't."

A gleam entered the reverend's eye. "Perhaps we can reach an accommodation for next week?"

"No," Solomon growled. "Today, if you please."

"Impossible!"

"But he's a marquess," Charles pointed out, perplexed by the man's intransigence.

"Splendid, my lord!" the reverend clapped and tipped his head toward Solomon.

Frustrated and anxious to be with his intended, Solomon wondered what his next move would be.

Heaving a sigh, Charles dug into his waistcoat for a coin purse and placed three golden guineas in the reverend's conveniently outstretched palm.

"I'll see you tomorrow morning at ten o'clock," said the reverend with a satisfied smile.

Tired and poorer, the two men left St. George's.

Tooling his curricle, Charles said, "You want to pick out a ring for her?"

"Oh, God, it's never ending. I just want to be with her, not do—" he waved his hand, "the rest of this."

Charles offered to send a wedding announcement to be inserted in *The Times*.

"Pick out the ring then go to Philomena."

"Very well," he snapped. "By all means, let's get on with it."

"Have you told her of your title, Laz?" Charles asked, turning the curricle toward Rundell & Bridges, the famed jewelers.

"No, although it wouldn't surprise me if Nancy has told her by now," he said grimly.

Charles sent him a questioning glance, and Solomon quickly explained, "When Philomena dined at your house last evening, Nancy overheard the servants discussing me being a lord, so the faithful companion knows."

"Do you think she'll squeal?"

"Yes. Nancy's devoted to Philomena, like a mother hen with her chick."

Charles whistled then ushered Solomon into the store, paying a street urchin to hold his horses.

"Jewels," Charles advised. "Something expensive ought to do the trick."

The clerk, following Charles's lead, suggested purchasing an emerald cut diamond, but the price far exceeded anything Solomon could afford. He shook his head and asked for something less expensive.

"Mistake," Charles warned.

"Shut up," Solomon replied.

Charles picked out a square-shaped agate stone, which had a beveled edge. "What color are her eyes?" he asked.

"Hazel, but I think Philomena would prefer a simple band of gold."

Neither Charles nor the clerk approved, but Solomon had too much pride to reveal that he didn't wish to use Philomena's dowry to buy her ring. Today's loans from Charles would have to be paid from his bride's fortune, and that rubbed against the grain.

It was late afternoon before an out of sorts Solomon called upon Philomena at the Bristol. The hours intervening since he'd said goodbye to her last night and this moment had stretched out too long. His hope that she hadn't removed from the Bristol was nearly desperate.

Feeling a cur, he knocked on her door, just as any young buck would approach an opera dancer backstage after her performance. He did not wish to sully his fiancée's reputation then remembered they were to be wed on the morrow.

She cracked the door open but, upon identifying him, relaxed and opened it wide. His heart lightened immediately upon seeing her, but then he frowned, noting the bruise blossoming on her cheek.

Grimly, he said, "I wish I'd struck him harder."

Following his concerned gaze, she lightly touched the spot. "Oh, forgive me! I meant to wear some rice powder to disguise the discoloration."

He touched the back of her hand and promised, "You don't need to hide your injuries on my account. I'm only sorry you were hurt."

"And you. How are your knuckles this morning?"

He smiled, showing the back of his hands and the skinned knuckles. "A little stiff."

Her smile faltered, as if she couldn't think of anything to say.

"May I come in?"

"Nancy isn't here."

Solomon welcomed that tidbit of news but noted his bride's discomfort. She stood awkwardly hovering over the threshold, uncertain whether she should invite him into her sitting room or join him in the hallway.

Little wonder he'd made her self-conscious. With a flash of insight, he understood her strange request that he hide behind the folding screen last evening. Because he'd accused her of being unchaste, Philomena was now determined to be a pattern card of respectability.

That would not do. He had no wish to marry a prude.

"Just as well," he said, casually sweeping past her and entering the sitting room.

She swallowed audibly then shut the door.

"Lock it, please," he advised.

"Mr. Braxton?"

"I think we need to discuss some things, don't you? Privately." He laughed and rubbed the side of his nose.

Philomena turned the key then settled herself on the sofa and spread out her skirts.

Amused by her prim posturing, Solomon stood for a moment, drinking in her loveliness. A spiral curl brushed the soft skin of her cheek, and he wanted to wrap it around his finger to feel its texture. What would it be like to be placed in that silken prison?

"You've been present in my thoughts today. I've worried for your health. How are you, my dear?"

Her eyes gleamed, as if she were pleased by his concern. "I'm fine," she stumbled over the words.

He quirked a brow, and she expanded upon them.

"Nancy made up a balm this morning, and that helped prodigiously. So, did you arrange for the wedding ceremony?"

"Yes. Tomorrow at ten o'clock, St. George's. I'm sorry it couldn't be sooner. Do you wish to invite anyone?"

Philomena shook her head. "Only Nancy, of course."

He eyed her before sitting next to her. As soon as he settled into the sofa, he smelled the scent of cloves from the ointment Nancy had created. It was unusual of Philomena to use a spicy fragrance. Without realizing it, Solomon had grown accustomed to the floral perfumes she favored.

"Today you smell like mulled wine," he said. "What scent do you typically wear?"

Solomon lifted her hand and toyed with her fingers while she held her breath. He glimpsed the shock in her eyes as he pressed a kiss onto the back of her hand.

"I vary my perfumes," she admitted. "Enjoying a different one daily."

"But you prefer floral?"

"Yes."

"As do I." His arm wrapped around her shoulders, and he brought her closer to him. "However, that clove scent is quite delicious. Won't you incorporate that in your repertoire?"

Her gaze latched onto his mouth, as if she awaited the words which would drop from it. When she spoke, her voice was breathless.

"If you like."

Solomon took her hand, gripping it loosely.

Staring at the link hands in her lap, she said, "If we are to marry tomorrow, now would be a good time to share any secrets."

His heart stopped as he wondered if she already knew his true identity and the history between their fathers.

"My middle name is Louise, which I despise. Blue is my favorite color. I cannot abide cruelty or deception, and my favorite dessert is strawberry tarts. Oh, and I am not *enceinte*."

He glanced at her mischievous expression. After a few seconds, he asked, "Louise, eh?"

She performed a dramatic shudder of distaste, which made him chuckle.

"Last, but not least, I prefer walking barefoot," she said breathlessly.

He brought her hand to his lips and dropped a kiss into her palm then pressed another onto the pulse point in her wrist. He heard her quick intake before he leaned back and answered in the same spirit.

"My middle name is Phillip. Green is my favorite color. I cannot abide cruelty or deception, either, but my favorite dessert is macaroons."

"I can make macaroons," she offered.

He cupped her chin, careful not to touch her bruised cheek. His lips touched on her winged brow, tracing its shape before pressing against her eyelids. Softly, he brushed the tips of her long, dark lashes, enjoying the tickling sensation against his bottom lip. Lazily, he trailed kisses along the slope of her cheek until he reached a sensitive spot behind her ear.

Her breathing hitched, and a small puff of air stirred the hair at his temple.

Philomena loosened her hand from his to cup the back of his neck. She toyed with the hair at his nape, spearing her fingers through it, and pleasure coursed through him.

Marveling at the combustible qualities of this kiss—mindful that it wasn't technically even a kiss yet—Solomon murmured, "You were right. We do suit."

Lowering his mouth to hers, he meant to give a gentle kiss, but those intentions burned to a crisp as she responded like a dream. Her mouth opened like a flower receiving the morning's first rays, inviting him to deepen the kiss. Solomon did, tasting the richness of her even as her warmth and spicy scent enveloped him in an intoxicating haze. He shifted his weight on the sofa, his body arching over hers as he pressed her against the sofa. Before he considered the wisdom of his next act, he kissed her again. At the start, he'd been intrigued, but now he was engulfed. Passion exploded between them like dry kindling in a hearth. Philomena's lashes fluttered as she moaned deep in her throat. He could get used to hearing that sound. It was appealing.

Finally, he could admit the impatience he'd felt at the archbishop's, the church, and the jeweler's was prelude to anticipating holding a warm and willing Philomena so closely. He was tempted to ease her back and toss up her skirts then take her. Solomon wanted to drive himself into her heat, lose himself in her arms.

"Solomon, there's something I must tell you—"

Too stunned to hear her words, Solomon pulled back. *My God, would I take my bride on the sofa in her sitting room?* No, that was not how a young woman would wish to experience her first time. Pressed against her, he could feel the ebb and flow of her breath, how it rumbled through her chest then thickened her voice. She'd implored him for another reason.

My God, he'd been on the verge of taking her as if she were some light-skirt, and not as his wife, to whom he should show the utmost respect. Appalled how he could have forgotten himself, he pulled back to allow some cooling distance between them. His hand shook as he raked his hair, and he cast her a rueful glance.

He stood and began pacing to work off the steam of his desire. Muttering, he said, "I, too, have things to say, only I cannot quite bring them to mind for some curious reason."

Philomena returned her slippered feet to the floor and smoothed the nap of her skirts. He noted her hands weren't steady as she went about the mundane process of setting herself to rights.

Huskily, she asked, "So, your middle name's Phillip? I thought it was Lazarus."

He frowned, not following her meaning. Solomon might as well have become drunk from her kisses because his usual intelligence had slowed to a near-standstill.

Prompting him, she said, "Charles and Winsome called you 'Laz,' which I thought was short for Lazarus."

"No. It's Lazonby." As soon as he said his titular name, he felt a weight shift from his shoulders. He hadn't liked allowing Philomena to continue believing he was a simple Mister Braxton.

She giggled then said apologetically, "Well, I can certainly understand why you'd prefer Solomon to Lazonby! Truthfully, it's not any worse than Lazarus, though."

"Thank you," he said dryly. "Lazonby is my title."

"Your title?" She took back her hand. Wide-eyed with dismay, she asked, "Are you a peer, Solomon?"

"Yes."

"Oh." She sat back in the corner of the sofa, as if she'd encountered a foul smell about him.

"There's nothing wrong with being a peer," he said, rather snappishly. How many women would have married him for his marquess title alone? Dozens? Hundreds? Yet Philomena Lower acted as if the rank were a contagion.

Waving her hands helplessly, she said, "I… I didn't know."

"Tomorrow morning you'll become a peeress."

More color leeched from her face. "But I don't want to be a peeress!" Too late, she clapped her hand over her mouth. "I mean, I do want to marry *you*, be your wife, but not the other."

Wryly, Solomon said, "I'll never have to worry you married me for my title."

Biting her lip, she queried, "What is your title, anyway?"

"Marquess."

"Excuse me?"

"Are you well?" he asked, amused.

"A marquess?" Her voice was unnaturally high, and her hands fluttered like a flock of startled birds flushed from their nests.

Surely there was nothing so terrifying about being a peeress that warranted this panic-stricken response?

She searched the room then beckoned to her kitten. Philomena scooped her into her arms and stroked her furry coat.

"What's wrong with being a marquess? Or a marchioness, for that matter?"

"Nothing. For you. But for me? It's ridiculous. My father owned a button factory, you see, so I know nothing about proprieties or proper addresses. There must be a hundred things I should know, only I'm too ignorant to even know what those are!"

"Time enough to learn later," he assured her.

Here her hands tangled together, and she looked miserable. "It's not so easy. When I came to London for my season, Father hired an older woman to chaperone me. She wasn't related to us, but she had a sterling pedigree and was in desperate straits, financially. She agreed to 'sponsor' me as her niece in exchange for my father paying all the expenses. He was ambitious and wanted me to marry well."

"Naturally."

Philomena didn't look as convinced.

"He only wished me to marry well for his own sake. My father was not interested in his offspring," she said dryly. "Anyway, Matilda took me to a ball at an earl's residence. I stood behind the wall of palms…"

"Were you shy?"

"I was at seventeen."

"I wish I'd been there to see it."

"No, you don't!" she urged, gripping his arm. "It was awful. Men spoke of the Long Meg Heiress. They agreed my looks were unfortunate, but my dowry was lovely."

Solomon caught his breath at the bleakness in her eyes. "There's nothing wrong with your looks! You're striking and regal. Their unkind words were unjust, and you shouldn't heed them."

She made a casual wave of her hand. "I've heard unkind words before. That's not a problem."

Before he could remark on that astounding revelation, Philomena sadly shook her head. "I could never fit into your world, Solomon. They'd never allow it."

"Come here," he said, opening his arms to her. He was gratified that she immediately set the kitten aside and crossed the room. Like a small, trusting child, she buried her head against his shoulder, and he let his arms enfold her.

"I can feel your heartbeat," she whispered.

Philomena might appear like an Amazon warrior, but she was a sensitive soul. That slight from years ago had been cruel, and it had hurt her.

"Mena, you minx," he said fondly. "I am a marquess. No one tells me what to do. If I marry you, rest assured it's my wish to do so. None will gainsay me."

"Will you like being married to me, Solomon?"

She was like a child, one who was eager to please and win his approval. What a fine wife she would make.

He should tell her about Olivia and Willy. After all, Philomena would be living with them. He should probably admit to his father's lost wager while he was about confessing.

But none of that mattered when Philomena's head was pressed in the curve of his shoulder. Her long lashes fluttered giving just a hint of the woodsy, green eyes behind them. Then she moistened her lips, and all thoughts fled. He kissed her instead. Just as he'd managed to quiet his passionate arousal, she touched his lips and his body leapt into flames.

The next half hour passed so pleasantly Solomon looked forward to spending the next few decades with Philomena. He'd not taken her maidenhead, but his blood remained warm as he strolled to the Drydens. After they married tomorrow, he would explain the wager—and Olivia and Willy's existence. Best not to overwhelm her. Solomon wanted Philomena to enjoy her new home, not dread it.

Chapter 11

By the time morning came, Philomena wondered why she hadn't told Solomon she was no longer a maiden. As her future husband, he deserved to know, but she was afraid of his reaction. If he withdrew his offer, that guaranteed she'd either marry Herr Schuler or live alone for the rest of her life. Neither prospect appealed.

Solomon had been furious when he thought she was *enceinte,* and she agreed it would have been dishonorable to marry one man with another man's child planted in her belly. That wasn't the case, though. Her deflowering happened years ago. There was no chance she carried another man's baby.

Whether to tell or say nothing? The question plagued her. What finally tipped the balance against full disclosure, oddly enough, was her stepmother, Clarissa.

How many times had she told Philomena she was bad luck?

To be consistent, if Philomena told Solomon of her affair with Randal, wouldn't she also have to voice her suspicions that her relative conspired with Mr. Peck to kidnap her? Without proof, Solomon might think her paranoid. Worse, how mortifying was it to declare her stepmother wished her harm? Lastly, might Solomon think she was bad luck after all these tawdry truths were out? He would be eager to be rid of her, and that left Philomena nowhere.

The abduction plot had been uncovered and failed. She would marry tomorrow and secure her fortune. Surely, those occurrences would end Clarissa's conniving? She could stay mum and avoid embarrassing herself. Why speak up and jeopardize her chance for happiness?

Besides, after yesterday's kissing session, it was clear she and Solomon were well-suited. They shared a strong attraction. He had been tender, but he had also been enthusiastic. She did not think he feigned his delight. Recalling some of the liberties he'd taken, Philomena no longer fretted about her lost maidenhead. Solomon had proved himself a man of the world with all the usual, healthy appetites. He treated her as an equal, as a person who knew her own mind. She and Solomon could have a happy marriage. All the makings of a good union were there.

Philomena was more concerned about learning how to be a marchioness. She had been sincere when she told Solomon she was ignorant of high societal mores and didn't know the first thing about how to conduct herself as a peeress. Frowning at her reflection, she recalled how he'd assured her she could learn the role. Perhaps she was creating mountains from molehills?

Thrusting her shoulders back, she resolved that neither heiresses nor marchionesses were nervous nellies. Today Philomena Lower looked like any stylish, wealthy, young woman in London, and that image surely would not discredit Lord Lazonby.

She'd purchased this new gown of pale blue silk. The sleeves were pleated from the elbow to wrist. Tiny seed pearls ringed the plunging neckline, and a large pearl nestled between her breasts on a delicate, golden chain. The fabric of her bonnet matched the dress, and a finely netted veil also had seed pearls.

Donning her specially dyed gloves, she thought the guineas she'd spent for the outfit would prove worthwhile if Solomon's eyes lit up when he saw her. Wrapped up in such giddy thoughts, Philomena was eager to marry Solomon Lord Lazonby. Even though she'd been severely hobbled in her husband hunting, she couldn't help but congratulate herself. Despite the pressures of a deadline, Philomena believed she'd chosen an excellent spouse.

She and Solomon should have a happy marriage.

When she looked at Solomon, she saw a man, not a marquess. Strangely enough, when Solomon looked at her, she felt *seen* as a person; she didn't think he saw her merely as an heiress. He seemed happy in her company, as though he enjoyed her presence, unlike her father and Clarissa, who bemoaned it.

She and Nancy walked to St. George's, and Philomena believed the soles of her feet scarcely touched the pavement.

Solomon was waiting for them outside the church, holding the Drydens' son, Nicholas. He was pointing at a passing carriage, and the toddler seemed enthused by its progress, chuckling at the turning wheels. Solomon would be a good father to their own children, unlike her own father had been to her. On the street outside the church, Philomena's heart warmed that she might soon carry Solomon's child. Would he be a doting husband, as well as a kind father? Watching him with Nicholas, Philomena felt those hopes were justified.

Wearing a sapphire-blue jacket of Bath superfine, an ivory cravat, and pale-yellow pantaloons, Lord Lazonby commanded attention from passersby. His waistcoat was made of ivory silk and trimmed in navy. The jacket showed off his broad shoulders. The cravat provided an excellent contrast with his dark looks. His lordship's handsomeness stole her breath.

How could she, Philomena Lower, cursed with bad luck, have been so fortunate to land this man as her husband even as the odds were so stacked against her? A smile broke out on her face, and her heart flipped. Her good fortune was enough to make her feel giddy. It was all she could do not to dance a jig up the church steps.

He turned into the church and handed the toddler off to some woman, a nanny, she supposed. It was rather deflating that he hadn't seen her, nor did he appear to have been waiting for her at the church's steps.

"There's his lordship," Nancy said.

Spying them, Solomon gave a brief, unsmiling salute before leaping onto the dais.

Her joy appeared one-sided.

Reeling from that blow, Philomena dawdled in the doorway, suddenly assailed by doubt.

"Come now, Mena." Nancy's words were brisk, as if she'd sensed nothing amiss in the groom's greeting.

Philomena took a calming breath then entered the church.

Charles Dryden greeted her with a wide smile, motioning her to remain in the vestibule while he sat his wife, children, and governess.

He returned from the pews and issued a hearty greeting. "Good morning, Miss Lower, Miss Nancy. You both look lovely. Arianna has just informed me, Miss Lower, you look like a princess who's stepped out of her book of fairy tales."

Smiling at his warmth, Philomena extended her hand and gripped his tightly.

"Oh, thank you for saying so, Mr. Dryden! I am excessively nervous today, and that was exactly the right thing to say."

"So is Solomon," he whispered, chuckling. "You will be pleased to note, however, that Winsome and I have remained remarkably calm."

Able to give him a fleeting smile, Philomena wondered if it were a good sign that both members of the bridal party were nervous.

Nancy preceded her and Charles down the aisle. Philomena's gazed fixed upon her groom, who waited, still unsmiling, next to the reverend.

Heart hammering, Philomena gave a quick, backward glance to the tall doors. She had this wild notion that Clarissa might try to prevent this wedding.

What occurred at the altar, Philomena only hazily recalled. She was poignantly aware of Solomon's quiet, somber presence. His voice, low and serious, recited the vows. The words, familiar and yet foreign, touched her, reaffirming the sacredness of her vows. She whispered the words, humbled by the moment.

After the vows were spoken, Solomon placed a golden wedding band on her finger. It was exactly what she would have selected for herself.

As the reverend announced them by their titles, they faced the congregants. Solomon beamed with triumph, while Philomena only felt relief that the ceremony was concluded without mishap.

Hand in hand, the bridal couple stepped out of St. George's church in Hanover Square, dazed by the afternoon sunlight. Standing beneath the portico, Charles clapped Solomon on the back while Winsome and Nancy took turns hugging them.

Solomon kissed the back of her gloved hand and grinned. One would think he'd emerged a victor after the spoils of war had been divided. She grinned as her memory flashed back to the excellent jab he'd delivered to Mr. Peck. Solomon had successfully flattened her former trustee.

Solomon slid his arm around her waist and tugged her against his side. Her heart rate increased, and giving into impulse, Philomena kissed his cheek.

He looked surprised. She laughed, glad she had thrown him off-balance.

She was safe, her fortune secured, and looked forward to their marriage. Perhaps all of Clarissa's scheming had come to naught; mayhap she actually had served Philomena a good turn.

"Ready?" he asked, waving toward the hotel.

"I am," she said, not believing her good luck.

THE PARTY FILTERED through the Bristol's pair of wide doors and meandered toward the private dining parlor Solomon reserved for their wedding breakfast.

Charles ordered champagne so frequent toasts could be made throughout the meal of carved ham, eggs, hot cross buns, and wedding cake doused in rum. Solomon enjoyed himself, disregarding the costs of these items and the expense of renting a private room. It was such a change, not having to worry about money. He could kiss his wife for that gift alone.

After the Drydens left and Nancy was safely seen to her new room, Solomon faced his hesitant bride, alone in their suite. He'd been anticipating this moment from first seeing her standing upright in her fashionable phaeton. With a shock, the idea returned that she had been brought into his life by the Fates.

Quietly, he strolled toward her, removing his cravat as he did so. He stopped and looked around the room. "Where's the kitten?"

"Nancy has taken her."

"What did you name her?"

She giggled. "Rascal. I was stymied, but you were right. She needed a name."

"I like it, actually."

The sight of her, tall and willowy with her bright, shiny eyes and the becoming flush on her cheeks, stirred him. Gently, he touched that cheek, hating when she flinched.

"Sore, eh? You hid the bruise quite well."

"I'm wearing rice powder. Nancy applied it with a rabbit's foot," she said.

"No one will ever hurt you again, Philomena," he promised. "You are mine to protect for the rest of my life. By the shield of Lazonby's winged lion."

"Thank you, and I you."

He chuckled. "You will protect me?"

Solemnly, she said, "If need be."

Placing his hand in the small of her back, he steered her into the bedchamber. "Don't be nervous."

"I'm not," she whispered.

Solomon removed the pins from her hair, letting it tumble to her shoulders where he fanned it. "You didn't wear your hair down."

"You meant that?"

"Of course I did." He cupped the back of her head and kissed her.

His kiss had originally been intended to wordlessly assure his bride he'd be a considerate lover, but it had been stupid to think it could remain so. After yesterday's interlude, Solomon's appetite had been thoroughly whetted.

Only the desire not to frighten her kept his passions in check. Solomon belatedly realized he'd been wrong to viciously pummel Peck in Philomena's presence. She had been horrified by the violence, and he didn't want his wife to fear him. That was the only reason he restrained himself now. A fearful bride could make this first, unpleasant joining even more painful.

She pressed herself against him, and he felt his body enflame. The passion was half a heartbeat away, and his flesh sizzled in anticipation. He deepened the kiss, wanting to taste her, teach her. His hands roamed over her form, molding her lithe shape to his. Cupping one of her breasts, he was pleased to find she was perfectly proportioned. His hand passed over her nipple once and she shivered with desire. Solomon found himself spiraling into wanting and needing.

"Solomon," she moaned, arching against him as her hands caressed his shirt off his back. She tugged it loose from his waistband, and he chuckled.

He'd heard virgins were unable to govern their passion, overwhelmed by emotions. Such was the case with Philomena. She was ardent and impetuous.

"Shh," he said, not wishing to rush through their first joining. Solomon wanted the experience to be good for her. He knew that not all of it would be, and he needed her to savor this part and remember it afterward, so when he took her maidenhead, she wouldn't feel bereft or cheated.

"I want you." Suiting deed to word, Philomena unbuttoned the fall of his pants. Her fingers were nimble—and experienced. He watched the quick work she'd made of unbuttoning his pantaloons. Philomena was unerring in the task, working without hesitation.

His blood turned to ice.

His bride was no shy virgin.

From that seed, a noxious weed quickly took over, sprouting all kinds of leaves and shooting upright with speed. Who was her lover? When did she have these relations? Could she even now be pregnant with another man's child? Did she, as he originally suspected, mean to foist that child onto him? As a possible heir to the marquisate?

Never!

He made a sharp inhalation, grasped her wrists, then placed them at her sides. "Enough," he said, harshly. "Enough."

He watched the light of desire fade from her eyes. No longer supple, her body had stiffened in alarm.

"Solomon? What's wrong?"

Viciously, he turned from her, too angry to be near her. "I asked you before but never received an answer, so I expect one now: are you with child, madam?"

As the silence lingered, he glanced over his shoulder.

She swayed, as if she would swoon, like some missish chit, which he knew very well she wasn't. Hadn't she slapped the fool out of him in Charles's drawing room? Then bit through Mr. Peck's flesh? Philomena Lower was no delicate maiden!

He swung around, grabbed her shoulder, then placed her, sitting, upon the edge of the bed. He quickly removed his hand.

"Speak!"

Philomena drew a shaky breath. "No. I am not with child, as I've told you before. I do not lie."

He recalled she'd said something to that effect the day before, but resentment washed over him as he recalled, too, how her father had swindled his own out of a fortune.

She ignored his scoff and continued, "No, I'm not a virgin. I lost my virginity years ago."

The words burned into him, eating at him like acid. In disgust, he faced away from her.

"You heard of my London season. I told you before what a disaster it'd been."

Philomena continued, "I'd been humiliated. My spirits were very low when I returned home. With age comes wisdom, and I can see I was very naïve and vulnerable. I fell head over heels for the first man who placed his heart at my feet."

Solomon remained quiet, sickened. He did not wish to hear his bride's recounting of her paramours.

Her tone pleading now, she said, "Please understand. I was so young. London's finest gentlemen had rejected me, saying my only attractive quality was my fortune. On the heels of that, an earnest young man approached me. Dashing, daring, and something of a Corinthian, he made me believe he loved me, that we would marry."

He couldn't ignore the pain in her voice. Despite his anger, he turned to her. He hesitated, on the verge of silencing her, but halted upon seeing Philomena's expression.

The planes of her face had softened in memory; her eyes welled. Plainly, she had loved that man. It nettled him.

"It was heady stuff, being pursued so avidly," she said wistfully. "Particularly after such a disastrous coming out."

Solomon made a sharp intake, not wanting to hear more. Gruffly, he said, "You need not say anymore."

She continued, as if she were lost in the daze of reminiscing and hadn't heard him. "He proposed. Like many young lovers, we anticipated our vows, but he assured me it was *pro forma*. Afterwards, he left me with the promise he'd ask my father for my hand."

Solomon frowned. As much as he disliked hearing this tale, he could find no wrong in what Philomena and her young sweetheart had done. It was a tale as old as time. Hell, he'd almost taken her yesterday on the sitting room sofa.

He faced her. "Were the banns called?"

"No. I never saw him again."

That shocked him.

"Who was he?"

"I'd rather not say." She bowed her head, clasping her hands before her.

"And since then?"

She gave him a puzzled look. "Since then, what?"

Enunciating with undue care, he asked, "How many lovers have you had since that first one?"

Recoiling in shock, Philomena paled and drew her hand up to her mouth.

His eyes narrowed. From her horrified reaction, she was either innocent or a consummate actress. Mockingly, he told himself his wife was no innocent, by her own admission.

Those moss-green eyes fired with flames of indignation as she shot at him, "None! Despite your ugly insinuations, I'm not a loose woman."

The word formed on his tongue in an instant, leaving his mouth. "Unbelievable."

Philomena gasped.

Silence hung between them, and he felt a tightening in his chest that warned him he'd just made a bad situation worse.

Quietly, she asked through trembling lips, "Are you calling me a liar?"

Solomon frowned, uncertain. It was a serious accusation to level against a person, particularly one's wife. He didn't undertake it lightly, but knowing human nature as he did, he found it ludicrous to think one could taste forbidden fruit and not hanker for a second bite.

A wave of color rose in her décolletage then speared up her throat. Stiffly, Philomena said, "I have answered you fully and truthfully."

Flinging her hand out, she went on the offensive and demanded, "If I asked *you* about your former lovers, you'd resent my prying!"

Perplexed, he asked, "What does that have to do with anything?"

"Only that I'm entitled to the same courtesy, and I resent your unfair treatment."

"How is this *my* fault? By your own accounting, you gave yourself to someone not your husband. Do you expect me to be grateful?" He threw his hands into the air and spun away from her. Stalking toward the window, he snapped, "Do you want the names of my prior lovers? Do you?"

"No," she said, her voice as cold as ice. "I am merely pointing out your hypocrisy."

"Hypocrisy?"

"Yes, hypocrisy!"

"It's different for men."

"It ought not to be."

"But it is." He pinched the bridge of his nose.

After a while, she asked wearily, "So, where does this leave us?"

He chanced a look at her. Philomena stood on the far side of the room, her shoulders curling inward.

How he hated it when she tried to make herself look small. Solomon frowned, thinking of what needed to be done next.

The solution was obvious and distasteful but necessary.

"We abstain from intercourse."

"What do you mean?"

"We'll have a platonic relationship until I'm certain you're not carrying another man's child."

"You won't take me at my word?" Her voice was quiet but raw.

That band tightened across his chest. It spurred him to go to her, to close the distance between them. Once he stood opposite her, he took her hand and held it loosely.

"I want to take you at your word," he assured her.

She raised her gaze to him then, showing that tender, hopeful light kindling in the depths of her eyes.

"But I cannot," he said, feeling like a murderer as he watched that light die.

She removed her hand from his grasp.

Her bowed head couldn't disguise the trembling chin and quick knuckling of tears.

Feeling the need to lessen her pain, he tried to explain, "I am a marquess. My primary duty is to ensure continuation of the bloodline. I must be certain any child of mine is a rightful heir."

She sniffed but kept her head lowered.

He preferred Philomena flare and glare at him rather than huddle before him like this. This situation was growing desperate. Now was not the time to discuss Olivia and Willy. That could keep until later.

Cajoling her with a light-hearted tone, he said, "Philomena, this isn't personal. It's just that we haven't known each other very long. Trust takes time, and I need that time."

"Take all the time you need," she said woodenly.

He should have been glad she agreed with him, but something about the way she said it made him wary.

"So, then it's agreed?"

"Yes, it's agreed."

Her voice sounded distant and cool. Briefly, her gaze touched upon him before skidding past, leaving Solomon frustrated.

He had every right to expect that his bride be virginal, yet somehow, Philomena made him feel as if he were in the wrong. Feeling this wedding night marked the zenith of missed opportunities, he bowed to her. "I'll leave you the bed."

She didn't acknowledge his statement.

He returned to the sitting room and stretched out on the sofa. The beginning of their marriage was not auspicious. Damn the man who'd taken her virginity, and damn the others who'd partaken of Philomena's delights. He wouldn't be one, at least, not tonight.

Staring at the closed door adjoining the two chambers and recalling her coldness, he conceded he wouldn't be able to make love to his wife for the foreseeable future.

He kicked the sofa cushion.

Chapter 12

When Philomena exited her bedchambers the next morning, she deliberately timed the event to take place after her husband's departure. He was the last person on the planet she wished to see, and she had no idea what to say to him.

Her husband.

She shivered. The man she'd married—Solomon Braxton Lord Lazonby—was a stranger. It had never occurred to her that he would still think she could be pregnant with another man's child. Nor had she imagined how much importance he'd placed on her being a maiden.

She'd never be able to see the world through an aristocratic prism where a woman's worth was tied to her fortune and chastity. Those historic remarks about her 'smelling of the shop' had been cruel but true. It was her grandfather who had purchased the title of baronet, an honor her father had inherited and never merited.

The gulf between their stations wasn't the only matter that distanced her from Solomon. The man clearly didn't trust or respect her. He thought her a light-skirt, and that filled her with shame. Clarissa and her father's mocking that she was bad luck echoed in her ears.

Nancy entered after knocking, her face wreathed in smiles, which disappeared once she inspected Philomena.

Rascal trotted in after her companion.

Philomena lifted her chin, and her lifelong companion gestured to the blanket left unfolded on the sofa. "What's this?"

Scooping up Rascal, Philomena found it easier to address her remarks to the kitten rather than Nancy. Calmly, she said, "Lord Lazonby has elected not to share my bed."

"What?"

Cradling Rascal, Philomena said, "I mustn't repine, because, as you once informed me, I have liberated my trust, which was the sole purpose of marrying."

"Sole purpose?" Nancy asked skeptically. Her gaze searched Philomena's, filled with concern.

Feeling her control slipping away, Philomena made a sharp nod.

"Oh, my little lamb!" Nancy's arms enveloped her in a fierce hug.

"No, don't." Philomena pulled away, sniffing. "It's taken me all morning to rally my spirits, and if you show me sympathy now, I'll turn into a watering pot."

Turning from Nancy's too-encompassing gaze, Philomena admitted, "He knows I'm not a virgin, and he's still convinced I'm carrying someone else's love child."

Nancy gasped, clutching her chest. "Devil take him! That was years ago. Doesn't he know how much you suffered?"

Coolly, Philomena replied, "I doubt my suffering interests anyone outside this room."

She moved to the dressing table, signaling Nancy to style her hair by handing her the brush. Moping, she complained, "I should have asked Herr Schuler to marry me."

"Don't go down that road," Nancy counseled, running the silver-plated hairbrush through Philomena's curls.

"What am I to do, Nancy?"

Her companion thought before she spoke, a rarity. Finally, she said, "You can't divorce him."

"No."

"Can't annul either, because you've no grounds for that, do you?"

"What kind of grounds?"

Grimacing, Nancy said, "I think you have to allege that one of the two of you cannot… um… well, cannot."

Philomena stared at her companion, trying to comprehend what she was saying until it struck her. "Oh!" she said, putting up her brows. "That's dreadful."

"So, an annulment will not serve," Nancy spoke tentatively.

Philomena frowned. "I see my mistake now. As soon as I discovered that stupid trust provision, I should have told Mr. Peck to go hang and give me the yearly stipend. We could have leased a cottage by the sea and lived peacefully, just the two of us. You'd have liked that, wouldn't you?"

Nancy shook her head. "Sounds dull."

That made Philomena laugh. Doing so brought her to the realization that life wasn't so terrible. She was young and healthy, as was Solomon. He overreacted last night, but so did she. Once they were calm, they could come together. In time, perhaps they would be able to laugh about their disastrous wedding night. In time.

She lowered Rascal to the floor, having come to decision. "I made a vow in church yesterday."

"Aye."

"It would be foolish to give up on a marriage after only a day," Philomena said.

"Very unsporting," Nancy agreed. "So, what if you have to wait a short bit to consummate your union? Time will prove his lordship bacon-brained. Give him a chance to get to know you better, to understand your character."

"He said he needed time. I suppose I must be patient and allow trust to grow between us."

"Fine words, Mena, and I know it won't come easily to you. Mark my words, though, the best things in life are worth the wait."

With these resolutions, Philomena chose to adjust her thinking. She must view Solomon's reluctance to consummate their marriage as a precaution, and not as a rejection. Although it chafed, she acknowledged she had under-estimated how jealously a marquess would guard his lineage. Her husband was simply performing his duty as he thought best—bacon-brained as that might be.

Philomena's newfound equilibrium lasted throughout the morning but vanished soon after her husband reappeared for luncheon.

He escorted her and Nancy to the lobby and ordered their meals. Philomena bristled but calmly replied that she was glad he did not order the beef tongue, as she didn't care for it.

"Would you prefer to order for yourself?" he asked, his dark brows lifting.

"Yes, until you learn my food preferences, I think that would be best, don't you agree?"

He accepted that cool suggestion with good grace but directed his next comments to Nancy, so Philomena wasn't sure if making her point had been worthwhile.

She suppressed a sigh, reminding herself that Solomon was just as new to this marriage business as she was and was also finding his way. She should have expected the first few weeks of marriage to take some adjusting. After all, they were practically strangers to one another.

"I met with Mr. Peck this morning." He withdrew a folded document and slid it across the surface of the table. "Marriage settlements have been approved."

"So soon?"

He shook his head. "I didn't wish to delay his departure to the continent."

"I beg your pardon? Is Mr. Peck not going to be tried?" She touched the side of her still-bruised face.

"No."

"May I ask why?" Aware of a hardening in her tone, Philomena could not change it.

His golden gaze flickered to her, and she received the strong impression he did not care to have his decisions questioned.

Did he imagine all this trust-building would be solely on her side? To use his word, unbelievable.

"It's not worth the scandal. Now that you are my marchioness, it wouldn't do to kick up a dust about Lady Lazonby's swindled fortune." He spoke the words with a tinge of bitterness.

"What's to become of him?"

"He wrote a confession." He indicated the paper on the tabletop. "In exchange for an agreement to never return to England. He and Lady Lower will sail for Italy later this week. Apparently, they are boon companions."

"So, he implicated Clarissa in this plot to deprive me of my inheritance?"

"No."

"Did Holden know, too?"

"I don't think so. If you wish, your stepbrother may reside with us at Lazonby."

"Holden intends to join the navy, my lord," Philomena murmured. "I would have preferred Mr. Peck face punishment. As the victim of his dastardly design, I should have been consulted as to my wishes."

She studied his countenance for a response to that, but he continued eating as if he hadn't heard a word she'd said. It angered her. Apparently, he *did* think she was the only one in this marriage who must prove herself trustworthy.

Nancy rested her elbow on the table, forgetting her manners. "My lord—"

"Never mind, Nancy," Philomena said, standing and throwing her napkin onto her half-eaten plate of food. "His lordship has already decided the matter and has indicated any information from me would be superfluous."

His golden eyes flashed in anger. Speaking in a clipped voice, Solomon said, "I shall be preoccupied with business for the rest of the day. Are there any preparations you wish made before we travel to Lazonby?"

Choosing to say nothing for fear she'd say too much, Philomena stalked from the dining room.

Nancy caught up with her, tugging on her sleeve. "Mena. Mena, please. You said you would be patient!"

"Odious, oppressive, obstreperous man," she muttered.

"You're being redundant," Nancy joked. "I think his lordship took those steps with a mind of protecting you. How could he know?"

"Precisely! How could he know without asking me? That's what bothers me the most. It's as if I don't exist."

"Mena!" her companion scolded. "That's unfair."

Philomena rolled her eyes.

Nancy reminded her that Solomon was a marquess, and as a lord, he was used to ordering people about. As a new husband, he failed to appreciate that wives should be consulted. "You must be patient, Mena."

Grudgingly, she agreed.

Several hours later, a knocking sent Philomena flying to her chamber door, hoping to find her husband and to apologize. Regretting her earlier rudeness, she flung the door open with eagerness.

"Is there a fire, sis?" Two pale blue orbs started from their sockets.

"Hullo, Holden. Won't you come in?"

Disappointed, she took a moment to master herself before following her stepbrother.

Nancy left, mumbling she had chores in her room to finish. "I'll ask staff to send up a tray."

"Thank you, Nancy."

Holden began, "Saw the paper. Can't say I'm surprised. Deuced clever of him, but I suppose all's well that ends well."

Philomena asked what he was talking about.

"Lord Lazonby. Marrying you. He and his friend, Mr. Dryden, dropped by the Marylebone residence last week, asking for you. Told me the whole story. I told him plain he should leave you be, but... ah, well! I daresay snagging a title has its compensation, and he's a fine figure of a man. No hardship to be with him, and I can see how his situation appealed to your quaint sense of justice."

Just as confused by the end of this speech as she was at the beginning, Philomena frowned. "What are you talking about? What situation?"

"Your husband's father and Sir John." He nodded to her, then the smile slid off his face. "Didn't he tell you?"

"Tell me what? I have no idea what you're talking about, Holden."

Another knock brought Philomena to her feet to answer it, with far less enthusiasm than she'd shown moments before.

The maid carried the tea tray, so Philomena directed her to place it on the table. After she departed, Philomena explained to her stepbrother, "Solomon and I married yesterday at St. George's. There wasn't much time to talk of anything."

Had it only been yesterday?

"Would you care for biscuits, Holden?"

"Er... gladly." He ran two fingers beneath his neckcloth. "I didn't mean to say anything. Forget it. Not my place. I came to congratulate you and tell you I'm going out to sea. On the HMS *Shannon*. Could you spare me a guinea 'til quarter day?"

"Naturally. Who's the captain?"

"Broke. He's a scrappy fellow, trains his crew to an inch, or so I've been told." Holden helped himself to the plate of biscuits as Philomena poured the tea.

Once he accepted his cup, Philomena asked again, "You met Solomon last week?"

He nodded, his mouth full.

"You told him to leave me be?"

Again, he nodded and uttered a muffled agreement.

"What occurred between Solomon's father and my own?"

Holden wiped a hand on his knee then swallowed. Looking miserable, he said, "There's no button factory, Philomena. I tried to tell you, but Nancy wouldn't let me speak. Remember? In your phaeton? On the way here?"

"I remember. What do you mean there's no button factory? Has it been sold?"

"There never was a button factory."

"What? That can't be! Father made his fortune—"

"He made his fortune by gambling and cheating people. Your husband's father was one of his plucked pigeons."

The words were succinct, but Philomena had a difficult time comprehending them. "Father cheated?"

"His lordship claims he had proof Sir John fixed a horse race at Newmarket. Wiped out the entirety of his father's fortune."

"Dear God." Philomena covered her mouth, feeling bile rise in her throat.

"He thought to lay it all out before you and Clarissa and see if you'd be willing to 'right the wrong,' so to speak. I told him Mother would never agree to that and he ought not to pester you with it, either."

"I see."

"Are you alright, sis? You're awfully pale. You know something? I don't really need the money, after all. I'll be reporting to the docks in two more days, and then we set sail for the Colonies on Friday."

Holden rose. Philomena gave him some money, but she had no idea how much. She thought she said all the proper things, wished him well, but she only recalled one detail of his leave-taking.

At the door, Holden said, "Don't look so sad, Mena. I'll visit whenever I'm in England, and not just for the money." He made a weak laugh at his joke.

To be polite, Philomena smiled.

Cocking his head, he looked at her with some concern. He chucked her chin, kissed her nose, then said, "Don't worry, Mena. Matters have a way of working out for you, sis."

"Do they? It feels as if I'm a magnet for bad luck."

"Course not." He hugged her one last time then was gone.

Chapter 13

It was the second day of their journey to Lazonby, and his bride wasn't blushing unless it was from anger. Solomon's glance flickered over Philomena's form. She was neatly dressed in a pale-green gown with darker green detailing, and she looked as pretty as a picture and as distant as the moon.

Since their wedding night, relations between them had soured rapidly. There was no pleasing the woman. He'd arranged for her former trustee to disappear in a manner that guaranteed he could never harm her again. He'd managed to chase the malevolent Lady Lower out of the country then offered to take in Philomena's stepbrother. He thought these acts would delight Philomena; instead, she had withdrawn from him and acted as if she held him in disdain.

Lord Lazonby was not used to being held in disdain, and the experience did not agree with him.

His wife had two temperatures: white-hot or icy cold. She was also an extremely stubborn, argumentative, and overly sensitive person.

Admittedly, he knew when he sold her phaeton, she might not care for that, but once he explained the impracticality of having an open conveyance in northern climes, he felt certain she'd see reason.

She had not.

What had he received for his long-thinking? Basilisk stares, monosyllabic answers, and an unrelenting view of her profile.

In all fairness, he'd been the one who decided there'd be no sexual congress between them, but it wasn't necessary to bar all intimate relations between them. He'd suggested a lovemaking that fell short of an actual joining, but Philomena practically singed his eyebrows when he offered that.

After last night's vehement rejection, he'd tossed and turned, sleeping little. However, this morning, he awoke, determined to restore them to friendlier footing. To that end, Solomon served her breakfast, heaping food on her plate. She'd ignored that, too, choosing instead to sip a cup of tea only. When he asked if she were an indifferent traveler, she gave him another sullen look and asked whether it mattered.

He took that as another dig that he hadn't consulted her regarding Peck's situation or selling her phaeton.

Wordlessly, he threw a beseeching look toward Nancy, but she didn't lift her gaze from her plate. There'd be no help from that quarter. The companion had maintained a careful muteness ever since leaving London.

Actually, both ladies' attitudes had soured toward him even before that. An arctic front had emerged two days ago, and Solomon wasn't sure he could weather the upcoming storm.

Well, he'd be damned if he lived under the cat's paw. He'd get to the bottom of this before the sun set on another lonely night.

"Care for a stroll, wife?" he asked as he pulled the new landau into an inn for their luncheon. He experienced another twinge in his shoulder, as he had on and off throughout the day.

"No," she answered.

Anticipating her, he captured her elbow and guided her steps toward the open field. "It's such a marvelous day. I insist."

She tried to break his hold, which only incensed his temper, and he tightened his grasp.

"You're hurting me," she said petulantly.

"Stop behaving like a child!" he hissed. All the same, his grip slackened.

He wanted to shake her, turn her over his knee, and spank that delectable bottom. Mostly, he wanted to hold her and kiss her, like he'd done the day before their wedding. It wasn't wrong to wish to cuddle with one's wife.

When they walked to the breast of the ridge overlooking the small town of Rugby, he released her and barked, "Out with it."

"What do you mean?" she asked coolly, averting her countenance.

He made a sound of exasperation and flung out his palm. "Philomena, stop this."

She darted him a quick glance.

It wasn't much, but it was something. It emboldened him to continue, "If Peck remained for his trial, it would have necessitated returning to London then testifying against the scoundrel. It would have made all the scandal sheets. Do you really want that?"

One shoulder lifted.

Pinching the bridge of his nose, he tried again. "I wanted the man out of the country, far away so that he could never harm you."

She lifted a brow. "Or where he'd never squeal on you."

His head jerked. "What do you mean by that?"

She folded her arms and lifted her chin. Those verdant, woodland eyes turned into chips of frost.

Had Philomena plunged an icy dagger into his heart, Solomon could not have imagined she could have wounded him more. His chest tightened, and his hopes for an amiable marriage dropped to the bottom of his belly. The tenderness and trust which had been written in her lovely gaze the morning they married might never have existed. He could have mourned their loss.

"You think I was in cohorts with Peck? Have I forever forfeited your trust in me?"

Philomena hastily looked away. "You married me for my money, and I find it no easier to trust you than you trust me."

She could have slapped him again, he was so stunned by her accusation. Staggering back, he clutched his chest, as if to ensure that a knife weren't actually planted there.

"I didn't marry you for your money—"

"Bah!"

His anger spewing to volcanic propulsions, he shouted, "*You* were the one to propose to *me*."

"Because I thought you were different."

"What the bloody hell does that mean?"

Wearily, she slumped. Her shoulders crumpled like a bridge swept away in the torrents of a flood. She brushed a stray curl from her still bruised cheek.

Philomena appeared so young, so untouched. No more than a small, frightened girl, who was alone in the world save for her loyal servant. His wife, infinitely dear and indescribably sad.

Throughout his life, Solomon had made mistakes while discharging his duties to his family and the marquisate, but none of those shortcomings were felt as keenly as the stunning revelation that he had failed his wife.

"Never mind. It doesn't matter," she said in a voice drained of emotion.

"If it didn't matter, I wouldn't be discussing this with you in the middle of nowhere now, would I?"

"I don't want to talk about this." She turned away from him.

"But we must," he said, touching her shoulder.

She shrank from him.

"Can you not bear my touch? Why do you act as if you hate me?" That thought, coupled with her suspicion that he'd colluded with her trustee, struck him like a blow. "My God, Philomena, *do* you hate me?"

Remaining silent, she gripped her chin to keep it from trembling.

Solomon inhaled sharply, sure that dagger had found its mark. A shaft of cold drove into his body, dispelling any sense of warmth or wellbeing, and his head jerked back from an invisible force.

Seeing his distress, Philomena reached for him.

"Do not!" he said harshly.

Pivoting away from her, he worked to control his temper by taking deep breaths. When he spoke, he stared at a faraway point, unable to bring himself to look at her. He carefully washed all emotion from his voice and said, "When we return to the inn, I'll write to Charles asking him to purchase your phaeton back. As to Peck, I don't know what's to be done about that. The man was to set sail yesterday. I suppose I could hire…"

He ran his hand through his hair. "No. It'll never do. For one, the price of hiring a Bow Street runner to go overseas would be astronomical, and the fellow wouldn't have jurisdiction in Italy at any rate, even if he could locate Peck."

"Solomon?" She sounded timid, unsure.

He closed his eyes, hating the hint of vulnerability in Philomena's voice, despising how his heart contracted in response to it.

"Leave Peck be. You were right about that, I suppose. I'm sorry for saying you conspired with him against me. I didn't mean it."

Solomon drawled, "I'm elated to hear it."

Philomena glanced at him, her mouth quirking a little.

"Humor, Philomena? It's inappropriate to be amused by the one you hold in contempt."

Her eyes widened in hurt, but it didn't move him. She'd flung enough arrows in his direction these past few days that he felt justified in returning a few volleys.

Too foul-tempered to accomplish anything else, Solomon returned to the inn, leaving her alone, as she obviously preferred.

She might have called to him. He couldn't be for certain it wasn't the wind he'd heard. Solomon wouldn't turn back. His wife had made her feelings perfectly clear. She wished to punish him for having sold her blasted phaeton. Well, Miss Lower would discover she could not treat the Marquess of Lazonby like an errant schoolboy!

Solomon did not share his luncheon with his traveling companions. Rather, he sat at another table and wrote the letter to Charles. He folded it, franked his name on the outside, then set two pence aside for the boot boy to send it on the mail coach.

The trio left the inn, speaking only of barest necessity. He bowed to the ladies, opened the carriage door, and shut it without saying a word.

"I've forgotten something," Philomena said.

Sighing, as if this were a great inconvenience to him, he re-opened the door, set down the steps, assisted her out of the carriage, then waited for her return. She did so, glancing at his face as she remounted the steps and entered the landau.

"Comfortable?" he asked with heavy sarcasm.

"Yes, thank you," she said in a small voice.

Furious, he slapped the steps into the closed position and hoisted himself onto the bench. Snapping his riding whip over the horses' heads, he gave the office to start. They left the inn yard with speed, and Solomon did not spare a backward glance for the little town of Rugby.

Within a few miles, his temper had cooled, and he found himself wondering if his wife weren't a heartless mercenary who favored possessions above people. Perhaps she just really enjoyed her phaeton?

It was grand with its color-coordinated spokes and upholstery. He'd kept her team of grays, so she had no complaint there, but her crane-neck phaeton offered a young spinster a taste of freedom she otherwise might never have had.

Unlike him, Philomena had not been used to deprivations for the past seven years. Possibly, she found it difficult to accept the loss of luxuries, just as he'd once done.

Mayhap the phaeton was a gift from her father, and she'd attached some sentimentality to it. If that were the case, he understood her resentment, and he had wronged her by selling it so cavalierly.

He frowned, recalling that Philomena had once confided that her father hadn't taken an interest in his offspring. He'd wanted her to marry well for his sake, not hers.

Sir John Lower didn't sound like the kind of man to inspire sentimental attachment.

By the time they put up for the night, Solomon didn't know what to think of his wife. If he wished to know her mind, he must ask her. He saw now that a husband must consider his spouse's feelings, and that he was no longer a bachelor with only his desires to consult. He should have discussed selling her phaeton.

Well, with any luck, Charles would be able to purchase it back and have it delivered within the month. Retrieving the phaeton would be a damned nuisance, but Solomon accepted that as part of his penitence.

He supped in the public parlor, having ordered two supper trays for Philomena and her maid. Solomon chose to eat his meal alone. Again. Two straight days of driving had left his right shoulder sore, and he was too tired for company of any kind.

The waitress was giving him heated, sidelong glances, swaying her hips in a provocative manner as she fetched his dinner. When she placed his plate and ale in front of him, she did so in such a way that her bosom fell right at his eye level. It was a glorious bosom, smooth and rounded with an intriguing shadow in its cleft. If his lips followed the shadowy trail, he might find momentary pleasure and release.

It had been a long time since he'd been with a woman. Longer than he cared to recall. He considered her soft, tempting form as he pushed away his half-eaten meal, speculating on the possibilities of mounting the nubile body.

Giggling, the waitress removed his plate, deftly leaving behind her key.

"Number 9, up the stairs and to the right," she invited in a breathy voice meant to entice.

Interested, intrigued, tempted—Solomon was no stranger to those stirrings in his loins, but it was the first time in his life when he was no longer free to pursue them. Recalling the darkened interior of St. George's church, the reverend's stentorian tones as he recited the wedding vows, and how a shaft of sunshine had highlighted the reddish glints in Philomena's curls, he pushed the key away.

"Thank you, darling, but I'm not alone."

Crestfallen, she made a moue with those full lips and said, "Oh, shame."

"Yes, isn't it?" he drawled, ruing the loss of what could have been a satisfying, vigorous exchange of pleasurable activity.

Suddenly, the waitress stilled then winced and backed away from his table.

He didn't have to turn around to know Philomena was behind him. He heard her low chuckle. Lifting his tankard, he hid another smile, this one of genuine amusement.

She tossed the letter he'd written to Charles Dryden onto the table then sat next to him.

"What's this?" he said, picking it up.

"It's not the phaeton. It never was."

Solomon pocketed the letter, trying to discern her meaning yet unable to do so.

"I thought the phaeton may have held sentimental value for you, having been a gift from your father."

She nodded. "It was a gift from Father, and I greatly appreciated it. It was wonderful to drive."

"Your eyes glow when you speak of it. Obviously, you enjoyed it. You should have it back. I would by no means steal your pleasure."

"As I have from you," Philomena gave a saucy look and jerked her head in the waitress's direction.

Not rising to that bait, he said firmly, "We are married."

"We are."

"So, where does this leave us?" he asked, repeating the words she'd said when he pronounced they would not consummate the marriage.

"As to the phaeton or the—" Philomena pointed in the general vicinity of the barmaid.

With a sharp exhalation, he stood upright then rolled his shoulder and flinched.

"What is it? What's wrong?" she asked.

"I told you before I couldn't abide deception, and you're deliberately being obtuse." Solomon clamped his hand onto the shoulder that pained him, his anger reanimating. "I thought it was Peck, but you said it wasn't. I thought it was the phaeton, but now you claim that isn't it, either. What am I supposed to think, Philomena?"

"You're hurt." Philomena bit her bottom lip and reached for him.

"It's nothing." Snarling, he turned away.

"Now who's being deceptive?" she said crossly, putting her hands on her hips.

He faced her and bowed. "You are correct. I apologize. My shoulder aches like the devil, and I would seek my bed."

Quirking his brow, he asked permission to leave. When she said nothing, he departed without a word.

Chapter 14

Philomena watched him leave, at a loss as to what to do next. She'd spent the entire afternoon thinking of their talk in that field. She re-played their acquaintance from the start. The salute in the park, the knocking of heads by the milliner's window. If Solomon had contrived these meetings, he was a wizard, not a fortune hunter. And to be so clever as to force her to propose to him within days of their meeting? Oh, yes. Solomon Lord Lazonby was a warlock among men!

She had presented, on a silver platter, the opportunity for him to regain his family's fortune. Of course, he had looked upon it as a godsend. Who wouldn't? Hadn't she considered him the answer to her prayers?

Regardless of whether Solomon married her for money or revenge, she had wed to liberate her trust, which was so near to his purposes as to be indistinct.

If Philomena could not accustom herself to a marriage of convenience, it would be better to live apart. Being at daggers drawn with Solomon created an unbearable strain. She wanted him, blushing in remembrance of how she'd confessed that on their wedding day. As angry and hurt as she was now, she still wanted Solomon, a man who despised her.

He should have left her in London, as she'd requested. Solomon insisted she and Nancy accompany him to Lazonby, and Philomena still didn't understand his reasoning. It was no secret that neither of them found this marriage convenient.

"It isn't safe," he argued, ignoring her arguments.

Since leaving Rugby, Philomena saw his reasoning for shuffling Peck out of the country, along with Lady Lower. It had been the better decision, actually, than the one she initially preferred. She wanted to see her former trustee hang. Having gained some perspective, she conceded it would do little good for Peck to stand trial. The outcome wouldn't immediately ensure her safety but would tarnish her reputation.

As Solomon's marchioness, she must be cognizant of that. She knew how zealously he guarded that title of his.

He had been the one to seek the airing of their differences, and she had been mean to him. Recalling his stricken expression when he thought she hated him—that she had wanted him to think so—fairly made her cringe. That had been unworthy of her, and it was untrue. She had been petty, so wrapped in her own wounded confidence that she had pretended the worse. Where had her better angels been when she'd chosen to make an ass of herself?

Such a bad decision. Now her husband didn't even wish to be in the same room with her. She had nearly driven Solomon into the arms of another woman within a week of being married.

Mortified, she turned and came face to face with the buxom waitress. There was no secret why she would have tempted her husband. Any man this side of the grave would have been willing to bed the woman. She had beautiful coloring and a figure which would make a Greek goddess cry with envy.

"We've argued." Why Philomena revealed that to the waitress, even she didn't know. Was it a plea to leave him alone and spare her embarrassment? Probably.

"Well, then you'd best make it up to your man, for he's handsome enough that any other wench will snatch him up without a second thought. Not that I would, but others might."

Shocked by such plain speaking, Philomena immediately understood that the waitress certainly would 'snap him up' if given a second chance, her denial notwithstanding. It was up to Philomena to make amends for her part of their argument. She was a grown, married woman and must behave like an adult rather than a spoiled child. She threw back her shoulders and lifted her chin.

"May I please have a clean towel and pitcher of hot water?"

The waitress handed Philomena a pitcher of water and instructed her to use the fireplace poker to warm it, then she placed a towel in her outstretched hand.

"I suppose I should wish you good luck," she said with a touch of envy in her tone. Shooing Philomena away, she said, "Off you go."

Philomena darted up the stairs and retrieved the jar of unguent and a packet of headache powders from her room. Grateful Nancy didn't question her actions, she skittered across the hallway and rapped on Solomon's door.

"Solomon? Open up. It's me. Philomena."

After a lengthy delay, she nibbled her bottom lip, afraid he would ignore her as she'd been ignoring him these past few days.

It was a salutary lesson, and she didn't care for it. They needed to get this marriage on an even keel. She determined she would do what she could to arrange matters satisfactorily for both of them.

He opened the door, his tall frame filling the space.

Philomena inhaled quickly, for he had already removed his cravat, exposing the bare triangle of skin at the base of his neck. It was oddly appealing.

"Yes?"

His voice wasn't cold, but it wasn't welcoming, either. She lifted the pitcher and towels. "May I enter?"

He said nothing but walked away, leaving the door ajar.

Quietly, she entered the room. Placing the pitcher on the hearth, she lay the poker's tip in the flames then hung the towel over the screen.

Pointing to the jar, she said, "I brought the healing balm Nancy prepared."

"Thank you."

"You've hurt your shoulder?" She pointed then felt foolish. Solomon would know where his shoulder was.

A crooked smile lifted one corner of his mouth, as if he'd sensed her awkwardness and found it amusing.

Then he stretched out his right arm. "Might have over-extended it when I worked over Peck. Aches prodigiously. We may have to hire a driver for the remainder of the journey. I don't know if I can take another day on the box."

She nodded, as if she'd expected him to concede that.

Blushing furiously, she tried to keep her voice steady as she said, "If you would... um... remove your arm from the sleeve?"

He stilled for a terrifying moment then lifted his black brows and said, "If you intend for me to apply the balm, I can tell you right now that I can't reach."

"No, of course not. I will—" She coughed into her fist. "Of course I'll apply the balm."

He tilted his head, warning her, "It would be better if I were to take off my shirt."

"If... if you like." She touched her cheeks, whirling about as she recalled the waitress's comment of him being a handsome man. To hide her embarrassment, she straightened the towel hanging on the fire screen.

Solomon removed his shirt then sat astride a slatted wooden chair, resting his forearms across the top. He groaned when he rotated his shoulder, and she forgot her embarrassment.

"Let me warm up the balm," she said, placing the poker into the pitcher then dropping the jar in as well.

Chatting to cover her discomfort, she said, "I found it offers more relief this way. Not that I used it like so on my face. My cheeks couldn't stand the heat generated by the pepper and cloves Nancy used, but it does provide some wonderful relief to…" Aware she'd nearly revealed how extensively Nancy had applied it to her backside, Philomena hastily amended her sentence. "Help your recovery."

"Philomena, you're prattling."

Solomon lowered his forehead to rest upon his forearms. He started when she dropped the warm towel over his shoulders. Beneath her fingertips, she skimmed the bunched-up muscles in his back. Like knots in a rope, the muscles had tightened. The constant strain of holding the reins all day would have exacerbated his tension to a painful degree.

Smoothing the warmed towel against his skin, she kept her touch light, allowing the heat to penetrate his skin and begin loosening the knots. Quietly, she moved the towel over his back and pressed it against his skin.

She returned the towel to the fire screen, allowing it to become toasty again. She used the poker to fish out the jar of ointment from the pitcher, jostling it when her fingers closed over it.

"Ooh, hot, hot," she squeaked to his low laughter as she removed the lid from the heated jar.

"Beast," she mumbled with a smile.

Philomena scooped a handful of the ointment and smeared it over his skin.

"Ahh! That is warm. Spicy, too." He straightened in the chair for a moment before returning to his sprawled position.

"It's the cayenne pepper." She said softly, concentrating on massage the knots out of existence. Using the heel of her palm, she put pressure on the lump until it finally gave way. He breathed a sigh of relief.

"Are you well?"

"Better." He made a low grunt, which she interpreted as an affirmative answer.

Alternating between the warming towel and the ointment, Philomena rubbed the length of his spine then over the expanse of his broad shoulders. Occasionally Solomon moaned, but otherwise she worked in silence and followed his scant guidance.

Her hands ran over his skin, tracing the contours, memorizing its texture and color. The tops of his shoulders were darker, as if he'd worked in the sun without a shirt. The shape formed a "V" as his wide shoulders narrowed to his waist. There wasn't an ounce of fat on him. His muscles had been honed into a lean strength that proved deceptive when covered by the layers of clothes society expected.

Neither she nor the waitress were blind to Solomon's handsomeness. Recalling how the female opera goers at the Pantheon had gazed at him with either smoldering looks or speculative glances, Philomena ruefully shook her head. None of them could appreciate Solomon's masculine beauty more than she did.

Save for the crackling of the fire and Solomon's occasional moans, quiet reigned in the room. It was not uncomfortable, but it was bittersweet. Their marriage was a disaster, and she honestly didn't know if it could be repaired. How did one grow trust? Neither trusted the other. He'd kept secrets from her, as she had done to him. Philomena was fast learning that secrets worked like poison in a marriage, killing intimacy.

Philomena had never touched a man like this before. Thinking back on her coupling all those years ago, she couldn't remember even seeing Randall's form. It had been so dark she hadn't been able to view his body. Maybe she had her eyes closed the entire time. She laughed at herself, at her shyness and gaucherie. Even without the benefit of sight, Philomena now had the advantage of touch. Randall's build had not been as powerful as Solomon's, his body not half as beautiful as her husband's.

"I'll drive tomorrow, so your body can heal," she decided.

"Like hell—I mean, no thank you."

Smiling to herself, Philomena pressed her thumbs along his spine from the top of his waistband all the way to his head. Frowning, she realized his knots had traveled to the left shoulder. "My, you are tense."

Again, he grunted for an answer.

She worked that side of his back just as she had the other, trailing her fingertips over his skin, smoothing in the scented ointment. Philomena hadn't been this close to Solomon since they had kissed in her hotel room.

A pang hit her. She had said she couldn't abide cruelty or deception, yet she had practiced both against her husband. At the very least, he had misled her about several things, but those were issues for him to answer on another day. This evening, she had to answer for her own errors.

Clearing her throat, she said, "My lord, I was not happy with your decision about sending my trustee away without a trial, but I realize now that was for the best."

"Thank you, my lady," he said quietly, his breathing even.

"Nor did I want my phaeton sold, but that's neither here nor there, truthfully."

Hearing no response from him, she continued. "What put me out of frame was Holden's visit."

"Holden? Your brother? When did he visit?"

"Stepbrother," she corrected. "He came the day our wedding announcement appeared in the papers. Once he saw it, Holden came to congratulate me. He said it was clever of you to marry me."

He lifted his head from his forearms. "Oh God, Philomena—"

"He... he said the marriage was a just outcome because my father tricked yours, and I'd landed myself a title."

Solomon stood, that golden gaze glowing with concern. "Listen to me."

She shook her head, anxious to tell him the lot of it. "Holden told me Father never owned a button factory. He said he made his money bilking others. I didn't know. Truly. I didn't know."

Thinking of how he must despise her father—and her by extension—agitated her. Despite Nancy's assurances, Philomena really was bad luck. She had foolishly trapped herself in a marriage with a person who would never trust or respect her.

She hiccupped.

"Please don't cry."

"I won't," she said, dashing at the fallen tears.

Heavens, this was even more difficult than proposing had been! She gave a watery chuckle.

He stretched out his hand but withdrew it without touching her. Helplessly, he stood there, hands on his hips.

Nodding as if she understood his reluctance, she said, "You reminded me to be honest, so I'm being honest."

She swallowed then draped the linen towel back onto the fire screen, letting it re-warm. With shaky hands, she secured the lid to the jar and placed it on the small table.

"What with discovering Mr. Peck's perfidy, Clarissa's involvement, and Father's criminality, I've had too many ugly revelations this week. I am sorry you bore the brunt of my anger."

Turning from him, she remembered the headache powders and pulled the packet from her pocket. "You should take this before retiring. It will help further ease your pain."

"Thank you," he said tightly.

This was more dreadful than she'd anticipated. Poor Solomon. He was so tense! She'd heard somewhere that lovemaking could relieve stress…

"Perhaps you should visit the waitress in her room. Such, ah, activities can help you relax."

He gaped.

She hoped her grin wasn't the travesty she felt. "I know you were tempted, and I suspect you'd find a hearty welcome there."

Solomon scowled. "Philomena, I did not marry you last week to cheat on you this week. Give me more credit than that."

Lifting her brow, she quizzed, "You didn't marry me for my dowry?"

"No!"

"To avenge the wrong my father had done yours?"

"No."

She nodded, noting the difference in conviction between his two answers. Softly, she reminded him, "You didn't marry me for love."

From beneath her lashes, she watched him struggle to answer, and she hated herself for putting him on the spot like that, but she also hated him a little bit, as well.

This was going from bad to worse. If she'd hoped to put their marriage on an even keel, she was wrecking that plan.

"Never mind," she said, walking toward the door. "You don't have to answer that."

"I married you to protect you."

To hear him say it aloud stung. She thumped her forehead against the back of the door.

"Philomena?"

"You don't need to protect me, Solomon."

"I disagree."

"Peck and Clarissa can no longer threaten me. You possess my fortune. There's no reason for anyone to harm me."

As she clasped the door handle, another thought occurred to her. Teasing, she said, "If anything, you're the one in danger."

"Me?"

Hearing his incredulity, she gave her first genuine smile in days.

"Yes," she chirped. "The wealthy are targets. Henceforth, you'll either be fawned over or despised for your wealth. You will never be wholly certain why a person seeks out your company."

His golden eyes narrowed to dangerous slits as he considered that point. He cocked his dark head to the side as he reminded her, "What an exasperating minx you are, Philomena. Do you forget that you will be right there alongside me? I will rely upon your judgment to sniff out those who try to take advantage."

"As to that, I won't be alongside you."

Solomon's gaze quickly returned to hers. Scowling, he demanded to know what she meant.

"After Holden's enlightening news, I wrote to a Chelmsford contact—under the trustee's name, of course. As a woman, I've no power."

"You're the least helpless female I know," he muttered.

She acknowledged that with a pert curtsey.

He smiled at her impudence. "At least, my face no longer stings from your slap, but Mr. Peck's ear may never grow back."

"It won't?"

"I don't know," he shrugged with a hint of irritation.

"Well, at any rate, I've ordered this man of affairs to sell the house in Chelmsford and its contents, and to forward the proceeds to Lady Lazonby."

He hesitated briefly before nodding sharply. "Very well. I see nothing objectionable about that."

She remembered her first sighting of Solomon and his jaunty salute of encouragement. She would return that favor for him now. She owed him that much for pummeling Mr. Peck. Possibly, he had saved her life that evening.

"What I propose, Solomon, is that you agree to house me and Nancy until I receive those proceeds."

"House you?"

"Yes. Once I receive the sale proceeds, I'll purchase a seaside cottage for Nancy and me. If you'd pay me a yearly annuity of three hundred pounds—"

"You expect me to pay you to live apart from me?"

She heard him approach. Whirling to face him, she pleaded, "But, Sol, that's what I would have received had we not married. You'll have the rest of the fortune, I swear. I'll sign whatever agreements you wish to that effect."

"Philomena Lower, you damnable tease! You come into my room, pretending to be some ministering angel then invite me to fornicate with the barmaid downstairs, and now you propose to live in some seaside shanty, as if it weren't the most blatant ruse one could imagine!" He pointed toward the door. "If you don't take yourself off at once, it will be very much the worse for you!"

Standing and shivering in the gale force winds of his fury, Philomena cowered. Like a hedgehog under attack, she folded inward, afraid she'd miscalculated again. How could she ever make him understand she meant no insult? Solomon seemed determined to expect the worst from her. Who was the one being churlish now? She was saddened he'd misconstrued her nursing as being a tease—heavens! He still regarded her as a light-skirt. Devastated he believed her desire to live apart was an excuse to be licentious with other men, she wiped more tears from her eyes. She cast him an accusing, mournful look before rushing to leave his room.

Something crashed against the door panel. It could have been a fist, a pitcher, or a jar of unguent.

Philomena had no idea.

Chapter 15

They made it to Lazonby without further incident, Solomon's shoulder feeling only slightly strained by the continuous driving. Philomena's once-off back rub had gone far toward healing him, even as she tore his masculinity to shreds. She again offered to drive for a stretch, but he'd ignored that suggestion, classifying it as yet another one of his wife's preposterous schemes. Like her dream of a seaside cottage, he disregarded it without comment.

Twice now she'd sought to be released from their marriage. She'd asked him to leave her and Nancy behind in London, then in Burton when she said she planned to live apart from him.

If Philomena Lower weren't fully alive to the consequences of swearing an oath before God and man, then… hell, he didn't know what then.

That was another thing about Philomena. She twisted, turned, and spun him in every direction so he didn't know if he was standing on his head or his feet.

He thought she had come to his room to make amends for her churlish behavior in that open field at Rugby. Smiling in reminiscence, he recalled how tender she'd been, how carefully she'd nursed him. She'd soothed his stiff back and shoulders. Somewhere along the line, the massage inspired him to hope they'd end the evening making love. He'd felt the familiar stirring in his lower belly, anticipating the end to a delightful ending. With Philomena in his arms, he didn't think he'd need clove-scented balm or deep, penetrating massages. He needed release. Sexual release. He'd wanted her so badly, he could shove aside his concerns about her already carrying a child. That was how much he desired his wife, damn her.

Those hopes died when she suggested he seek his ease with the waitress. Her lack of faith in him offended him. Deeply. His ire was so ruffled, he conveniently forgot he had been tempted to pursue pleasure with the serving girl.

They had resided at Lazonby for nearly a month, and during that time, matters between him and Philomena had remained as strained as when she'd left his hotel room in Burton. She treated him with civility and distance. Solomon was honest enough to admit that Philomena had merely followed his lead, but he justified his conduct. Although Philomena had insulted his pride by leading him on, then offering an open marriage, then declaring a separation all within the span of a few minutes, he behaved with dignity toward her. He congratulated himself that he hadn't shaken her until her teeth rattled, as he longed to do.

However, this charade of 'civility' would likely be the death of him. He couldn't bear it. It was like punching fog. There was no chance of hashing out their differences because Philomena refused to be drawn into any conversation beyond the commonplace. Unlike the first week of their marriage, when she believed he'd married her for revenge, she no longer treated him with cold disdain. No, the vixen had managed to make displaying good manners a method of torture. The courteous treatment was as bad as her icy disdain had been. Unremittingly, annoyingly polite, Philomena remained as distant as ever. This disinterested treatment was more than a husband could bear. He must be a masochist, but he wished her fiery temper would return.

Since meeting Philomena, he'd dreamed of making love with her. As the weeks passed and she grew farther from him, his dreams had intensified, but they had taken a frightening turn last night.

He'd pictured his wife tending a garden at a neatly kept cottage by the sea. As she pulled weeds, she looked straight at him with teary eyes and the accusatory look she'd had leaving his room at the Burton inn.

I wanted roses, but there are too many weeds. Roses cannot grow here.

He jerked awake, his heart pounding, his forehead covered in cold sweat. Flinging back the covers, he leapt from his bed and ran to the adjoining door between his chamber and hers. Silently, carefully, he cracked the door and peeped inside.

She slept, her brown hair curling around her head like the Madonna's corona. A stream of moonlight slanted across her bed, and Rascal lifted her head from its resting place at Philomena's side.

The kitten blinked then stared at Solomon, utterly still, as if deciding whether he was a threat. Rascal blinked again then lowered her head, snuggling for warmth.

He couldn't even arouse the cat's interest.

Returning to his room, Solomon frowned. He told himself it had been a stupid dream and meant nothing.

Except he couldn't discount it entirely.

The visions were so somber. Philomena's sadness had felt palpable, as if it reached from the ether and gripped him. He scowled, trying to recall the details. She'd given up hope of ever having a rose garden.

What could it possibly mean?

"Good morning, Philomena," he greeted her as he entered the breakfast room. "I don't normally see you in the mornings. What brings you out?"

She wore a faded, woolen dress, as she had every day since arriving here. Was it a sign her spirits were so depressed she couldn't bring herself to care how she looked? In London, Philomena had a wardrobe of fine gowns, tastefully trimmed, but those clothes must have vanished. He'd seen no evidence of such finery since she took up residence at Lazonby.

"Oh, I'm usually up before you, my lord," she said, brushing crumbs off her palms. "I take my breakfast elsewhere."

"Where do you go?"

She lowered her teacup, leveling a serious, questioning look upon him. She gave her head a tiny shake, as if she'd come to a metaphorical fork in the road and declined to tread down a certain path.

"Oh, here and there," she said airily then stood, ready to depart. "Have a pleasant day, my lord."

It might have been the longest conversation they'd had since arriving at Lazonby. They didn't share breakfast, and he usually worked through lunch. She declined afternoon tea, so he shared his in the kitchen with Olivia Rodgers, his housekeeper. From the first night, Philomena and Nancy had elected to take supper in her room. This was their first shared meal at Lazonby, he realized with a start.

Daunted by his bride's relentless cheerfulness, he girded his loins and cleared his throat.

Nancy entered the room, glancing warily from her mistress to him.

"Stay, if you will," he said.

The companion took a seat as Philomena made to leave the room.

Frustrated they'd both misunderstood him, Solomon stood and said, "Philomena? Would you please stay, too? I'd like to ask you some things."

"Yes, my lord?" Her brow arched.

It spoke poorly of their relationship that he couldn't divine if she were curious or skeptical of his interest.

Swallowing nervously, he quickly searched for something to say. "Do you… do you enjoy rose gardens?"

"Rose gardens?" She placed a hand on her hip and wrinkled her nose as though she were giving the thought consideration for the first time in her life. "I suppose."

"Would you... would you wish to plant one?"

"Now?" She frowned.

Had he once believed a rapport existed between them? That idea was sheer lunacy.

"If you like." He forced himself to stop grinding his teeth and to smile naturally.

"Willy and I are making a chicken coop today."

Rascal appeared, leaning against her skirts to purr until she picked him up.

"A chicken coop? Do you think that's practical? It gets rather cold here for chickens." He frowned, thinking of a myriad of problems posed by having a chicken coop.

She scratched Rascal's head, intent on the task. "That's what Willy said, but Mr. Coke wrote an article about it, and I think with an enclosed henhouse and a brazier..."

"A brazier?"

"A ceramic kiln, if you like, so the chickens wouldn't get burned."

"Don't you think a rose garden would be more pleasant?"

She wouldn't look at him. Rather, she lavished her blasted attention on that damned cat.

"Yes, my lord. If you would just tell me where you'd like it placed, and the kind of roses..." She appeared resigned and miserable.

The cat lunged out of her arms. Idiot Rascal.

He slashed his hand through the air. "If you wish to build a chicken coop with Willy, by all means, you should do that."

"No, no. A rose garden would be a fine feature for the estate."

"I'd hoped we'd create the garden together, you and I," he suggested, hoping to entice her.

It didn't work.

"Did you?" she said, rubbing fret marks deeper into her forehead. "If you'll excuse me, I'll inform Willy our plans must be changed."

Exasperated, he snapped, "Don't bother."

She glanced at him, her eyes widening in alarm.

God, he was making a mull of this.

Trying to be more cordial, he bowed to his wife then offered, "Shall we plant a rose garden after you've built the chicken coop?"

She curtsied then left, a frown still on her brow. Her slow footsteps sounded lethargic as she walked down the hallway.

Exhausted by that measly confrontation, Solomon flung himself into a chair and wiped the sides of his face.

Nancy fastened her gaze on her plate and continued eating in silence.

"My God, I could almost believe she actually intends to live in that seaside cottage." He gave a shaky laugh, if only to prove to the companion he was aware how silly that sounded.

"Believe it, my lord," Nancy said shortly.

His hands stilled before he lowered them from his face. "Nancy? Tell me what it is. What have I done so wrong?"

Pursing her lips, she shook her head. "Not my place, my lord."

Angered by that, he snapped, "And quit all this 'my lord' business. You used to call me Solomon, remember?"

"Aye," she agreed, rising from the table.

"Nancy, help me. Please."

She turned, hands on her hips, a pugnacious set to her jaw. "Help you what? Make Mena more miserable than she already is? I think not!"

"She *is* miserable, isn't she?"

"Yes, she is, little lamb."

He slapped the tabletop then rested his chin in his hand. Morosely, he said, "I thought we'd overcome that last hurdle in Burton when she finally told me what Holden said to her."

Heaving a sigh, Nancy poured herself another cup of tea and re-filled his. She sat down, took a sip, then motioned to him to continue.

"Philomena noticed I'd hurt my shoulder. She came to my room and gave me a massage. It was quite nice of her."

Nancy nodded, urging him to finish the story.

"Philomena admitted she'd learned of her father's duplicity from Holden. Her stepbrother thought I'd married her to even the score between our fathers. He congratulated her on snagging a title."

"She never cared for the title, my lord."

"I know that," he said, recalling her panic upon learning he was a marquess. She had made it plain she'd never desired to be a marchioness.

He rubbed the back of his neck, trying to remember their conversation in the Burton inn. "I told her I didn't marry for money or revenge. She pointed out that we hadn't married for love, either. When I admitted I'd married to protect her, she said she no longer needed protection."

Solomon swallowed the bleakness that statement engendered in him.

He flung his hand out. "That's when she told me of her absurd scheme to live separately. Says she wishes to purchase a seaside cottage, dammit—"

A V-shaped notch reappeared in Nancy's brow as she nodded slowly. "Says you deserve better, and we'll be just fine."

"I deserve better?" Solomon jerked upright. "What the—pardon me, what does she mean by that?"

"The lamb feels guilty that her father cheated yours. Convinced she spreads rotten luck wherever she goes. Of all the London bachelors she could have married, she chose the one her father fleeced."

"That had nothing to do with her. For Lord's sake! The man lied to her for years, claiming his fortune came from a button factory! Button factories don't even exist."

"Which makes her feel even worse, that she was so gullible," Nancy said, exhaling at the end.

He stared at the companion for several seconds before quietly asking, "Philomena blames herself?"

Nancy shrugged.

"So, that's why she's given up hope."

"Yes. Despite my constant yammering that 'twas the men to blame, she's convinced she's the one at fault for creating this disastrous alliance. Convinced she's bad luck, and you believe her to be a light-skirt, so she ought to leave before matters get worse."

"This is beyond anything." He scowled. "Disastrous alliance? Did she actually use that phrase?"

"Yes, my lord."

That stunned him. Solomon knew their marriage wasn't as it should be, but he wouldn't have labeled it a disaster.

He snapped his head toward the companion.

"You said the men were to blame?"

"Yes," she said crisply. "I'll grant you Sir John was a lout and a terrible parent to Mena, but was your own father any better?"

Solomon was taken aback. He was well aware of his father's shortcomings, but loyalty forbade he discuss them with others.

"For that matter, are you any better than they?" Nancy pointed an accusing finger at him.

"Explain yourself, if you please," he said tightly.

Nancy used her fingers to tick off her points. "Since the day Mena's mother died, Sir John did nothing but berate her. He's the one who planted this notion in her head that she's bad luck. The man wasn't just a cheat, my lord. He was cruel."

"My God."

She raised her second finger. "The London dandies cruelly mocked her looks. Her first suitor accepted the baronet's bribe to abandon Mena."

Solomon winced. "She's wondered about that."

"I should think so. Despite the constant belittling of her intelligence, Mena is a very smart woman."

"I don't belittle her."

"Don't you think chicken coops are impractical?" she parroted back to him before rolling her eyes. "I could have throttled you with my own hands for that."

"But... but..." Solomon sank back into his chair, shamed.

For a sensitive soul like his wife, of course she would shrink at perceived criticism. He gave himself a shake. Nancy was still rattling on, throwing her hands in the air.

"—careless, leaving his by-blow like that, setting the example for his son to follow."

"What are you talking about now?" Solomon asked, even though he had a fairly good idea.

"Clear as the nose on my face that Mrs. Rodgers is some kin to you. You've the same color eyes."

"True."

"Well?" Nancy lowered her voice. "Is she or is she not your father's illegitimate daughter?"

Softly, he said, "She is."

Nancy raised four fingers, having proven her point.

"But Olivia's an integral part of this household, and I won't have her disparaged—"

"Neither I nor Mena have said anything improper or unkind to the woman. Nor would we," Nancy said, soothing him.

He acknowledged that with a grateful nod, then he recalled the rest of her statement, and his eyes narrowed. "You said 'example for his son'? Did you mean me?"

She lifted her brows and raised all five fingers.

"You think I have a by-blow?"

Nancy scowled then demanded, "Isn't Willy yours?"

"He's not," he flatly declared. "He's my half-brother. My mother died after delivering my sister. My father took up with one of the village lasses. Olivia is the result. Willy's story is the same, except the woman and timing are different."

Suddenly, Solomon felt very tired. His fingertip traced a pattern in the tablecloth. "So, my wife thinks I have a natural son? And a mistress?"

The twist of Nancy's mouth provided Solomon with his answer.

He swore beneath his breath then bit out, "Brilliant. Marvelous."

Solomon understood why Philomena thought he'd forsake his wedding vows. Because they had not married for love. Because Philomena knew he was a healthy man with the usual appetites, and because she'd seen him reluctantly decline the waitress's offer for bed sport. None of these would instill confidence in a spouse's faithfulness.

Solomon wanted to bed Philomena. He had since first sighting her. Finding his nightly rest was damn difficult knowing she lay in the next room, but he didn't know if he loved the woman. He was growing used to her presence, as sporadic as that was in his life; in fact, Solomon thought he could become fond of her, despite her chilly exterior. Her idea of living separately did not appeal to him, but he couldn't articulate why.

Like a man walking in his sleep, Solomon exited the breakfast room and the house. He saddled King without calling for Alvin then left the stables for a gallop across the southern boundary.

Snippets of former conversations bombarded him, striking as quickly as King's hooves hit the ground. At the Drydens' house, Philomena said they would suit. He'd turned her down flat, not even bothering to spare her embarrassment.

At the Burton inn, Philomena said losing her fortune meant she would no longer be targeted. An image of Philomena hoisted over Peck's shoulder with her head slamming against the lamp post flashed in his mind. Her father, trustee, and stepmother had targeted and betrayed her.

In the field at Rugby, she'd said she thought he was different. He hadn't heeded the compliment she'd given him. Hell, Solomon had disappointed Philomena as much as the loathsome threesome.

Despising himself for his callousness, he dismounted and loosely held the reins so the stallion could drink from a running brook.

Looking back on the start of their journey from London, he understood the reasons for his wife's anger. Philomena had been humiliated and hurt. She acted as if nothing had mattered, when in actuality everything had mattered very much.

He scowled, tossing a stick into the brook and watching it make its way downstream.

It was more important to her that she build a chicken coop than a rose garden. Why? Because only idiots like him realized one can't eat roses.

Signs of poverty and neglect were rampant about his estate, even if Willy hadn't told Solomon's wife of their troubles. Of course, Philomena would know the tenants' needs were dire. She'd hope to ameliorate their situation by providing two food sources, chickens and eggs.

With a growl of impatience, he remounted.

He had rejected his bride on their wedding night afraid she was *enceinte*, dubious of her chastity. The Marquess of Lazonby had declared his bride wanting. He had hurt her feelings and hadn't relented. Unfortunately, this was an issue where he still had to hold the line, but he now understood why his marchioness preferred not to share her meals with him. Why would she seek out his company when all he'd done was fail her?

A very nasty question, one that had danced on the edges at the back of his mind for the duration of their month-long marriage, reared its head. He could no longer ignore it. Had he been less than a good husband to his wife because, subconsciously, he was punishing her for her father's sins? He had wanted to wreak revenge on Sir John; had he, however unknowingly, transferred that hostility toward Philomena?

He realized why he had squelched that question for the past few weeks. It was why he'd not sought out his wife's company, nor asked her to join him for meals, nor introduced her to his tenants.

Solomon had avoided Philomena. In the hope of what? Hoping she'd wish to live separately from him? Hoping she'd take herself off to some seaside cottage while conveniently leaving him her fortune?

Solomon shook his head, rejecting that idea as overly harsh. He might be a lousy husband, but Solomon wasn't a greedy person.

Cudgeling his mind for the reason he'd treated Philomena thus, he finally struck upon it. He'd treated his wife so distantly because he didn't want to be tempted by her again. He'd accused her of being a tease, but with the wide berth she'd given him since the Burton massage, that couldn't be true. Philomena had made no effort to talk with him, let alone flirt.

He was attracted to his wife, and he didn't wish to be. Worldly enough to know they had a unique chemistry together, Solomon was astute enough to enjoy the quickness of her mind and her dry sense of humor. The physical and mental connections were difficult to resist, and that terrified him. If he allowed intimacy to grow between them, without avenging the wrong done to his father, didn't that make him a bad son? Liking Philomena made him feel as if he were betraying his father.

The truth of that hit him like a blow to the mid-section.

What kind of man was he? Was he a fool? Being so caught up in being a dutiful son to his dead parent, he hadn't been a companion to his wife.

He'd self-righteously mocked his wife for taking her wedding vows too lightly. Philomena had been right to label him a hypocrite.

Turning the stallion homeward, Solomon spurred King into a gallop.

Solomon resolved to become a better husband to Philomena, if she would let him.

Chapter 16

At fourteen, Willy was all legs and elbows, but his lighthearted, playful nature was the antidote Philomena needed to chase away her blue devils. They had spent a great deal of time together since she'd arrived at Lazonby. She'd seen him taking off across a field that first morning, heading toward the home woods. A muzzle loading rifle strapped across his back, a bag of gunpowder tied to his belt.

She'd asked if he was going hunting, and he graciously invited her along. Philomena didn't for one minute think Willy actually meant her to accept his invitation, but they had formed a fast friendship since then.

Willy didn't flatter her or demean her with snide comments. He had declared, "Fine job," when she'd shot down her first bird but also ribbed her for her other stray shots. He'd laughed when she slid down the muddy bank then pulled her out before she fell into the pond. Frank honesty was the bedrock of her friendship with Willy. Although there was disparity in their ages, this was a friendship of equals.

Solomon had kept her at a distance ever since coming to Lazonby. He'd shown no interest in her, no inclination to consummate their marriage. Clearly, his loyalties were torn, leaving her to surmise his heart was elsewhere. Perhaps with that lovely housekeeper of his, Mrs. Rodgers? She was young and beautiful and convenient. What more could a man ask of his mistress? Philomena kept her suspicions to herself, though, refusing to share this even with Nancy. It was simply too degrading to discuss.

After wasting her childhood hungrily seeking her father's approval, Philomena was done with futile chases. She refused to pine for her husband's affection. If his heart belonged to another, as she feared, there would be no happy outcome for any of them. She consoled herself that once she received the sale proceeds from the Chelmsford house, she and Nancy could leave Lazonby, thereby ceding the field to Solomon's lover.

That day couldn't come soon enough, for it was a strain to be near Solomon. It was difficult to describe the distancing game they played with one another. He'd started it, but she'd allowed it. They could sit in the same room, but they might as well have lived in two separate counties for all the interaction they had. Marriage, she was discovering, could be a lonely enterprise.

She cursed herself for bringing such bad luck on his head, his lover's head, and her own.

To bide her time until her departure, Philomena determined to be cordial toward Solomon, even if it killed her. She had two reasons for that course: first, she did not want the marquess to think her ill-bred; secondly, it was not his fault if Solomon loved another. He'd married her to protect her, saving her from danger. How could she resent him for that?

This morning found her bickering with Willy over measurements, enjoying a friendly squabble for its own sake. The topic under debate concerned mathematics.

"You're mad," her companion cried, flinging his palms in the air.

Willy looked so much like Solomon at that moment, Philomena laughed.

He ignored it, intent upon proving his point. Willy used a nail and scratched numbers into a board.

"To calculate the surface of the rectangle, you must add the lengths of the four sides together, in which case—"

"In which case the lady's right."

Philomena spun around.

Solomon leaned against the doorframe of the barn, a crooked grin on his face. He wore buckskins, a homespun shirt, and ancient, scuffed boots. The smell of horse and leather wafting about indicated Solomon had completed his morning ride. The breeze ruffled the raven strands of his hair.

The Marquess of Lazonby was the most handsome man she'd ever beheld.

The sooner Philomena moved into that seaside cottage, the better for her peace of mind. Oh, how his lover must resent having to share him even this much!

"How long have you been there, my lord?"

"Long enough to know it may take you two years to build this chicken coop, and then we'll never get to that rose garden."

Was he serious about the rose garden?

"Two years?" Philomena scoffed. "Three days, at the most."

"Two if you don't need a roof," Willy chimed in.

Philomena rolled her eyes, feeling a lightness in her spirits already. "We must have a roof, Willy. The foxes, remember?"

"That's right." He snapped his fingers then pointed at his dark head. "Got the details all in here, Laz. Don't worry about a thing."

Solomon sauntered toward them, pulling a pair of gloves from his back pocket then handing them to her. "Here, my dear. I wouldn't want you to get a splinter."

Surprised by the endearment and his thoughtfulness, she took the gloves without thinking. She glanced at him, saw him smiling at her, then quickly looked away. His presence unnerved her, and she could only pray they appeared like a normal married couple to Willy. Philomena didn't wish to embarrass herself or her husband in front of the youth.

"Thank you," she murmured. Trying to cover her blush, she asked coolly, "Are you here to help or to supervise?"

"Help."

"Very well. Let's get started." Determined to act businesslike, Philomena pointed to the structure she and Willy had already made. "Our next move is to create cleats for the resting cradles."

Solomon nodded then jerked his head toward the youth. "Willy? Do you want to do that whilst Philomena and I build cradles?"

"Fine."

Willy marked the level lines, while she and Solomon moved to the scrap pile of lumber. Philomena brought some boards to the cutting block where her husband stood.

"I thought we'd use these to create boxes," she said.

"Fine. How many do you want?"

"A dozen to start with, I think."

He whistled. "Twelve's a lot."

"We can scale up or down as the need drives." She lifted her chin in the air, daring him to argue with the sage advice of Mr. Coke.

He pointed at her and grinned. "You're adorable when you do that."

Philomena glanced over her shoulder, wondering what Willy was doing that drew such praise. The youth was eyeing the level. Shrugging, Philomena didn't know what was so adorable about that. Perhaps Solomon was teasing him.

Solomon grunted then said dryly, "Just hold it steady, won't you?"

She was completely flummoxed by his affability, and it slowly dawned on Philomena that good manners dictated that Solomon behave agreeably in Willy's presence. Once she unraveled that mystery, she relaxed.

Philomena measured short boards for Solomon to nail into the long plank, creating nesting cradles for the hens. Once the cradles were made, she and Willy hung a shelf on the cleat then set the cradles on it. They worked through luncheon but took a break for afternoon tea.

"Today's Wednesday, isn't it?" Willy asked Solomon, who nodded.

"The vicar and his wife will be dropping by for tea. I'm surprised he's waited so long to visit. Must be restraining himself out of respect for the newlyweds," Willy teased, handing Philomena the hammer.

She pounded in the last two nails then returned the hammer.

"Go on and change, Mena," Willy said.

"You don't think this dress is good enough to greet the vicar?"

"No. Unless you're a heathen."

Philomena playfully smacked Willy's arm. She froze, though, when she saw Solomon's lips tighten. Obviously, he did not care for his marchioness's frivolous conduct.

Subdued, she and Solomon returned to the house, leaving Willy in the yard.

"You mentioned something about a brazier?" Solomon asked.

"Yes."

"I believe you wanted a ceramic one? Shall we go to Penrith tomorrow and purchase one? We can take the wagon." Seeing her hesitate, he added, "This way you can pick out the hens and rooster you'll need to populate the coop."

"But the coop's not ready."

He waved off that concern. "Willy can work while we're gone, and if he doesn't complete it, we can keep the chickens in their cages until it's finished."

"Yes, all right. Shall I ask Nancy to join us?"

"It's a pity, but there won't be enough room for a third person. I've ordered a plow, so we'll collect that, too."

"Fine."

He made a sweeping bow then said, "I'll meet you in the drawing room at four o'clock for tea, my lady."

Philomena cleaned and, unable to locate Nancy, changed from her work gown into a cinnamon-colored day dress. Trimmed in brown velvet, it complimented her curly hair, which she wore in a simple style tied at the nape. For weeks she'd dressed in warm, serviceable gowns, so Philomena enjoyed wearing something more fashionable.

She hoped Solomon would enjoy the pains she'd taken with her appearance. It would be nice if this newfound sense of camaraderie continued between them, but Philomena wouldn't wager on it. She didn't have that kind of luck.

Taking a deep breath and giving herself a quick go-over, Philomena resolved that she'd do her part to maintain the friendly truce.

At tea, Philomena met the vicar and his wife, Mr. and Mrs. Watson. They were middle-aged with lined faces and reddened hands, which revealed their lives had not be easy. In awe of the young marchioness, Mrs. Watson teetered while executing her low curtsy. Quickly, Philomena caught the woman's elbow to prevent a fall. Not wishing her guest to be embarrassed, Philomena then drew Mrs. Watson's arm through her own and led her to the sofa, prattling about the weather.

"What a fine day to pay a visit. His lordship has tried to warn me that Cumbria's weather can be harsh, knowing I am used to Chelmsford's more moderate climes, but he has yet to convince me. Do you suppose I have arrived to view the best offerings of the year? Or are the seasons markedly different?"

The vicar and the marquess shared a look while Mrs. Watson made a faint demurrer.

"Cumbria's winter will not compare well to Chelmsford, I imagine," said the vicar with a twinkle in his eye. "Although I think she outshines Essex during the summers."

"I see you have the requisite tact required for your profession, Mr. Watson," Philomena said.

He acknowledged the compliment with a smile.

Mrs. Rodgers brought in the tea tray, greeting the vicar and his wife. Philomena's hackles rose, as they always did in that woman's presence, although she'd done her best not to show it.

A small conversation broke out among them as Mrs. Watson asked after a man named John. The housekeeper softly replied, while Philomena remained quiet, not knowing the person. Throughout the course of their conversation, it became clear that John was Mrs. Rodgers's husband. He was away at sea on a merchant ship. Solomon had taken Mrs. Rodgers into his household during her husband's absence so that she wouldn't have to live alone. Philomena had no idea. Was it possible Olivia Rodgers wasn't Solomon's lover?

Pouring the tea, Philomena asked Mrs. Watson if she could recommend people to serve Lazonby. "We need to hire more staff."

"My lady's right. If you know anyone who's willing to work, please have them come for interviews on Friday. If that suits you, dear?" Solomon folded one long leg over another and addressed his wife.

"Yes, my lord."

"Good," he said.

Talk became general after that, and Philomena enjoyed the Watsons' company. The vicar was a solid man with a level head on his shoulders, and Philomena thought his parishioners were lucky to have such a practical leader. His wife, chuckling at jokes she must have heard a dozen times before, impressed Philomena as a good helpmate.

Before taking their leave, Mr. Watson asked her if she shared her husband's musical talent.

Philomena stared blankly at the marquess. "Talent? Are you musical, my lord?"

Solomon chuckled. "Our marriage is so new she hasn't discovered all my secrets."

"I know your favorite color is green and you love macaroons," she teased.

"There is nothing more a good wife needs to learn about her husband than that," the vicar quipped.

After the Watsons left, Solomon said, "Come with me."

Curious, she followed him to a large, domed room. Its walls were bare, once painted a bright green, and there were faded patches where paintings had been removed. Occasional chairs, in need of reupholstering, were scattered around a large piano near the window, and a broken music stand leaned against the back wall. Voluminous blue silk, faded from the sun, served as drapes. This room, like all the others at Lazonby, had been neglected, and its ambience saddened her.

Waving toward the instrument, he asked, "Do you play?"

"A little," she said, suddenly shy.

"Will you play for me?"

"Is there any sheet music?" Her gaze scanned the piano but didn't find any.

"No. Do you have any piece memorized?"

"No."

Solomon placed her on the bench then sat next to her. He didn't wear cologne, but he must mix his shaving cream with castile soap and honey, for she smelled their lingering scents. It was subtle and clean, and she vastly preferred that to the concoction her father used.

"Then I shall play for you."

He played *Eine Kleine Nachtmusik,* and he played it beautifully. If anything, Mr. Watson had understated her husband's talent. He had a real gift. While he played, she stole glances at his profile. His hands moved over the keyboard, his eyes closed, and she sensed he became lost in the piece. Solomon had a deep love for music, she saw that now.

Philomena watched Solomon, turning over in her mind what she knew of him. Kind. Musical. Unable to let go of a grudge. Attractive to women, with his black hair and eyes the color of a sunset. He fought like a lion not because of a violent nature but to protect. Solomon Braxton, Marquess of Lazonby, was complexity redefined.

She recalled he had once pledged to know all her secrets, even the number of freckles sprinkled across her nose. Remembering their night at the opera, she could scarcely believe it had happened during her lifetime it felt so distant.

"Sing for me, Mena," he invited at the end of Mozart's piece.

"Oh, no." She shook her head. "I can't sing."

"You can talk, can't you? You can sing."

She laughed. "No, really, Solomon. I can't carry a tune in a bucket."

"Please? Sing with me."

He began a Scottish melody, *Robin Adair,* as she clapped along. He sang the first verse in a smooth baritone and the second in a falsetto, which sent her into reels of laughter. Caught in his enthusiasm, she joined in singing, *Oh, I can ne'er forget Robin Adair.*

She dropped her face into her hands, mortified as that last part echoed in the chambers, loud and off-key.

"Philomena," he choked, gasping with mirth.

Peeping between her spread fingers, she half-expected Solomon to send her from the room.

"Philomena, look at me."

"I told you I couldn't sing."

"You are refreshingly honest, which is more important than being able to sing on key, anyway."

Prying her fingers from her face, he peered at her, his expression uncertain.

She tapped his shoulder. "You're quizzing me!"

He saw that she wasn't offended by his teasing, and his shoulders began to shake with laughter. Still holding her hands, Solomon made a slight effort to maintain a straight face, but the battle was lost before it began. He threw his head back, his hilarity erupting. He gasped through fits of laughter. Like a contagion, his mirth spread to her until Philomena gave a peal of laughter and clutched her stomach.

Solomon stood, wiped his eyes, then said through a wide smile, "Your laughter is one of my favorite things about you, Mena."

Philomena blinked, sobering immediately.

"I want you to be happy here and laugh every day," he said softly.

As that was highly unlikely, she chose her words with great tact. "While I remain here, I wish to be happy, as well."

His eyes gleamed with mischief as he prodded, "Still planning to remove to that seaside cottage, I see. Won't you reconsider?"

She shook her head. "It's for the best."

"I understand why you think so," he said slowly. "After our day together, I rather think we could rub along nicely. If we put our minds to it, no doubt we could have a good marriage."

Cocking her head to the side, she asked out of curiosity. "Why? You already have my money, there's no need—"

"Damnation, Philomena."

She jumped at his violent cursing.

Inhaling deeply, Solomon glared at her and ground out, "There's more to you than your fortune, just as there's more to marriage than this."

"I know there's more to marriage," she said quietly, rising from the piano bench. "You were the one who placed that stupid condition on ours."

"Stupid?"

"Yes, stupid." She skirted past a shabby chair, lifting her skirts. "If I were pregnant with another man's child—which I'm not—it'd be considered yours anyway because we're married. If I delivered another man's male child—which I won't—the world would view him as your heir, like it or not."

"You don't understand my need for a legitimate heir." Scowling, he paced in the opposite direction, roughly moving chairs from his path. "You don't understand."

"I understand you don't trust me! You don't respect me and think I'm a light-skirt even as you—never mind."

His gaze sliced toward her, as sharp as a knife. "None of those things are true."

Flummoxed, she waved her palms. "Confess, Solomon. You never intended ours to be a real marriage."

"It isn't that. All I asked for is a little time."

"There's no shame in recovering your swindled fortune, but there's no need to continue this charade, either. We'll both be happier—"

"For the last time, Philomena, I did not marry you for your money." He picked up a chair and shuffled it aside with slightly more force than was necessary.

Biting her bottom lip, she watched the chair teeter before falling backward.

"Do you believe me?"

"It's time for dinner, Solomon. We can discuss this later."

"My God." Clutching the sides of his head, he asked, "Do you think I don't want to consummate this marriage? Do you think it's been easy for me to lie awake in my lonely bed?"

She laughed.

He lowered his hands and stared at her. "Why are you laughing?"

Rolling her eyes, Philomena scoffed, "Your lonely bed."

He advanced on her, menace in his golden eyes. "You think I share my bed with another? You believe that's the reason I've not bedded you?"

Remembering her promise to do her level best to maintain their truce, Philomena mumbled, "It doesn't matter what I think. It's time for dinner."

Wearily, she walked toward the door, but Solomon reached it before she did. She turned to face him, on the verge of asking his intentions, but he placed his hands on either side of her head and used his body to form a cage around her.

He bit his words out. "You'll agree, dear wife, that it is *bad ton* to bring one's whore into one's ancestral home?"

Trying not to flinch at the vulgar expression, she said levelly, "If you say, my lord."

"Would you agree that I have conducted myself in the well-established mode of a gentleman, ma'am?"

Arching her brow, she clarified, "When you're not tossing chairs in music rooms or throwing levelers at felonious trustees?"

He frowned.

"Yes, I'll agree you generally comport yourself in a gentlemanly fashion."

"Thank you," he gritted out.

Staring into his golden eyes, Philomena felt mesmerized, unable to look away. Time stretched out as their gazes snagged. The combination of castile soap and honey wafted to her, enticing her. His utter stillness reminded her of a predator whose senses were sharpened by a hunt.

Solomon leaned in and nipped her earlobe then soothed it with a flick of his tongue. He nuzzled in the sensitive hollow behind her ear, causing the hair at her nape to rise. Delicious ripples shivered over her. Anticipation sizzled in the atmosphere. Spellbound, Philomena felt her breath hitch.

"Just where would I keep this fancy piece you believe I have?" His voice was dangerous and low. Philomena was thrown off by his uncertain mood, even as his mouth trailed a fiery path from her jaw to brow. Her knees wobbled.

"I don't know."

He kissed her temple, moving closer. "Not in the house, not on the estate."

"No. Perhaps in the village?"

Flames burned in his eyes as he gripped her chin in a tight hold, forcing her to look directly at him. "Stop it. I don't have a mistress."

His denial only mystified her more. Philomena had her courses a fortnight ago, although she wasn't certain Solomon knew. How could he still suspect her of carrying another man's child? Did he refuse her because he still believed she was a tease? A light-skirt? Was that why he'd kept her at arm's length? If he didn't already have a lover, why wouldn't he consummate their marriage?

His hands clamped onto her hips, slid down then cupped her buttocks. He brought her hips to his, pressing his warm length against her belly, giving unmistakable proof of his arousal. Was that for her sake or his mystery lover? Cocooned in the heat radiating off his body, Philomena blindly wondered if the distinction even mattered. Her other questions remained unanswered. Her curiosity vanished in the shimmering warmth building between them. Did it matter who Solomon loved when she was the one with him now?

The small voice in her head which argued that, indeed, it did matter, was pointedly ignored. Her lashes drifted closed, and she surrendered to the fluttery sensations coursing through her blood. She wanted this. She wanted him. Philomena slumped against the door and linked her hands behind his neck. She lifted her face, begging for a kiss.

With a muttered imprecation, Solomon gathered her tightly against him. His kiss was long and hard, his tongue spearing into mouth as if his patience had snapped. He devoured her mouth, pressing her against the door as he worked out his fury in that punishing kiss.

Her anger flared. Years of resentment for being belittled and despised erupted. Always she had been treated as an afterthought, her father moving the family according to his needs, never her own. His flaws had been exacerbated by his second wife, who encouraged him to speak disparagingly of her until her self-esteem had been whittled down to a toothpick, and the London dandies made clear even with her newfound fortune that she still smelled of the shop and would never be acceptable.

Philomena was more than their taunts. Never had she been unkind to anyone, yet she had been made to suffer for others' cruelty. Wasn't her own husband among those who resented her wealth, who hated her father? Sir John robbed his family, but her father stole from her, as well, and not once had anyone sought to address that injustice! Was she expected to quash herself, biting her tongue in resignation at an heiress's lot? No more. Not ever again.

Solomon kissed with ravaged intensity, so Philomena responded in kind. She returned his lustful ire, kissing him with a cutting savageness that would make him forget about any other woman, that would drive him to his knees to admit he wanted her, a baronet's daughter. She would mark him with her passion, sear him with her lust, and ruin him for any civilized female. As if someone had set off a powder keg, the heat between them exploded.

He shoved aside her bodice to cup her breast, molding it to suit his needs.

She moaned, not sure when his anger turned from punishing her to pleasing her, but it had. Her hands gripped his waist, then traveled lower to his buttocks, just as he'd done to her. She gripped the firm, round bottom, impressed by its similarity to steel.

The Marquess of Lazonby would soon discover, if he hadn't already, that she would meet his demands, step by step. She felt his chest rise and fall in an arrhythmic fashion as his breathing grew ragged. A thrill of triumph coursed through her chest at the realization that she had done this to Solomon. Philomena Lower, worthless heiress, had rocked him off-kilter.

The music room filled with the sounds of groans and pants. They murmured nonsensical words to each other. The lofty chambers grew so unbearably hot, Philomena wondered if cinders rested beneath her gown. Her entire body was aflame, their mutual desire spiraling into a bonfire which would consume the whole house and burn it to the ground.

When Solomon brought her breast from her gown, she sighed as the cool air rushed around it, but the relief was brief and transitory. He caressed the flesh, kissing it until her body spiked with fever. In her most secret spot, heat pooled there, churning and roiling as passion blazed everything in its path like a wildfire out of control.

She moaned, hungry for more pleasure, an empty vessel save for desires.

The dinner gong sounded again, shattering the moment.

Solomon whispered her name, easing apart from her. Hastily, he tucked his shirt into his waistband, and she marveled at his quick recovery. She remained leaning against the door, doubtful if her legs could carry her weight.

He turned away, casting a hand in her general direction with a harsh instruction to tidy herself.

She wanted to cry.

Philomena wished to run outside and howl at the moon. She would enjoy flinging herself on the damp grass and beating her breast in shame as her fevered senses cooled, leaving her with the taste of ashes in her mouth.

Shaking her head, she shoved such maudlin, dramatic proclivities from her mind, knowing very well she would do no such thing. Nothing had changed to merit such desperate measures. Her plans of relocating remained. Her goal of maintaining a friendly front with her husband had not shifted.

Even after that earth-shaking exchange, her situation had not shifted.

"Dinner awaits, my lord."

"You'll dine with me tonight?"

She paused, not wishing to guess the reasons for his invitation, if it even was an invitation. Lifting her chin in defiance, she nodded. She would not hide from Solomon as if she were a coward.

Until these past few minutes, today had been her best day at Lazonby. Because he had put himself out to be good company, as he had that night at the opera. When Solomon was with her, really with her, her senses sharpened, as if she were coming awake after a long slumber.

"In case you're not clear, I very much wish to bed my wife. I never intended ours to be a permanently sexless marriage, you know. Only delayed for a few months. Now, are you ready to go into dinner?"

He extended a hand, and she studied it, wishing her ability to think wasn't so jumbled. She'd been right. Nothing had changed. He still regarded her as a light-skirt, a tease, someone who could satiate his bodily needs while he kept her at arm's length.

She would accept that challenge and issue one of her own.

"Yes."

"Excellent," he said.

He had no idea.

Chapter 17

Dinner was pleasant as he exerted himself to be a better companion for his wife. They conversed about the progress of the chicken coop and discussed other investments they needed to make beyond purchasing a brazier to ensure its survival.

"Amongst the Lazonby tenants," asked Philomena, "is there a little boy or girl who could collect the eggs and feed the chicks?"

Solomon considered the possibilities, rattling off the names, which led him to briefly describing the estate families.

"I should introduce you to my tenants. After all, they should know their marchioness."

For the sake of keeping their fragile peace, he said nothing to Philomena's skepticism. Her reluctance to meet his tenants was yet another reminder she considered her residency temporary. That bothered him more than it should, he owned. When he'd asked her to reconsider, and she'd refused, citing that living separately was 'for the best,' he'd been tempted to shake her.

That and her mistaken belief that he consorted with another had maddened him, causing him to act like a crazed lunatic. What was worse, Solomon couldn't summon the tiniest shred of remorse, either, because Philomena's passion had matched his own. He'd acknowledged they had unique chemistry, but even he hadn't known its incendiary nature. How could he ever kiss another woman after having kissed Philomena? Others paled in comparison.

He had never met a person as exasperating as his wife, and yet... he couldn't deny that he found her imminently kissable.

She was probably right, though. If she removed to a seaside cottage, she might finally find some peace. Philomena could relax, away from people who constantly judged her and found her wanting. Perhaps she'd meet a country gentleman, a scholar or vicar, who could become a companion to her.

"My lord?"

He gave himself a shake, halting the drift of his thoughts, and addressed his wife. "Beg your pardon?"

"You've spilled your wine."

Incredulous, he stared at the large red stain spreading on the tablecloth and shook the droplets off his hand. He mumbled his apologies.

Thereafter, their discussion passed to improvements of the manor house. Solomon had definite plans for the changes he wanted, but his wife, contrary creature that she was, questioned his reasoning in some instances. She had this annoying habit of spying the disadvantages in his schemes. He was forced to defend his choices, but he wasn't always successful. Throughout the meal, it was just as often that her point carried as did his.

He should resent it. After all, as a marquess, he was not used to losing arguments, but he found this experience invigorating. Because their final solution improved the estate, he heeded some of her suggestions.

Nancy had been correct when she'd told him Philomena was a very smart woman. His tenants would benefit from having such a strong-minded marchioness. Smiling wryly to himself, Solomon acknowledged he might benefit from having a strong-minded marchioness, too.

Solomon appreciated how she defended her positions. He also appreciated the soft, errant curl that fell on her forehead and which she frequently brushed aside. It reminded him of her stubbornly persistent personality.

His wife was also clever with finances. When she suggested dyeing the silken drapes of the music room and reupholstering the chairs, he grew curious.

"To what purpose?"

"Because you play so divinely, we should invite the local gentry and allow you to perform."

"No," he said firmly.

Smiling, she countered by saying, "Yes."

Eyeing her with exasperation, he said, "Nobody wishes to be entertained by a marquess."

"Of course not," she promptly agreed.

"Mena, you minx," he half-laughed.

Grinning, she carried on. "But they do wish to be entertained by someone so uniquely gifted. Honestly, Solomon, I don't know why you didn't perform in all the capitals. You could have gone on a worldwide tour and made a fortune."

"Are you mad?"

"I should have thought that was evident when I proposed." Her dry retort made him laugh aloud.

She continued, "You are talented, and it's criminal not to share your gift."

Pleased and humbled by her praise, he was aware she'd re-worked her magic. Philomena had twisted his thinking in every which direction, so he didn't know if he was on his head or his heels.

"If you're sincere, I will consider it."

The smile that spread across her face caused his breath to hitch. Earlier, he'd marked it as transformative, but this surpassed the former. The luminosity of her countenance, mixed with the sparkling good humor in her eyes, did something strange to his heart.

After the meal, they retired to the drawing room. Sparsely furnished with serviceable, yet drab and mismatched furniture, the room's sole advantage was being clean. Seeing it through Philomena's eyes, he grimaced.

"What's the matter?"

"It's just occurred to me how little comfort or beauty my home offers. Without rugs and wall hangings, it's not only chilly here but dismal."

"Perhaps we can find a rug in Penrith tomorrow?"

Nodding, he agreed, "That would be nice. If we were to re-decorate this room, what color should it be?"

"What color would you like?" She gestured back at him, as if it were his decision to make.

An arrow of regret sliced him. Philomena wasn't planning to make Lazonby her home, so why would she care about color schemes? He'd forgotten, after the intellectual exercises for improving the estate, that their futures were not necessarily entwined.

Ignoring the loneliness that thought engendered, he explained, "I'd like you to refurbish the house while you're here. Regardless that you will soon remove elsewhere, this is work that needs to be done, and I can think of no one better suited."

Her hazel eyes narrowed upon him while he strained to keep his expression impassive.

If he introduced her to tenants, neighbors, and villagers, would she form personal attachments to the estate and not wish to leave Lazonby? It was definitely worth a shot. If she restored his manor home, the fields, and home farm, that could also delay her departure.

In short, Solomon wasn't above manipulating Philomena to gain more time with her. He had to convince her to give up this stupid plan of living apart. She didn't need to live in a backwater seaside cottage with some tepid suitor. Philomena was a woman of strong passions. She needed a real man who could match those. If it were only a matter of being near an ocean, he'd take her there for a holiday.

Idly considering what a belated honeymoon could be like, Solomon imagined making love to Philomena in the salty air beneath an open sky.

"Why are you smiling in such a mysterious fashion?"

"I'm just picturing this room returned to its former glory," he lied. "It would mean a great deal to me if you were to be a part of that restoration."

Recognizing his stubborn wife wouldn't easily drop her plans of living in a remote cottage, Solomon realized he'd have better success if he attacked the problem diagonally, rather than directly. Tucking the corners of his smile back in, he poured a drink from a new bottle in the freshly supplied wine cellar and brought it to her.

As she sipped her ratafia, he tried not to smile at her nervousness. It was time to put him and his wife out of their misery. His body cried out for a good bedding, and the anticipation that had simmered in his loins for the past month was boiling over after their delightful interlude in the music room.

"You were right earlier," he said.

"If you could please be more specific, I'd be overjoyed."

Smiling, he prompted, "About my faulty reasoning regarding consummating our marriage."

She lifted her brows.

Leaning forward in his chair, he carefully set his drink on the floor and began a somber, if somewhat terse, explanation. "Mrs. Olivia Rodgers is my half-sister, and Willy my half-brother. They're illegitimate."

She inhaled sharply.

"Even before my mother died in childbirth, my father took lovers. After her death, that practice continued, unabated. It wouldn't be a stretch to say he enjoyed half the females in Cumbria."

"Oh, Solomon. I am sorry."

He acknowledged her answer, but the anger toward his father re-surfaced, and he didn't bother to hide it. It felt cathartic to finally reveal this to her.

"Father littered the neighborhood with his by-blows. His carelessness has hurt his children; the illegitimacy makes their lives more difficult. It's a mark of shame none have earned. In the end, he died from the pox."

She flinched then reached for him, as if to console him. "What a dreadful way to die! Illegitimacy is unfortunate, as well, and with so many... well, it doesn't appear your father's licentious behavior left you unscathed, either."

Surprised by the astuteness of her observation, he merely nodded. "Now you see why I'm so..."

"Obsessed with the legitimacy of your heir?"

Giving her a sardonic smile, he gently corrected, "Concerned, more like."

Nodding slowly, Philomena said, "It makes sense now that you've explained it. Thank you. That couldn't have been easy."

Grateful for her understanding, Solomon sat beside her on the faded sofa and picked up her hand. "Now that we've leapt that hurdle, I lay myself at your feet. You've won this particular skirmish."

"I have? How remarkably clever of me."

Quickly, he planted a kiss on the tender skin inside her wrist. "Yes, isn't it, though? As you said, even if you were carrying another man's child, the world would consider it mine."

Solomon placed his hand on her abdomen, as if she were, indeed, carrying a child.

"There's no reason we shouldn't have a full marriage and begin it immediately."

He lowered his head, intending to kiss her, but she scrambled off the sofa.

Astonished, he croaked, "Philomena?"

She stood, eyes wide, clutching her hands. "I can't. We can't."

"Of course we can," he promised. "It will be very good. For both of us."

"No." Her head shook quickly, back and forth, in jerky little movements.

"It won't be good?"

She groaned then snapped, "Not that."

"Then what? Why shouldn't we enjoy each other to the full? There's no reason to deny ourselves." He stood and approached her.

Philomena took both his hands, her eyes looming large. "But there is," she said, her voice throbbing with emotion.

"There is what?"

"There's a reason we shouldn't have a full marriage. You still don't trust me."

Solomon didn't deny it. To swallow her story that she had been with a man—once—seven years ago then remained celibate? He was a man of the world and knew better.

Still clutching his hands, she argued—did she ever cease?

"You don't trust me because I was the one to propose, and I did so within days of meeting you. If we… um… consummate our marriage, and I quickly become pregnant or deliver an early baby, you'll always doubt you're the father. You'll always resent me for that 'coincidence' and won't *ever* trust me."

"That's not true, Philomena."

"If those things came to pass, that would be dreadful."

"I wouldn't say dreadful. Life happens. People adjust." He shrugged.

"No."

From the mulish expression in her eyes and the jut of her determined chin, Solomon knew all hope was lost. He'd never persuade his wife this didn't matter, because she was correct in her predictions. This mattered a great deal to him.

Heaving a sigh of frustration, he asked, "So, where does that leave us, Philomena?"

"I don't know."

PHILOMENA VISITED HIS dreams again. Dancing on the edge of a plot of brown, loamy soil, she flashed smiles at him over a bare shoulder. Her gown whipped in the wind, outlining her slender form. She was beautiful and tantalizing and barefoot.

Come plant roses with me, Mena.

He lifted a bucket filled with plantings, trying to entice her.

Grinning, she shook her head then flitted to a cottage. He followed, but the home disappeared in the mists.

Coming awake, he flipped the covers back and put his feet on the cold, wooden floor. Sitting with his elbows on his thighs, he clutched his hair, wondering what it all meant.

His gaze lifted to the adjoining door between his chambers and Philomena's. The closed door mocked him.

He slipped from his bed and stole into Philomena's room. For a while he stood over her, wondering if she dreamed of planting rose gardens with him or of living with Nancy in that blasted seaside cottage.

The lines and angles of her face softened in sleep. Her bruise from Peck's mishandling had completely faded, but Solomon's anger had not abated. Sending the man to Italy had been too kind. He ought to have seen him tried and hanged instead.

Grabbing Rascal by the scruff of her neck, he moved the cat to the foot of her bed then quietly peeled back the covers. By slow, cautious increments, he slid in beside her.

Philomena stirred, and he held his breath. When she did not awaken, he closed his eyes. Solomon did not touch her. Lying next to a rose-scented Philomena, feeling the warmth of her body—it was enough.

Later, Solomon stirred, discovering his body curved around Philomena's as she slept in his arms. His slight smile broadened. After weeks of curiosity, he finally gave into the longing and touched Philomena's curls. He coiled one around his finger, stretching out the length then allowing it to bounce back into its spiral shape.

Her lashes fluttered and she yawned, looking very much like Rascal had when he'd moved the cat from her spot on the bed. He stilled, catching his breath, unsure how she'd react to finding him in her bed.

She snuggled closer, and he exhaled.

"I'm a great admirer of curly hair, Mena."

She lifted her face, rubbing her moss-green eyes. "Am I dreaming?"

"I've been thinking, Philomena, about a middle ground..."

"Yes?"

"Yes. As your husband, I want to be your friend and champion."

She made a husky sounding chuckle. "Champion? Like the knights of yore?"

"Yes."

She whispered, "I've never had a champion."

"Then it's time that changed."

Her lips slowly curled, forming a smile of pure loveliness.

"And lover. I want to be your lover."

Her gaze met his, confusion shimmering in the depths of her eyes. "But last night we agreed—"

"Yes, but we gave up too quickly. We didn't discuss the possibility of pleasing one another without congress."

"You mentioned that once before..."

He nodded.

Burying her head against his chest, she admitted, "I was too angry to listen."

Gently, he tipped her chin so he could see her face. Then he kissed the end of her nose. His finger touched on a freckle as he counted, "One, two, three, four, five..."

She giggled. "Are you counting my freckles?"

"Shh. Don't disturb me." One hand roamed over her back as he kept counting.

Strangely, Philomena lay passively as he caressed her. Odd behavior for a woman he knew was no wilting flower. Bending his head, he kissed her softly at first then more deeply as her shyness evaporated. Philomena gave kiss for kiss, touch for touch with unstinting generosity after that initial hesitation.

Making small sounds in the back of her throat, she sent his temperature rising.

Sliding his hand beneath her shift, he cupped her breast. Testing its weight and shape, he explored at his leisure. His thumb brushed her nipple, teasing until it peaked. His lips soon followed, and he suckled at her breast, dimly aware of her sharp intake. She squirmed and shivered, and her response delighted him.

Solomon wouldn't hurry this. His mouth lingered on her skin, tasting its sweetness.

"Mena, your skin's as soft as a rose petal."

She lifted her hands briefly before dropping them to her sides, as if she didn't know what to do with them. Intrigued, he watched her lashes flutter as she moved her legs restlessly.

"Touch me," he whispered.

"Where?"

"Anywhere."

Tentatively, her fingers skimmed his hair. Solomon leaned into the caress, which emboldened Philomena.

Thrusting her fingers through his locks, she massaged his scalp. He smiled against her nipple then massaged its mate. Solomon leveraged himself onto his elbow before taking her mouth in a deep, hot kiss.

His manhood hardened, and he muttered, "I need more of you."

Gripping her waist, he rolled onto his back until she sprawled on top of him. He stroked her smooth buttocks and pressed against her belly, so she'd understand how much he wanted her.

"Solomon," she gasped then scrambled off him. In her haste, she fell off the bed and landed on the floor with a *thud*.

"Are you all right?" he asked, leaning over the edge.

With her hair falling into her eyes and her limbs askew, she made an endearing picture.

Grinning down at her, he watched as she gingerly came to her feet and glared at him.

Now he was certain she'd suffered no ill side-effects from her tumble. He patted the mattress, inviting her to come back to bed.

"You… you're ready to mate," she blurted.

Agitated, she rose then stood by the window with her arms folded over her chest.

"Yes," he agreed. Frowning, he asked, "Does that frighten you?"

"No. I mean, not really, but you did say—" Here she wagged her finger in an accusatory manner. "You said we would not have congress."

How he didn't dissolve into peals of laughter, Solomon never knew. Leaving the bed, he padded across the room, approaching her from behind. He took her by the shoulders. When she didn't resist, he nuzzled her neck.

Skimming his lips against her warm skin, he said, "I am ready to mate, but at two-and-thirty, I can restrain myself."

His hands slid from her shoulders to her front then skimmed down further. "We won't join, but we can find much pleasure together, if you wish."

Through her linen shift, Solomon rhythmically pressed her core with the heel of his hand. "Say yes, Mena."

She nodded.

Triumph surged through his veins. He lost no time seducing his wife. Already it felt as if they'd wasted a lifetime. Solomon lifted the hem of her shift and found her delicate channels. Sliding his finger inside her, he groaned at the tightness.

"You're so sweet, Mena."

How it happened next, he could never really recall because he lost his head. He placed Philomena against the wall then dropped to his knees. Remnants of her delicate perfume commingled with her natural scent, creating a fragrance of rose and salt. He parted her pink folds, thinking they were similar to the flower's petals, and kissed them.

Philomena's knees buckled, and she clutched his shoulders for support.

His tongue darted in the channels, making short, quick movements, which caused her to sharply inhale. She began to knead his shoulders. Her fingernails scratched along his back but not hard enough to draw blood. She moaned and shivered, mumbling incoherently.

Solomon had glimpsed flashes of his wife's passions, but he had under-estimated her explosive response. She reacted like an untried maiden, as if she were new to sensual experiences and held in their thrall.

It was a matter of personal pride that she climax.

Her breathing hitched, and she murmured his name, over and over. It was a silent plea, begging him for release.

Wordlessly, he guided her to the floor. His mouth never left her petal-soft core. He suckled the tender nub, changing the rhythm and pressure. His hand worked in tandem with his mouth, and he was gratified when she arched off the floor.

Panting, shuddering, high with color, Philomena became a new creature whose face softened as her eyes grew dewy. Solomon had once imagined how she would look at this moment, but those imaginings were not worthy of his new reality. She had never looked more beautiful than she did now, lying naked on the floor, her long legs bathed in morning sunshine.

"God, you're beautiful, Mena."

His voice was unusually low. Solomon had never intentionally pushed the limits of celibacy, but he suspected he was precariously close. He stood then helped her upright.

The throbbing in his own loins made it impossible to dally. Solomon kissed her forehead then left, tossing over his shoulder a reminder that they would soon leave for Penrith.

Striding into his chambers, Solomon saw to his needs then quickly dressed and rushed through breakfast, anxious to get on the road, itching to spend the day with Philomena. He drank his coffee so fast it scalded his tongue, then he hurried to tell Alvin to harness the team.

Crossing the muddy foreyard, he paused at Philomena's window to holler, "Hurry up, slugabug."

She poked her head through the open window and waved.

Grinning broadly, he saluted her with his driving whip. "I told you I wanted to get an early start to Penrith."

"Nancy and I can't decide what I should wear. It may take hours before I'm ready." Her grin belied her words. She stepped in front of the window, tying the ribbon to her bonnet, fully clothed.

"If you aren't the most hoydenish—"

"Nonsense. Whoever heard of a hoydenish heiress?"

Despite his lips twitching in humor, Solomon deliberately made his voice stern. "Alvin's hitching the wagon. Get a move on."

He tossed the wire cages Alvin had constructed the day before onto the bed of the wagon then tied them down. Solomon loaded two more lengths of rope and a jug of cider Olivia had sent from the kitchen.

When Philomena appeared, she looked young and fresh, dressed in her green traveling gown. He helped her onto the wagon's bench. When she was settled, he flicked the whip, and the grays pulled out of the yard at a trot.

"My wife does me credit."

"Thank you. You look well yourself," she said. Her words came out nearly in a squeak, and her cheeks flushed. She folded her hands in her lap then flexed her fingers and refolded them. Philomena gazed off to the side of the road, as if she searched for something interesting among the hedges.

Was she embarrassed by his lovemaking? He frowned, realizing it must be so, but that didn't fit with what he knew of her past. Perhaps she was unfamiliar with his particular technique.

Glancing down at the new jacket Schweitzer had made for him in London, Solomon realized it had been nearly a month since he'd worn it.

"We needed reminding to wear our best clothes," he said.

"Yes."

"Perhaps we should plan a dinner party and show off our finery? Or host a ball?"

"The house isn't ready for such events. We don't even have a full staff, remember, but I intend your piano recital to be our first social occasion."

He sighed, as if it were a great burden he carried, but secretly he was pleased she hadn't forgotten. Philomena seemed to genuinely appreciate his musicality. It'd never occurred to him to play for others, but he found himself looking forward to the opportunity.

"It would be a nice way to thank our community after all the years of hardship."

"Yes, and you'll be splendid."

She clapped as she spoke, unable to contain her enthusiasm.

He smiled for no reason.

"Tell me," she said, tucking her hand into the crook of his arm. "Once the chicken coop's finished, what other projects do you want to accomplish on the farm?"

Not since his father's death had Solomon had someone with whom he could discuss these matters. They fell into discussions similar to the previous evenings where there was give-and-take on various approaches.

"I want to install a mill and wheelhouse. That would serve as a draw to this area, providing the village with more workers and employment."

"Would you also build a school for the village?"

He stared blankly at her. "I never thought of it."

"But surely you wish the tenants and their children to be educated, don't you?"

Chuckling, Solomon said, "I'm not opposed to the idea. It just never occurred to me."

"So, you'll do it?"

"Once we have enough pupils."

She clapped her hands. "Good. If we start building a schoolhouse now, and interview for a schoolmistress, perhaps by September…"

"Slow down, Philomena," he cautioned, comprehending his wife was not the kind of person to let the grass grow beneath her feet.

"What do you mean?"

"These past years, Lazonby has suffered a steady decline in tenants. With the crop failure of last year, we've barely survived. My first order of business is to put food on the tenants' tables, repair the cottage roofs. This revitalization plan, financed with your fortune, needs to be put into effect wisely. I must prioritize the projects, and there are many of them."

"I see. So, your first job is to see to the farm?"

"Yes."

"To grow the crops needed for milling. So that's why you want a plow?"

"Yes, for the upcoming planting season. We've lived on a steady diet of oats, barley, and turnips. Mr. Coke suggests expanding those selections, alternating yearly crops to replenish the soil, so I also want to purchase seed for wheat, rye, and beans."

"What about a greenhouse?"

"Like a forcing house?"

"Yes."

He frowned, adding up the costs and his long list of improvements, which grew longer the more he thought of it.

"I don't know where I'd place that in the list of priorities," he confessed.

"What are some other priorities?"

"Re-gravel the drive and village road, so it'll be easier to bring the crops to market."

Tapping her chin, she observed, "Once the coop's finished, can we expand the farm and bring in some pigs and dairy cows?"

"I don't see why not. In fact, that's a very good idea."

"Between the new crops, new livestock, and the game in the home woods, you needn't worry your tenants will starve now, even if there is another crop failure."

Unable to speak, Solomon waited for the constriction in his throat to ease. As if sensing his mood, Philomena patted his knee.

He gave her a sideways glance, horrified to discover she looked on the verge of tears.

"Oh, I am sorry my father was so wicked," she said, her voice breaking. "He did so much harm to your people. Of course you're grateful they'll eat better."

His heart swelled. "It was your father's perfidy that robbed the marquisate, but it's your generosity that will restore it."

Those moss-green eyes widened as her mouth formed a circle. "I always thought I was bad luck."

Chortling, he said, "No. You may sing off-key, but I wouldn't change a lovely curl on your head."

They entered into Penrith, laughing.

Chapter 18

Of course, the marquess was well known in Penrith, and Philomena had seen ample signs of Solomon's love for his community, but the exuberance with which he was greeted astonished her.

In keeping with his impeccable manners, he introduced her to the shopkeepers and townspeople. Once the greetings were completed, though, Philomena and Solomon became busy with some serious shopping. At the mercantile, they paid for the plow and brazier. Once those items were put on the wagon bed, there was room to spare, so they purchased three woolen rugs for the bedrooms.

In the midst of their purchases, Solomon mentioned that Lazonby needed laborers to gravel the road and drive. An older woman, overhearing this welcome news, hurriedly left the store, muttering that she'd send her son, Johnny, to his lordship on the instant.

The atmosphere in Mr. Tibbs' general store, already enlivened by Lord Lazonby's presence, buzzed with interest, and a small crowd formed around the marquess. Solomon answered a host of questions, repeating the plans they'd discussed during their drive to Penrith.

It annoyed her that Solomon hadn't adopted every one of her suggestions. Stubborn man, but in a flash of insight, she realized her husband had been forced to be self-reliant. After her father had swindled the previous marquess out of his fortune, Solomon had witnessed the diminution of their tenants, prized possessions, and even his family.

Solomon couldn't be managed by a strong-willed wife, and although Philomena recognized this attribute would mildly inconvenience her, she respected him for it.

On the heels of that epiphany, another knocked her with the force of one of Mr. Peck's blows. She loved Solomon. Her heart flipped in her chest, and her stays suddenly felt uncomfortably tight. A wave of heat rushed upward from her half-boots to the roots of her hair. She loved him. How had this happened? Why hadn't she noticed this was where her emotions had been leading her?

All the anger she'd experience while kissing him in the music room, all the joy he'd brought her this morning— merely two sides of the same coin. Ever since she'd been heartened to see that encouraging salute of his in St. James Park, Fate had been wrapping invisible ribbons around her, binding her to Solomon. It was inevitable that she fell in love with him. Of course it was.

This discovery was too fragile to be experienced in the middle of a crowded general store. Philomena shuffled aside, mumbling that she wished to select fabric to replace the music room's drapery. "So the piano recital can go forward," she said, uncertain whether Solomon heard her in the melee.

Sightlessly, she pretended to inspect the bolts of fabric, while her mind whirled with this newfound information. Could they make theirs a real marriage? Was it possible all those buoyant hopes she'd carried on that walk to St. George's Church could bear fruit? Solomon had no lover, as she'd imagined, and he appeared sincere in wishing to make theirs a real marriage. Did she dare hope?

Blood thrummed through her veins as the possibilities unfolded in marvelous study. She was so enraptured by these prospects, Philomena didn't notice the fair-headed gentleman until he spoke to her.

"Philomena Lower? Could it be... by the heavens, it *is* you!"

She didn't recognize the voice, which was hardly surprising since she'd heard nothing from him for seven years. Whirling around with a smile of greeting, Philomena stiffened upon seeing who spoke to her.

Randall Scott. She faced her erstwhile suitor, the one who'd claimed her heart, hand, and maidenhead.

The Fates sent a stinging reminder of her bad luck and the warning that believing in fairy tales was unwise.

"Hello, Mena," he said, leaning in as if he wished to create an aura of intimacy.

His hair was still blond, but there was less of it. The pink of his scalp was visible when he bowed. His nose resembled a red bulb, and he'd added at least a stone since she'd last seen him. Given his air of dissipation, Philomena doubted he could pursue any of the Corinthian activities he'd enjoyed while they'd been acquainted.

Quickly, she stepped backward. "Mr. Scott! What a surprise. How do you do?"

Before answering, he allowed his gaze to roam her form from top to bottom, lingering on certain parts.

She bristled, not caring for the proprietary gleam in his eye.

When he answered, he grinned slowly. "I do well but not half as well as you, apparently. The years have been kind to you, Mena. You're stunning."

Not caring for flattery, she turned the conversation away and asked, "Do you live nearby, Mr. Scott?"

His eyes glinted with sardonic humor. "You don't believe me, but I'm in earnest, Mena. You look lovely."

"Thank you, Mr. Scott." Again, she addressed him by his surname, hoping he'd take the hint and refrain from using her Christian name in public.

That hope died on the vine.

"Oh, Mena." He made a sorrowful shake of his head. "What happened that you can no longer accept a compliment?"

She almost snapped that it was his treachery that happened, but she remained mute, opting to uphold the decorum expected of a marchioness.

"You used to be quite fond of me, and I of you."

Randall lowered his voice, speaking so softly she was forced to lean in to hear his words. Immediately, she regretted it because his breath smelled bad.

Philomena wished Nancy were here. She would know exactly how to handle Randall's unwelcomed flirtation.

From the corner of her eye, she spied Solomon conversing with the older woman who'd dashed off to retrieve her son. Relieved that Solomon was oblivious to her predicament, Philomena focused on the bolts of fabric.

"That was a long time ago," she said.

"Yes," he said near her ear.

She batted her hand as if she were swatting a fly and 'accidentally' struck his cheek.

"Excuse me. I had no idea you were so close."

He gave an injured look but stopped crowding her. "What brings you to my fair city?"

"I'm shopping."

"Clearly. I've a better idea how to spend our time. Let's remove to the inn, partake of luncheon, then reminisce about old times. You can tell me how your family's doing and all that."

"Thank you, but no. I can tell you everything right here. Let's see, my father passed away last year. Holden's off to join the navy under Captain Broke, and Clarissa sailed for Italy last month."

Philomena stretched her lips and bared her teeth. She side-stepped, thinking to brush past him, but he gripped her upper arm.

Her gaze fixed upon the spot where he grabbed her. In a low undertone, she said, "You will release me, Mr. Scott."

"You're angry with me, aren't you, Mena? I don't blame you, I suppose. Your father never gave you my letters, did he?"

Shrugging out of his hold, she asked, "Your letters?"

"I wrote to you for months, but your father must have intercepted them. I suspected as much."

Whispering fiercely, she said, "I never received your correspondence. In fact, Sir John told me you failed to appear at the meeting."

"He lied." Muttering an oath, he grabbed her upper arms and gave her a little shake. "This is impossible. We must talk, Mena. Give me a chance to explain—"

"No." She broke his hold, embarrassed by this public display. "The past no longer matters."

"Of course it matters. *You* still matter to me. Please, Mena—"

"Have you selected the fabrics, my dear?"

If Philomena swallowed her teeth in surprise, she wouldn't have wondered at it. While Randall distracted her, Solomon had approached them. How much of their conversation he'd overheard, she didn't know, but she was acutely uncomfortable having the two men meet.

She *was* cursed.

What other conclusion could she draw when Randall's untimely appearance threatened to shatter her hopes of forging a real marriage with Solomon?

Philomena's gaze flickered to her husband's bland expression. The stoic show worried her. His impassiveness boded ill, but she wasn't certain if it would be directed to her or Randall.

Solomon draped an arm around her shoulder, bringing her into the side of his body in a hair-raising move. He'd only done that once before—after they left the church where they married. This was different from that, though. This moment wasn't one of jubilation. No, her husband's act now was territorial, claiming her as if she were a mere possession.

Philomena stiffened. As much as she scorned Randall's empty flattery, she didn't care for Solomon's possessive air. Resisting the temptation to walk away from both men, she instead performed the introductions.

"Mr. Scott, this is my husband, Lord Lazonby. Solomon, this is Mr. Scott."

Practically purring, her old suitor said, "Randall, if you please, your lordship. Mena and I are old friends."

Solomon ignored his outstretched hand but placidly remarked, "It's always pleasant to meet an old friend, but we're unable to linger. I have need of my wife at the moment, so please excuse us."

Philomena did a quick intake.

Mr. Scott's lips curled in a mocking smile, but he took his dismissal with equanimity. "It was a pleasure to meet you, Lord Lazonby. I hope you cherish the prize you have in your wife."

Randall's words made her flinch, but she allowed him to kiss the back of her hand. It would be impolite to refuse, but heat suffused her cheeks as her resentment nearly choked her.

"Goodbye, Mr. Scott," she said.

"Goodbye, sweet Mena."

Clenching her fists in impotent rage, Philomena turned her back to the departing figure.

"Are you well, Philomena?" Solomon asked quietly.

"Yes." Closing her eyes, she prayed he wouldn't press her for any details. She did not want their newfound amity ruined, and she rather thought telling Solomon he'd just been introduced to her former lover would do that.

"Have you found anything for the music room?" he asked.

Grateful for the reprieve, Philomena placed her hand on a random bolt of fabric. "What do you think of this?"

"That?" Solomon pointed to the material. "Are you serious? Mayhap we should send to Liverpool or Manchester for swatches if nothing here suits our tastes."

Philomena looked at the fabric then shuddered. She had stupidly picked puce, a reddish purple that wouldn't blend with anything in the house. Giving him a nervous smile, she lied, "I was quizzing you, Solomon."

Her eyes darted as she hurriedly surveyed the offerings. Her glance lit upon a sky-blue fabric, and she touched it and said, "Actually, I meant this one."

"That's perfectly acceptable," he agreed.

After a small discussion, they selected more fabrics for the bedroom hangings.

A timid woman stepped forward, holding the hand of a small girl, who coughed. The woman curtsied then waited to be recognized. Her daughter curtsied, too, then coughed again.

"Hello," Solomon greeted the females, offering his linen handkerchief to the girl.

"My lord, if I may offer my services? I'm a seamstress. If you plan to make curtains, as your lovely wife said, I can sew them and embroider the hems."

She curtsied again, revealing her nervousness in addressing a marquess. Her barefooted daughter dutifully mimicked her.

The girl looked to be no older than four years, but the sound of her cough was very phlegmy.

The mother was pale, her face pinched from too much worry and too little relief. Both were thin—painfully thin. Philomena feared a strong wind could lift the pair and carry them for miles.

"We don't have accommodations..." Solomon began, frowning then glancing at Philomena.

"Please, my lord. We can sleep on the kitchen floor, if necessary. I'm a widow, and my name is Ivy Smith. Cora's my daughter. The shopkeeper, Mr. Tibbs, will vouch for us."

Philomena touched Solomon's forearm, and he swiftly glanced at her, a troubled question in his eyes.

"Do you have a sewing kit?" Philomena asked Mrs. Smith.

"Yes, ma'am." The woman bobbed her head in answer.

"Will you fetch it, please?"

Audibly swallowing, Mrs. Smith said, "It's at home, two miles away. I'd have to leave Cora here. She couldn't walk four, or rather, six more miles today."

Crestfallen, the woman turned away, tugging on the girl's hand. "Come away, Cora."

"Please stay," Philomena said.

Turning to the shopkeeper, Mr. Tibbs, Philomena asked for a needle and thread. "Mrs. Smith, will you show me an example of your work while Lord Lazonby takes Cora to purchase a sweet?"

At the word 'sweet,' the girl brightened considerably.

So did Solomon.

Hand in hand, he led the girl to the candy counter and allowed her to choose something. Those round eyes widened even more, and a flush of pleasure entered her cheeks, giving Cora a temporary, healthy glow.

Mrs. Smith quickly threaded the needle the shopkeeper had provided, flashing a quick grin at Mr. Tibbs's whispered encouragement.

Mrs. Smith set a row of perfectly even stitches. With deft movements, she then drew the thread through the fabric until a flower emerged with petals and leaves.

Before she inspected the work, Philomena had determined to hire the woman. The health of Mrs. Smith's child would never improve if she walked barefoot in the cold mornings.

Since her arrival at Lazonby, Philomena had not ventured to the kitchens or the servants' quarters, assuming she wouldn't be in residence long enough to involve herself in domestic matters. Now, she was angered by her short-sightedness. Ivy and Cora would need a place to sleep, as would the other staff members Solomon thought to interview tomorrow and whomever he'd hired today.

They would have to prepare for the new staff in a hurry. Looking at Cora, she frowned, wondering how the pair would make their way to Lazonby, fifteen miles hence.

Solomon and Cora strolled up to them. The girl admired her mother's handiwork, while the marquess offered Mrs. Smith a peppermint from his bag.

"Care for one, my lady?" he asked, holding out the bag to her.

"Thank you."

He inspected Mrs. Smith's needlework, his jaw working as he chewed on his peppermint.

Philomena blushed, recalling how Solomon's mouth had worked on her this morning. What ecstasy he'd wrought with his mouth. She had no idea these were the sorts of intimacies that could occur in marriage, but she grew warm, remembering them. Her cheeks heated as she realized how very much she looked forward to more of Solomon's wickedly delightful lovemaking.

"Very nice," he murmured, so busy inspecting the handiwork that he didn't notice Philomena's flushed countenance, for which she was grateful.

"What do you think, my lady? Should Mrs. Smith become seamstress for Lazonby?"

Once more, Mrs. Smith's daughter latched onto her hand, and the pair waited, tense and anxious.

Solomon had an amused glint in his eyes, as if he were well aware Philomena would offer the job to Mrs. Smith.

"It's not just drapes that we require but also new uniforms for the incoming staff and bed linens. There are several chair covers that need to be replaced, so if you're versed in needlepoint as well..."

"I am, my lady."

"Aye," piped up the grandfatherly shopkeeper, clearly an advocate for the widow. "I know for a fact Mrs. Smith has sewn the vicar's new robes and mended his others. He's very particular, our Mr. Gaines."

"Excellent." Philomena addressed the widow. "Mrs. Smith, would you like to work for the marquess?"

"Yes, ma'am." She curtsied.

So did Cora.

After exchanging a look of amusement with Philomena, Solomon asked the widow when she could begin.

Mrs. Smith's face clouded. "We need to return to our home, pack a few belongings, then travel to Lazonby. I... I can't say when, my lord."

"I can take you, Mrs. Smith, day after tomorrow, if that suits," offered Mr. Tibbs, the shopkeeper.

"Thank you." She smiled her gratitude toward that worthy merchant.

"Marvelous." Solomon dropped a guinea in the widow's hand and extended his arm. "All that remains is to purchase some cough syrup for your daughter."

Mrs. Smith's smile broadened.

Philomena watched her husband escort the widow and her young daughter to the apothecary's. Whatever remnants of irritation she'd felt toward him vanished. She was devoutly glad she'd found this prince of a marquess.

Chapter 19

Their shared luncheon was delicious. Solomon had taken his madam wife to a private dining room in the Penrith posting inn to dine on pheasant, green beans, cheese, bread, and a cherry tart with clotted cream. While he'd eaten with relish, he noticed Philomena had not.

Ever since meeting her old friend, Philomena had been distracted. She'd sat through the meal mumbling to herself and making notes. His wife had transformed into a Nervous Nellie, worrying about readying Lazonby for the incoming staff. She muttered about cleaning the servants' quarters, irritated with herself that she wasn't certain where they were or their dimensions.

It might have amused him, watching Philomena brood, but he also wondered if her recent loss of composure wasn't related to meeting Mr. Randall Scott again. How important had the blighter been in his wife's history?

"It will all work out, Mena," he told her, not for the first time.

"How like a man!" she retorted cryptically.

"Really, my dear, you're worrying over nothing. All this can be handled by Olivia and Willy."

She continued to jot down errands on her to-do list, not even glancing his direction.

"Mena, how well did you know Mr. Scott?" He kept his tone light, as if he were simply making conversation rather than being so curious he thought he'd go mad.

She shrugged, and her gaze returned to her list, but she murmured, "He was a suitor, but I haven't seen him in years."

"What happened?"

"What happened?" she repeated dumbly, shuffling through her notes.

He lifted his brow and waited.

The silence finally penetrated his wife's concentration, and she presented a furrowed brow when she finally looked up. Philomena sat in confusion before comprehension dawned. Her eyes widened as she asked, "Oh, what happened to Mr. Scott's pursuit?"

"Yes."

She chuckled. "It died. One day he attended me, and the next day–poof! He was gone."

Solomon's heart stilled. Was Randall Scott the dastard who had defiled Philomena then abandoned her once he received her father's bribe? He watched the passing emotions cross her face. Gentle humor gave sway to a wistful sadness.

"You were disappointed," he said, experiencing a sudden and inexplicable tightening in his chest.

Frowning, she contemplated her answer before slowly replying. "For a while, I was. I was very green and very young, remember." Flashing an irreverent grin, she quipped, "He was more handsome then."

This was worse than he thought. She was making light of her youthful flirtation. Had Philomena been in love with that nodcock?

Clearing his throat, he then asked, "Was Mr. Scott your first suitor?"

"As a matter of fact, he was."

Thankfully, his wife's gaze had returned to those damnable lists, for Solomon was certain his expression would betray his disgust at that man's actions.

"I wonder if I misjudged Mr. Scott."

"I doubt it," he muttered.

"Beg your pardon?"

"Nothing. In what way do you think you misjudged him?"

"I don't know that I have," she corrected with a schoolteacher's precision. "With his abrupt departure, I thought my father interfered in the relationship, perhaps threatened or bribed him."

Solomon held his breath as his wife danced on the edge of that sharp knife of truth.

"However, this morning, he told me he'd sent letters. Letters that would have explained why he left so abruptly. Needless to say, I never received them, but if he explained his absence, I wish I'd learned of it."

"It was a long time ago," he said. "Does it matter to you? Does he still matter to you?"

"It matters if I've wronged him," she said gently. "But no, Mr. Scott no longer matters to me. That was over years ago."

"I understand."

She smiled then swerved into a different subject by asking, "Did you ensure Cora took the syrup?"

He declined to immediately respond.

"Well?" she asked.

Her lips, the color of a ripened peach, pursed, and he couldn't resist the temptation to kiss them until they softened. He leaned forward and brushed his mouth against hers in a soft salute, intending a brief buss, but Mena touched the side of his face, and he went up in flames.

Her rose-scented perfume wafted to him, teasing his senses. As wonderful as she smelled, he knew holding her would be even better. A strong compulsion gripped him, and being a man of action, he swiftly stepped around the table to draw her into his arms. With her arms outstretched, Mena seemed to have anticipated him, and a thrill of delight passed through him because she'd read his intent.

They kissed deeply, and he held her close to his heart, as if she were the glue that kept his mind, body, and soul together.

"Mena. My Mena."

She purred in the back of her throat, and her fingers toyed with his hair.

What he would have done next he never discovered, for the landlady's son entered the room.

A little squeak came from Philomena as she jumped out of his arms.

Damning the youth's timing, Solomon walked to the window and waited for him to clear the empty dishes.

After the door shut behind him, Philomena giggled.

Smiling, he swerved his gaze to her.

"He saw us! Mercy, I've never been so embarrassed." To prove it, Philomena fanned her red cheeks.

"Serves him right for not knocking."

Chuckling at her heightened color, he paused, wondering how she could appear so innocent yet be experienced. Sometimes Philomena baffled him.

Abruptly, he said, "A man can kiss his wife in private, Mena, and yes, I personally observed Cora drink the cough syrup."

"What?" She gave herself a shake, retracing their previous conversation. "Oh, yes. Thank you."

Tilting his head, Solomon considered this Randall Scott. Mena couldn't be infatuated with the blighter, otherwise she'd never respond to him as she did.

Solomon paid the shot on that cheerful thought, then they parted ways—Solomon to collect the livestock while Philomena shopped for food to feed all the incoming employees.

The butcher directed him to the paddock behind his store. After paying for two cows and pig, Solomon and the butcher tied the animals to the back of the wagon. The butcher returned to gather the chickens in the cages Solomon had brought, but he was stayed by an interesting sight. Across the alley from the livery, he spied Mr. Scott joining a woman dressed in high fashion.

Scott's companion possessed the typical coloring of a British female, but it was her outfit that drew the eye. Her bonnet, tilted at a roguish angle, was flamboyant, and he doubted another woman could have worn it with aplomb.

"Dear sissy!" Mr. Scott greeted the female with his arms outstretched.

She whacked him with her parasol and snapped, "Stop! You know I hate it when you call me that."

Mr. Scott chuckled. "I've just met Mena, so stop your frowning. Our trip has already borne fruit."

Solomon's ears perked up when he heard his wife's name on the man's lips. He strained to hear their conversation, but the butcher returned, hauling the crate of chickens.

"My lord?"

The interruption prevented any more eavesdropping, but Solomon's mind turned over the phrase, 'our trip has borne fruit.' That stayed with him as he finished the rest of his chores, the faint ominous tone spurring Solomon to write to Charles Dryden. He'd ask his friend to make inquiries of Mr. Randall Scott—and his sister, whose identity remained unknown.

They departed Penrith with his wife full of ambitious plans for improving the household, which he doubted she could accomplish before hying off to her stupid seaside cottage. At least, he hoped so. He never wished Mena to put that plan into action because the idea of her living elsewhere irritated him. From her enthusiasm and innate understanding of the tenants' needs, he couldn't have imagined a better mistress for Lazonby. He must persuade her to change her mind. The estate needed a caring marchioness.

Speaking over the din caused by the animals, Philomena loudly repeated herself on their return journey. All of a sudden, for no particular reason, their gazes snagged, and they began to laugh at the absurdity of their situation: a pair of aristocrats shouting to be heard over chickens, pigs, and cows. She held her belly and leaned against him. Solomon couldn't remember the last time he'd laughed so hard.

Perhaps it wasn't only for his tenants' sakes that he wished to persuade Philomena to stay at Lazonby.

Upon arrival, it was pressed upon Solomon how he routinely under-estimated his wife to his peril. Philomena was determined to get to work as soon as she alighted from the wagon. Calling for Nancy, she entered the house, while he unloaded the livestock and brazier.

Foregoing her afternoon tea, Philomena commandeered Nancy and his half-siblings to prepare a room for Mrs. Smith and Cora. The four cleaned a large room at the back of the house, aired the bedding, and scavenged to find sufficient furniture to accommodate the modest needs of the widow and her sickly child.

They enjoyed a simple dinner, pushed back half an hour so Philomena could change into a clean gown. In the midst of sharing an amusing anecdote, he darted a glance at his wife. With her head cradled in her palm, and her elbow propped on the table, she had fallen asleep listening to his tales.

"You poor thing." Solomon chuckled, scooping her from the chair.

Philomena nestled into his arms then blinked drowsily. "I'm sorry, Solomon. What were you saying?"

"Nothing of import." He smiled, striding from the dining room as a sense of well-being settled into him, liking the weight of his wife in his arms. Glancing down at his burden, tenderness stirring in his breast, Solomon wondered when Mena had grown on him.

Lazonby didn't just need a marchioness; he needed a wife.

Suppressing a sigh, he also acknowledged he needed a good romp in bed. He wanted a lover, and he wanted it to be Mena. Damn the circumstances that made it impossible for him to claim her as his own. At times like these, it was very difficult to hold the line.

Nancy wasn't in Philomena's chambers, so the task of undressing her fell to him. His smile broadened then disappeared. Staring into the face of a sleeping woman, Solomon felt the sting of disappointment. He was too much of a gentleman to press his wife for favors tonight. Damn him for being such a randy fellow.

Carefully, he placed Mena on the bed and gently removed her garments so as not to disturb her sleep. Once she was in her linen chemise, he loosened its ribbon then glimpsed her long, lean thighs. The tender skin had begun to pebble in the cool air, so with a great deal of regret, he covered her with a blanket.

Quietly, he stood over her, his hands on his hips as his appreciative gaze passed over his wife. Although they had a uniquely flammable chemistry, it wasn't only lust Philomena inspired within him. There was something more. Solomon hoped that, whatever it was, it would prove sufficient for them to have a successful marriage. He wanted to build a future together, which would be impossible if she lived in some far-off cottage by the ocean.

What did Mena want?

Who was this Randall Scott, her old friend from the past? Why had his off-chance remark to his sister cast such a pall upon Solomon's day? Turning on his heel, he went to his study and wrote to Charles.

Traipsing back upstairs to his bed, he debated for a moment at the head of the stairs. Should he go to his room or return to Philomena's?

If she left Lazonby, he'd have to get used to an empty bed again, and Solomon enjoyed sleeping next to a warm, soft body.

"No sense depriving yourself."

Quietly, he entered her chamber, undressed then joined her.

Immediately, she snuggled against him then mumbled something.

"Mop first? No, dust. The dust will fall everywhere and make another mess. What about the mattresses? They'll probably need new straw."

His belly shook with repressed laughter. His wife was no curse, she was a blessing.

Chapter 20

Three days after their excursion to Penrith, Nancy appeared in Philomena's chamber, carrying a breakfast tray.

"Good morning!" her companion greeted her.

Philomena's brows arched at the cheery greeting. Nancy was not, and had never been, a morning person. Even simple conversation was beyond her before breakfast. At that time of day, the best her companion usually managed was a series of grunts.

"Good morning," Philomena replied, curious as to what had caused such a transformation in Nancy. "You seem especially cheerful. Have you been awake long?"

"Well, Rascal woke me, so I was letting her out to do her business when a man and his two sons came looking for work. I chatted with them until his lordship arrived to interview him."

Philomena blushed, knowing she'd been the reason Solomon had been late this morning. He had come to her bed each night, and while he initiated her to the pleasures of the flesh, they had yet to become one. What began as pleasurable lovemaking was becoming torturous. Each time Solomon left, she was only partly satiated. Her body coiled into a compressed spring, as if she were wound so tightly she'd soon explode.

Solomon's ministrations left her panting for more. It seemed every morning he drove her into a fevered pitch then left her doused with a bucket of cold water. The journeys to ecstasy were delicious, but the abrupt endings would drive her mad. The only reason she hadn't lost her temper was because Solomon was also gratifyingly frustrated.

Pointing to the tray Nancy had placed on the bedside table, Philomena asked, "Is that chocolate?"

"Yes. I'm awfully glad you were able to purchase some in Penrith." Nancy poured the small pot of hot chocolate into a dainty teacup then stirred the mixture. She tapped the spoon on the edge of the china then picked up the cup and saucer.

Reaching for it, Philomena marveled, "Me, too. How I love my morning chocolate!"

"Being without for the past month has been a hardship," Nancy said, closing her eyes as she drank. "I don't know when I became so spoiled."

Philomena's smile faltered, and her hand fell away. Sighing, she poured what remained in the pot into a second cup for herself.

Nancy's lips stretched in a dreamy smile, and she sighed deeply.

"Oho," Philomena said, her senses sharpening. "You've taken a fancy to someone. Who? No, don't tell me. Let me guess."

Like a satisfied cat lapping at its bowl of milk, Nancy smiled.

"Can't be Willy."

Philomena laughed, hearing Nancy's indignant harrumph. "No, all right then. Let's see... there are so few possibilities. Alvin? The groom?"

"A fine man, to be sure, and if I were forty, I'd set my cap on him."

"You're eight-and-thirty!" Philomena sputtered.

"I am not," Nancy hotly denied.

Philomena's fine eyebrows drew together as she performed some mathematical calculations. Nodding at herself, she said, "You'll be eight-and-thirty within three months."

"Still..."

Suppressing her smile for Nancy's persnickety reaction, Philomena asked, "Oh no! You've not fallen for the vicar, have you? Nancy, he's a married man! Happily married, I might add."

"Don't be daft, Mena." Nancy scowled. "No, it'll do you no good guessing because you've not met the man."

"Oh. Well, that wasn't very sporting of you."

"But I did mention him, for he was the laborer I let into the house this morning."

"What's his name?"

"Mr. Maclean. He's Scottish, a widower, and has two sons. I hope his lordship hires him."

Frowning, Philomena murmured, "Where could a family of three live?"

Nancy shrugged.

"We've readied the attics for the staff Solomon's hired—a butler, two footmen, three maids, and a housekeeper, so now I suppose we'll have to clear out the rooms above the stables."

"Can't put a family in the stable barracks."

"No," Philomena fretted. "Of course not. I suppose I'll have to find an empty cottage on the estate?"

"That'd be lovely," Nancy said. "Just don't place him too far from this main house, my dear."

"I'm anxious to meet this Mr. Maclean. Speaking of men, you'll never believe who I met in Penrith the other day."

"You met someone you know in Penrith? Why didn't you say so? Who was it?"

"Randall Scott."

Nancy's cup rattled in the saucer. "I must have misheard."

Smiling ruefully, Philomena said, "No, you heard correctly. I met Randall in the general store."

"Why didn't you tell me this sooner?"

Philomena shrugged. "I forgot. In the midst of preparing for the staff, it slipped my mind."

"Well, well, well. That proves he's not important to you. Was it awkward?"

"Yes. Can you believe it, he tried flirting with me, and with Solomon in the store to boot!"

"Did you set a flea in his ear, Mena?"

"No. If anything, it was quite the reverse."

"How so?"

"He told me he still cared for me, and that he'd sent me letters to explain his disappearance."

Nancy's mouth knotted in a sardonic twist.

Philomena hesitated, mortified to speak her secret suspicions aloud. "Randall said he'd ask Father for my hand, and based on the strength of that promise, we anticipated our vows. Afterward, Randall disappeared. I've always suspected Father paid him to do so."

Chewing her bottom lip, Nancy asked, "I am right, aren't I? You don't still care for Randall?"

"No, you're right. That's long past." Philomena sat at her dresser and retrieved her hairbrush. "He behaved very possessively toward me, and it made my skin crawl. Furthermore, his hair's so thin he may go bald in the next half hour."

Nancy laughed, as Philomena intended.

Her companion put her empty cup on the tray then came to stand behind Philomena. Taking the brush from her, Nancy took over the chore of styling Philomena's hair.

"You're happy with his lordship?"

"For a marriage of convenience, it's proven maddeningly inconvenient."

"You've fallen in love with him, haven't you, Mena?"

"No, I haven't. He doesn't love me."

Ignoring her companion's healthy skepticism, Philomena bid Nancy good morning then left.

The past few days, Philomena had been busy with preparations for the incoming staff. She'd helped scrub floors and sweep cobwebs from the servants' quarters in the attics and found a great deal of satisfaction in seeing their remarkable progress. She had not had to perform domestic chores in the years since her father had become wealthy enough to hire staff, and she found she enjoyed the physical activity. Granted, Philomena would not wish to do this every day, but for the time being, she found it rewarding.

Willy had cut straw and helped Nancy re-stuff the mattresses, while Philomena had mended bedlinens and Mrs. Smith had sewn curtains from the old drapes in the music room. Mrs. Rodgers had overseen the re-dyeing of the silk, and there was enough left over to re-upholster the sofa for the drawing room.

She met Willy in the foyer. He had a small purse on him and carried a packet of letters. Little Cora was dangling from his arm, begging to ride along with him.

"No, Cora. It's much too far. I'm going to Carlisle."

"Were you planning to ride?" Philomena asked.

"Yes."

"Instead of riding, would you take the wagon and fetch some woolen blankets and pillows for the attic rooms?"

"All right," he agreed then wagged his finger at the little girl. "But I'm still not taking you with me."

Cora's lower lip jutted out, and Willy's eyes enlarged before he quickly told her, "It's too dangerous, and you'd be bored with the drive. Would you like it if I brought you back a sweet? Or a dolly?"

The girl's jaw dropped, and she whispered, "A dolly? Of my very own?"

"Your very own," he promised. "Besides, I need you to remain here and meet the Maclean boys."

Willy glanced at Philomena. "Laz hired Mr. Maclean earlier this morning, so we have three new tenants on the estate. Did you know?"

"I suspected as much from what Nancy told me. Do you know where his lordship intends to house the Maclean family?"

"One of the vacant estate cottages, I suppose. They're already plowing the north field with Solomon."

Until her husband hired enough field hands and gained more tenants, he labored alongside the workers. Philomena suspected he received satisfaction from seeing the fruits of his endeavors, just as she did. They were odd ducks for a marquess and marchioness, but at least they matched.

Hearing the new family was already at work, Philomena frowned. "Didn't Solomon take the Macleans to their home so they could unpack before they began work?"

Willy chuckled. "I don't think so. They came with only the possessions on their backs. Seemed eager to start."

Groaning, Philomena realized her plans for the day had shifted. "I really wanted to work on the music room, but my time would be better spent preparing a cottage for the Scottish family."

"Yes," Willy said, heading out the door. He stopped and lifted his head. "Oh, Mena?"

"Yes."

"Were you aware Laz pawned his signet ring to finance his London trip?"

"Why, no, I wasn't."

"I only bring it up because I pawned it for him in Carlisle—"

"And you might as well redeem it today while you're there?"

"Yes."

She clapped. "Good thinking! I'm so glad you told me. Yes, by all means redeem it, but allow me to return it to him, please? I want it to be a surprise."

He grinned and gave her a salute.

Shaking her head, Philomena marveled that Willy would become irresistible to women within a few short years. She couldn't be the only female who found jaunty salutes so enticing.

"Buy at least twenty blankets and pillows, if you can!" she hollered after him.

"Don't forget my dolly!" Cora reminded him.

He lifted his hand in acknowledgment then rounded the house. Philomena stared down at Cora, whose uplifted face wore an expectant expression.

"Shall we go tour the cottages?"

"Please!"

They popped into the apartment off the kitchen to check in with Mrs. Smith then admired her close stitching on the clothes she'd finished for the butler and footmen, who would begin work tomorrow.

"When you begin on the maids' dresses, would you also sew one for my companion, Nancy?" Philomena asked the seamstress. "And before you begin, please ask the females which fabric they prefer. I see no reason they shouldn't have their choice."

"Yes, my lady." Mrs. Smith chuckled. "There's certainly a wide variety for them to pick their favorite."

Grinning, Philomena asked, "Which will you choose?"

"Me?" The young widow gaped then shook her head as if coming out of a daze. "I never dreamt—"

"Of course you and Cora must have new gowns."

"I'm getting a dolly!" the little girl informed her mother. "Willy's bringing it back. He says it'll be my very own."

Staring dumbfounded at her daughter, Mrs. Smith dabbed her eyes before giving a watery chuckle.

Four days of medicine, food, and rest had banished Cora's earlier illness. Mrs. Smith had used his lordship's guinea wisely, buying new shoes for them both, along with the cough syrup.

Sniffing, she said, "I'm so grateful to you, Lady Lazonby."

"I hope you'll both be happy here. Coming Cora?"

Taking the marchioness's outstretched hand, Cora skipped along at Philomena's side, with Rascal trailing behind them.

They wandered, exploring the new chicken coop and pigsty, waving to Alvin the groom, who led one of the cows from the stall back to the pasture. The first estate cottage was occupied by the Bransons, a family of eight. Cora shyly waved to the daughters of the house while Philomena introduced herself.

After a short visit, the trio followed a dirt trail to an empty cottage Philomena intended for the Macleans. Rascal allowed Cora to carry her.

"The roof needs rethatching," Philomena muttered before shoving the door open.

Its hinges protested, giving an agonized wail, which caused Rascal to leap from Cora's arms.

Philomena grinned at her indignant companion. "Do you wish to remain outside with Rascal while I inspect the place?"

Shaking her head violently, Cora tightened her clasp on Philomena's hand. "No. I want to stay with you."

"You're much braver than Rascal."

Hand in hand, they inspected the cottage. The living space required a good sweeping, but it was dry and free of mouse droppings. Some of the furniture must be replaced or mended, she noted, jotting down other items on her list. They'd need candles, food, and blankets immediately. The mattresses were so lumpy, the Macleans might be more comfortable sleeping on the floor until she could have them re-stuffed.

Before leaving, she opened the windows to air the house. The maids would need to give it a thorough cleaning, and she would have Nancy bring the necessary items this afternoon. Perhaps her companion would have to make two trips?

Philomena grinned, knowing Nancy would thank her for that.

"There's a lot of work to be done," said Cora, casting a dubious eye over the interior of the cottage.

"Quite a lot," Philomena agreed, happy to be a part of restoring the Lazonby estates. Glad she was no longer a harbinger of bad fortune.

Chapter 21

Solomon was nervous. He'd never played in public before, at least, not on such a grand scale as this. Sitting on the piano bench, with the tails of his newly tailored coat splayed to his sides, he couldn't quite believe the size of this crowd. How had Mena managed to create a fete out of thin air?

Lazonby had never celebrated the end of planting season, but from the number of smiles he saw on the people's faces, Solomon knew this was the start of a tradition. With the variety of new crops already planted, and the additional livestock and tenant farms, he prayed his home was on the cusp of a new era of prosperity, and he had his wife to thank for that.

Mena had persuaded Mr. Watson to loan the church pews for the piano recital in exchange for a donation to repair the roof. Nancy had spent the past week instructing the Maclean lads how to reupholster the dining room and music room chairs. Tenants had built benches and tables, while Mrs. Rodgers and the newly enhanced kitchen staff had filled those tables with numerous dishes to create a dizzying buffet.

The celebrations had started this morning with foot races and archery contests for the townspeople and tenants. Throughout the day, people mingled on the terrace, played cards, talked to their neighbors, or strolled Lazonby grounds. By afternoon, his lady wife presented silk ribbons to the winners of the morning games. Lifting his tankard of ale, Solomon joined in saluting the winners to a round of hearty cheers. Unable to contain his joy, he'd kissed Mena at the ribbon ceremony, and the cheers grew louder. All of Lazonby adored the new marchioness, as did he.

These past few weeks, she had loved him every night. She was so eager to explore their relationship that Solomon could hardly restrain himself from taking her. Mena's responses had been untutored, but as a lover she was playful, inquisitive, and unstinting. She hadn't known the first thing about sexual awakenings until he ignited those fires within her. His wife was an innocent for all practical purposes. The man who had taken her maidenhead had not thoroughly performed the job, and no one else had followed him, Solomon slowly realized. His cynicism had blinded him to his wife's chastity, but now she fit so nicely in his arms, he couldn't imagine sleeping without her. She had become essential to his continued happiness.

Solomon was to provide the evening's entertainment; as the people shuffled into the music room, his chest swelled with pride for Mena's accomplishments. This room showed the most startling transformation in the house. Cream walls, ivory plaster, and icy blue upholstery set off the room's natural elegance, but Mrs. Smith had embroidered the drapes with the Lazonby crest. After the fifth mixture, the painters matched the precise shade of blue of the chairs to the ceiling. At the center of the room stood the gleaming piano, and the chairs and benches circled it.

The windows were open, and a light breeze cooled the heat of so many bodies. Even with the scramble of seating for which Philomena had bartered, some men were standing against the walls. If anyone had told Solomon four months ago that his house would be overflowing with drink, food, song, and well-wishers, he never would have believed it.

Laughingly, he addressed the crowd. "Lady Lazonby has wrought a small miracle in bringing us all together like this. I wish to express my thanks for her hard work."

Wearing a pink satin gown with a pearlized overskirt, Philomena looked young and fresh. Her curly hair was cut shorter, with a small rosebud pinned above one ear.

Philomena looked exactly as a marchioness should look—regal and kind. She beamed at the applause that followed his remarks and pressed her hands together. Their gazes met, and a bubble of happiness rose from within him, something light and delicate yet steadfast. He had to give himself a shake to remember his next words.

"We wish to thank you for coming to Lazonby, and we hope you've enjoyed yourselves. I also wish to express my gratitude for your continued friendship, and I ask that you accept my gift of song for that appreciation." He paused briefly, before announcing, "*Für Elise* by Ludwig van Beethoven."

Solomon intentionally started with the simplest of pieces, and within a few measures, he found his nerves had settled and he played for the sheer joy of it.

When he finished, he looked to Mena to see her response. Smiling enthusiastically, she clapped, and he grinned before introducing his next piece.

"Georg Friedrich Handel's *Wassermusik*." This, too, he performed flawlessly, as if the Fates smiled upon him.

At the end of the recital, Solomon stood to thunderous applause. His mood was one of elation, and he beckoned Philomena to join him. The clapping accelerated, and shouts were sent up.

Shyly, as if she were bewildered by this enthusiasm, Philomena took his hand and performed a graceful curtsy as he bowed.

"You did this, Mena," he whispered in her ear. Then he loudly hailed his wife by clapping and saying, "Bravo!"

He allowed her to relish in those golden moments then took her hand to lead her to a private alcove where he intended to spend the next half hour kissing her senseless, but this was not to be.

Revelers swarmed them, claiming their attention, complimenting his talent. Willy pried Philomena away with a request from the kitchens, and reluctantly Solomon released Mena so she could perform her duties.

Solomon watched her slender form as she hurried away and felt a pang at being separated. Tonight, he would not stop their lovemaking. This night, he intended to consummate their union, proving how completely he loved and trusted her.

Shrugging off his disappointment, Solomon then engaged in conversation with another of his guests. There was such an atmosphere of bonhomie that nearly an hour had passed before he searched for his wife again, wondering at her long absence.

Setting down his champagne, he went to look for her.

"Willy, where's Mena?"

His brother's cheeks were slashed with color, and his eyes were fever-bright. Willy flung his hand out, knocking Nancy inadvertently.

"Whazzat, Laz? Sorry. So sorry, Nance."

The mortified look on Willy's face deepened beneath her maternal glare.

"My God, you're as drunk as a wheelbarrow," Solomon said with a laugh.

Giving him a silly grin and saucy salute, Willy said, "Correct!"

Turning to his newest tenant, Mr. Maclean, Solomon asked, "Would you see that Willy gets to his bed? I'm afraid he won't be able to maneuver the stairs in his present case without assistance."

"Certainly, my lordship." The Scot nodded, good humor lighting his eyes.

"I'll help Willy, too," Nancy volunteered.

Together the pair tried to discreetly escort Willy from the room. Their subtlety was wasted by his brother's cheerful waves to the rest of the room.

Shaking his head, Solomon watched them depart, but before he could resume his search for Mena, he was waylaid again as some guests were taking their leave.

"Where is her ladyship?" he inquired of a new footman whose name escaped him.

The man looked about, as if the marchioness would suddenly appear in his range of vision. Did he not think Solomon could do the same?

"Never mind," he snapped. "I'll find Mena. If you see the marchioness, tell her I'm looking for her."

"Yes, my lord."

Solomon returned to the music room, but she was not there. He walked through the entire lower level, barely keeping his stride in check as he hid his agitation.

Still no sign of Mena.

Hoping he might find his wife on the terrace, Solomon searched it out only to surprise the couple who were taking advantage of the dark corner as he'd planned earlier.

"Nancy! Mr. Maclean, beg your pardon."

Swiftly, Solomon returned to the drawing room, hands on his hips, thinking of all possible places his wife could be hiding, for certainly she had stayed out of sight long enough that her disappearance must be intentional.

Philomena must have a headache. Although she had never been prone to the ailment, he supposed the tensions of throwing this elaborate party would have caused one.

Deciding to allow his wife to recover her spirits in the quiet of her own room, Solomon then joined another group of landowners and lost himself in agricultural forecasts.

The next morning came far earlier than he would have wished, and far too late.

The new butler, Woodsworth, pounded on his chamber door in a most unseemly manner. Intending to put a flea in the man's ear, Solomon donned his worn robe and yanked open the door.

"What is it?"

"Forgive me, my lord, but I just found this near the coal room."

"A ring box?" Solomon opened it, confused to discover his signet ring. He hadn't thought of asking Willy to redeem it since returning from London.

"Where did you say you found this?"

Miserably, the butler said, "Near the coal room. Lord Lazonby, I also found this."

The man pulled forth a mutilated rosebud and hank of brown, curly hair.

Solomon shoved Woodsworth aside and raced to Philomena's room. The curtains were drawn so the room was dark and airless. A chill slithered up his spine as he viewed the empty bed with its pillows and counterpane in pristine condition.

Philomena had not slept here last night. And she sure as hell hadn't slept with him, so where was she?

The ring box fell to the floor, slipping from his nerveless fingers. Running his hand over his chin, Solomon dimly noted his knees weakening.

"What did you say?" He turned, frowning at the butler, who had repeatedly said something to him.

"Shall I call upon her maid?"

"No, I'll do it." He strode from the room and rapped on Nancy's door, waking her as rudely as Woodsworth had him.

Bleary-eyed, she leaned against the doorjamb and blinked. "Yes, my lord?"

"Where's Mena?"

She blinked again then perfected the owlish impersonation by uttering, "Who?"

"Mena," he said distinctly. "Mena's gone. Do you know where she is?"

The woman rushed past him, ignoring his warning that she wasn't in her room. When Nancy whirled about in the empty chamber, her eyes sought his, and he read the confusion there.

"Where could she have gone?" Her hands flailed; she was at a loss for an answer.

Tight-lipped and worried, Solomon returned to his chambers and dressed. Then he searched the house, starting with the coal cellar. He found nothing. He walked around the chicken coop and barnyard, wondering if she'd taken some maggoty notion to visit the animals.

He returned to the house, climbed the stairs, then woke Willy.

"Do you know where Mena is?"

Clasping his head, Willy urged him to lower his voice, which Solomon did with exaggerated patience.

"Mena's missing. Do you know where she is?"

"What? No." Willy groaned, leaning back on his pillow.

Solomon shook his shoulder. "You were the last to see her, dear brother, and if you don't come awake right now, I'll toss you in the pigsty."

Willy sat upright, adjusting his eyes to the glare of the morning sun. After rolling his head, he knuckled away the sleep from his eyes and said, "Start again. Mena's missing, you say?"

"Yes." Solomon stood and tossed the ring box down on the bed. "Woodsworth found this and a hank of her hair with the rosebud by the coal cellar."

Swiping the box, Willy opened it and smiled at the signet ring. "I told Mena you pawned your ring to finance the London trip, so she asked me to redeem it. She planned on giving it to you last night."

"What time did you last see her? And where?"

Willy crunched his nose as he recollected the hazy details. "I saw her after you played, around eight o'clock?"

"Yes. Go on."

"I had to bring her to the kitchen. There was a squabble with one of the merchants."

"Who? What merchant?"

He shrugged. "I don't know."

"Would Olivia know?"

Swinging his legs off the bed, Willy said, "Let's ask her."

But Solomon wasn't going to wait on his unsteady brother. He found Olivia in the kitchen, but she wasn't aware Philomena had even spoken with a merchant.

One of her assistants, overhearing their conversation, piped up that a wine merchant had asked her ladyship to go outside with him and inspect the next crate.

"He said he worried about the champagne being inferior and wanted to know which she preferred be used for her guests."

"She went alone?"

"Well, the man said he'd hurt his back and didn't wish to haul the champagne inside if it wouldn't suit…" The young maid trailed off, trembling at her employer's wrathful look.

Solomon barked out the question, "What did this vintner look like?"

Swallowing audibly, she said, "Tall, brown hair. Ordinary."

Willy rushed into the kitchen with the head groom, Alvin.

"Laz. There's something we need to tell you. In private."

Alarmed, Solomon led them to the narrow corridor leading to the back stairs.

"You tell him," Willy nudged the groom.

Looking extremely self-conscious, Alvin had removed his hat and twirled it by the brim.

Solomon's nerves tightened in his belly, and he simultaneously wished to loosen Alvin's tongue and stopper him from speaking his next words. The small hairs rose on the back of his neck as he awaited his groom.

"Found a dead body outside the gates—"

Solomon staggered, supposing he referred to Philomena.

Willy shook Solomon's arm and sharply said, "It's not that."

"We discovered a man's body. Probably in his early thirties. He'd been shot."

Weak with relief, Solomon felt a buzzing in his ears.

"Describe him," Willy said.

"Brunette. Not handsome but not ugly, either. An—"

"Ordinary fellow," Solomon finished for him.

"Yes, sir," said his head groom.

"Must be the vintner," Solomon muttered. "Mena went with him, so where is she now?" Wiping his forehead with a shaky hand, he noted Willy and Alvin exchanging a significant look.

"She's been taken," Willy said gently.

A wave of heat passed over Solomon so that he briefly wondered if he'd shortly faint.

His groom pulled from his coat pocket a folded note, splattered with blood. "It was..." He cleared his throat, "pinned to his jacket, above the bullet hole. He was shot in the heart by the look of things."

Slowly, Solomon unfolded the note. His fingers smeared the blood droplets, and a scrap of material fell out. The pink satin fluttered to the floor like a flower being tossed aside.

The note read:

We have the marchioness. If you wish to see her again, alive, you must slip £2,000 into Mr. Sonders' coffin.

Chapter 22

Philomena stirred then immediately wished she hadn't. Her head pounded. Her shoulder ached as if it'd been wrenched, and a handkerchief had been stuffed in her mouth. It had the sickly-sweet taste of opium. She yanked the cloth from her mouth, coughing at the dryness it left behind.

Scooting backward, she maneuvered her shoulder against the cellar's cool wall and groaned in relief. The movement triggered a nauseous feeling, so she took deep breaths until it passed. Once she steadied, she took stock of her surroundings. She was underground in a small, dim room where the ceiling tapered to the ground. At the opposite end stood a wooden door so old and weather-beaten, it appeared to be silver, not brown. A barrel, a few cloth rags, and a handful of root vegetables were scattered throughout the cellar.

She rubbed her forehead, trying to coax the memory of how she had come to be here, but the details eluded her. Scowling, she concentrated harder. The laudanum had clouded her mind. She took another deep breath, hoping to clear the cobwebs.

Recall came in flashes so disorganized she couldn't fathom their meaning. A handsome man grinned as he played piano. A flushed youth. Her companion, Nancy, blushing in pleasure, delighted with her new gown, but who were those men?

The youth resembled the dark-haired man playing piano. Perhaps they were brothers? Perhaps they were *her* brothers? She did not know, but Nancy was her companion and would search for her.

She looked at her left hand, which bore no ring. If she were married, she'd have a ring, she felt certain of that.

"How long have I been here?"

Tentatively, she touched the back of her head. Among the tangled, matted hair, her fingers felt a tender spot. It was crusty, and she drew her hand away to discover her fingers stained with blood.

Someone had struck her. She didn't know who or why or when. She looked toward the handkerchief that had been stuffed in her mouth, searching for answers. It was a plain linen square, free of embroidery. The handkerchief could have belonged to anyone, male or female.

"Never mind how I got here," she muttered, annoyed with herself. "How do I get out?"

Thoughts whirled in her head at a dizzying speed, and soon she trembled. An uncomfortable warmth passed through her body, and she barely crawled to the corner of the room before retching. Wiping her mouth with the tattered hem of her satin skirt, she squirmed back to her spot and leaned against the wall. She hadn't the energy to escape just yet. She would gather her strength then strike out later, if her family hadn't arrived by the time she awoke.

Satisfied with that plan, she slept propped against the cool, earthen wall.

The next time she woke, the room was just as gloomy. Without being able to track the sun, it was impossible to guess the time, but from the stiffness in her limbs she supposed she'd slept for several hours.

Moving slowly, for she didn't wish to be sick again, she stood and leaned against the wall. Agony radiated from her shoulder and head, and the pain caused her to falter. Groaning, she crumpled to the floor and pressed her cheek against the dirt, finding relief in its coolness.

Philomena slept again.

When she awoke, rays of sunshine shone through the narrow slats of the root cellar's door. She crawled to the door and pressed her hand against it. The wood was ancient and thin and might give way with a forceful kick.

It was a pity she was so weak she might not be able to easily escape. Mildly cursing, she used one hand to unfasten her petticoat then ripped the material. Once she had a strip, she knotted the ends together and slipped the loop around her neck, occasionally whimpering in pain. With her arm hanging in the sling, the tightened muscles in her shoulder began to loosen from their knots.

She congratulated herself on not being sick again, but the exertion wasn't without price. Feeling faint, Philomena sat again and waited for the dizziness to pass.

She awoke later, having dozed. Her head still ached. The sun's rays had grown dim. Taking advantage of the dying light, Philomena crawled to the other side of the root cellar and groped in the dirt until her hand clasped a carrot and turnip. Gingerly, she munched on vegetables, listening to the eerie silence broken by the unnaturally loud sounds of her chewing.

Philomena pressed her face against the door, squinting through the cracks and into the twilight. Outside the door was a set of wheel tracks.

"Hello? Is anyone out there?"

She waited in the gloom, uncertain whether she actually wanted to hear a reply. Whoever kept her in here meant her harm. What would she do if that person returned?

"My family must be rich," she told herself. "If my abductors wanted me dead, they would have killed me by now. No, they have kept me alive for a reason. Perhaps they intend to ransom me then return me to my family?"

Reaching toward the gash in the back of her head, Philomena wondered if her assailant really had meant to keep her alive. The blow to her head could have been lethal. Her abductors hadn't tied her hands or feet, as she'd supposed would occur in a standard kidnapping. Had they already presumed she was dead and therefore didn't need to be restrained?

She'd been gone at least a day. Poor Nancy must be worried half to death. Her brothers, too.

Philomena nibbled on a turnip and drank some ale, which was in the barrel, feeling the ache in her head ease.

As dusk passed into night, she propped herself against the door and squinted through the openings. It would do her no good to try to escape when she was so weak, and it was too dark to get her bearings. She could become hopelessly lost. The smarter course would be to stay in the cellar overnight, gather her strength, then strike out in the morning if her family still hadn't fetched her.

Anticipating that homecoming, she wasn't certain if she would fall upon her brothers' necks or scold them for having taken so long to rescue her. She fell asleep, promising to do both.

The next morning, Philomena woke to birdsong, an encouraging sign. She rose to her feet without teetering, which she interpreted as another good omen. She stuffed her sling with the remaining carrots and turnips, took a long drink of ale, then examined the door with a critical eye. After testing the slats' solidity, she kicked at the weakest ones then snuck her hand through the splintered remains and lifted the outside latch.

Once she swung it open, she crouched near the doorway, hidden by the long grasses, afraid her escape would be noticed. Nothing disturbed the bird's chirping, so she poked her head out to survey the landscape.

It was quite a jolt to view the unfamiliar scenery. The terrain was unknown to her with the tall grass, but she approached the modest house with stealth. Crouching beneath a window, she peeked over its sill. The interior was empty. She moved to the next window and peered inside.

This room was sparsely furnished, the grate in the fireplace without kindling.

Searching for answers, she entered the cottage, determined to look about quickly then leave. A pot of vegetable stew sat near the brick hearth, its surface covered in crusty scum. It had been left unattended for quite a while. She took a deep breath and ventured upstairs, flinching with every squeak on the stair treads.

There were two bedchambers, so she searched the first, finding rumpled sheets and a valise with scattered personal belongings. There was a hairbrush with long strands of blonde hair. A lady then? Packed in the valise was a cotton shift trimmed in lace, so an affluent lady, perhaps? Spread over a chair was a blue carriage dress. As she touched the wool, it struck her that this was a fashionable garment—how she knew that she didn't understand, but the accoutrements strewn haphazardly about the room reinforced that perception. There were kid leather gloves, dyed to match the traveling outfit, and matching headgear with a heavy veil.

Her female abductor had planned to depart from this place with her identity obscured, Philomena realized, hurrying to survey the next room.

Everything here was as neat as a pin. The bed was made, and a valise was packed with a man's comb tucked into a pair of slippers, while a neatly folded silken robe nestled next to them. Laid out on the bed, as if in anticipation of his return, was a dark outfit with a black waistcoat and clean linen shirt. The beaver hat, gloves, and cane awaited their master's return as a golden pocket watch kept time on the highboy dresser.

She studied the pocket watch, fascinated by the monogram on its back, RJS. This timepiece identified her kidnapper, whoever RJS was. Tucking it into her bodice, she fled from the room as fast as she could, fearful the pair would return.

She did not take the main road, which ran next to the house, but headed east over the fields, hoping to elude discovery. Philomena walked swiftly, anxious to put distance between her and that place.

Mid-morning had brought her to the small village. She made her way to the church, stole into its gloomy interior, then quietly found a pew. She prayed for a while, but soon dozed.

"What have we here?" a masculine voice asked.

Philomena lifted her lashes. The moment she saw the stranger's face, she shrank back and raised her hand as if to ward off a blow.

"Please don't hurt me!" she cried.

"Don't be frightened of me, child. I won't hurt you." His eyes warmed with concern and his gaze flickered to the blood splatters on her gown. "It appears someone has, though."

Philomena lowered her arm, flinching as her shoulder shifted against the back of the pew. "Yes. I think somebody tried to kidnap me."

"You think someone tried to kidnap you?"

"Well, I know they did, but I do not know why."

He frowned then introduced himself. "I'm Mr. Manfred, the reverend of New Rent's congregation, and you are?"

"Philomena Lower. I'm from Chelmsford, but I don't live there anymore. Could you take me to see a doctor? I've hurt my head and shoulder."

"Nay, miss. We've not even an apothecary in New Rent, but my wife can tend your wounds, if you please."

He helped her to stand, but her knees seemed to turn to liquid, and she slid back to the pew.

"I will have to carry you, miss."

She nodded.

Mr. Manfred picked her up and carried her from the church to the rectory. A maid opened the door, having seen him coming, and exclaimed, "Dear heavens! What's this?"

"Fetch your mistress, Mary. This lass requires our assistance." Straining under his burden, the reverend staggered into the parlor and placed her on the settee then wiped his brow. With a breathless laugh, he assured her, "My wife's a known healer in the area. She makes marvelous possets."

As he finished, that good woman appeared at the door, her eyes widening in dismay. "Mr. Manfred! I could hardly understand a word from Mary. What's all this?"

"Mrs. Manfred, I found this waif resting in the church. Her name is Miss Philomena Lower, and she's been injured."

The motherly Mrs. Manfred leaned over her and *tsked* as she inspected the back of her head.

"You have a deep cut, my dear. It may require stitching."

The reverend departed, leaving his wife and Mary to clean the head wound, but he shortly reappeared with a glass of brandy and advised her to drink it.

She did so, but the brandy made her head swim, Propped up against the arm of the settee, she gestured that she was ready for the next stage.

Mrs. Manfred held the needle over a candle's flame then threaded it.

"This might pinch," Mrs. Manfred said.

The first stitch caused her to wince, so she steeled herself for the second, third, and fourth. By the time her companions knotted the silk thread, her teeth ached from biting back her cries.

Mary used a shawl to bind her arm to her side to immobilize her shoulder, then Mrs. Manfred allowed her to drink a soothing cup of tea.

Philomena thanked them for their assistance, glad to have the extra cloth supporting the back of her elbow, and dashed away the few tears that had trickled down her cheeks.

"I'm certain I have family. If you could help me find them, I'd be grateful."

"Rest, my child." Mrs. Manfred covered her with a blanket, and they left the parlor, allowing her to sleep on the settee.

"Thank you," she mumbled.

Before sleep claimed her, something tugged at her memory. Like a branch that snagged on its descent from a tree, the motion was arrested, and she could not call forth any details. That broken branch, that slipped memory, remained frustratingly out of her reach.

She made a sound of vexation then, with a huff, rolled onto her side and caught her breath. There she lay, thunderstruck by a startling discovery: she was an heiress.

Chapter 23

As soon as he read the ransom note, Solomon ran to his study and opened the safe. Feverishly, he counted out two thousand pounds in bank notes and coins.

"Laz," Charles said, his voice cracking as he leaned against the doorjamb.

Red-eyed, Solomon lifted his gaze to his friend. Stating, rather than asking, he said, "You heard. How?"

"I'm no clairvoyant," Charles said, sauntering over to the sideboard and pouring two shots of whisky. "I inquired into Lady Lower's background and discovered she has a brother named Randall Scott, whom I believe you mentioned was a former suitor of your wife's. I also learned the merry widow didn't leave for Italy with Mr. Peck, so I rode my horse into a lather rushing here to tell you, only to discover I've arrived too late."

"Lady Lower worked with Peck to have Mena abducted in London," Solomon said.

"To clear her path to Sir John's fortune."

"With Peck out of the way, she turned to her brother for assistance in her schemes?"

"With the same goal in mind, I daresay," Charles said. "To ransom her and gain a fortune."

Solomon agreed before downing his whisky. "If those dastards hurt her…"

"Woodsworth mentioned something about finding a corpse?"

Solomon nodded. "We were hosting a fete for the townspeople and tenants, celebrating the end of planting season. From what I've gathered, Sonders—the dead man—pretended to be a vintner. He must have lured Philomena from the kitchen on the pretense of her inspecting the champagne. A scullery maid saw that interaction, but nobody's seen Mena since that time."

"This happened during the party?"

"Yes."

Charles nodded, thinking aloud, "Sonders took advantage of the chaos during the revelry. As he was just one more face in a crowd, his presence wouldn't have been remarkable."

Running his hands through his hair, Solomon scoffed, "And like an idiot, I thought she'd retired from the party due to a headache. I should have realized Mena would have at least said goodnight before retiring."

"When did you notice she was missing?"

"This morning."

As Solomon spoke, he inwardly lashed himself for this unforgivable oversight. If only he, rather than Mena, had gone to the kitchen. If only he had noticed her disappearance sooner. If only he could have followed their tracks.

If only...

A vital part had been ripped from his chest. Until Philomena was restored to him, Solomon knew he'd never feel whole. For weeks, his heart had hinted he loved Philomena, but he'd only acknowledged it yesterday. It didn't matter that her father had swindled his foolish parent. It didn't matter she'd not come to this marriage as a maiden. Even with her flaws, Philomena was perfect for him; she was all that mattered.

Taking a seat in one of the easy chairs, Charles sprawled his long legs before him.

Mr. Woodsworth entered silently, bearing a tray of eggs, bacon, kippers, and coffee.

"Any word yet?"

"None, my lord."

"Thank you, Woodsworth."

Marshalling his spirits, Solomon turned to Charles and said, "I fear I've taken your presence for granted, old friend. Why have you come?"

"You needed me," Charles said with a shrug. "I left Keddington yesterday. Winsome will follow with her maid, while Mama will stay with the children."

"Good," Solomon said absent-mindedly. "Did you confirm that Peck left England?"

"Yes. His name was on the passenger manifest."

"Thank you."

Solomon stood and poked his head through the door to ask the butler to fetch Nancy. Once he'd done that, he returned to Charles and said, "Mr. Scott was a former suitor of Mena's. He appeared in Penrith recently, and met Mena."

"Odd timing that his path should cross hers," Charles murmured.

"Yes."

A pale, shaky companion appeared at the door, her tear-stained face revealing how Philomena's kidnapping had affected her.

"Should I call the doctor for you, Nancy? Have Mrs. Rodgers make you a tisane?" Solomon asked.

"No." Nancy dabbed her eyes, sniffed, and made a valiant effort to gather her composure. "What can I do? Give me a task, or I'll lose my sanity."

Hugging her briefly, Solomon ushered her into the study, re-introducing her to Charles Dryden.

Nancy whispered a greeting and twisted her handkerchief.

"Mr. Peck, Philomena's former trustee, has departed for the continent," Solomon said. "Lady Lower, however, did not."

"But that was the agreement," Nancy argued.

Nodding, Solomon continued, "Before departing, Mr. Peck gave a sworn statement in which he incriminated Lady Lower in the conspiracy to deprive Mena of her fortune."

"They wanted to keep Mena in the dark as to the marriage condition in her father's trust. We only found out about that by accident."

"Yes."

Angrily, Nancy dashed tears from her eyes. "Mena suspected as much."

"Charles has just uncovered that Randall Scott is the brother to Lady Lower—"

"What?" Nancy gasped.

"You didn't know?"

"Never!"

Nancy sat down hard in a chair, frowning at the mangled linen square. "They must have conspired to steal that blasted fortune all these years!"

"Explain, please," Charles said, his voice gentling.

Glancing at him, Nancy frowned again before blowing her nose. "After Mena's disastrous season in London, she returned home in a very vulnerable state. Mr. Scott appeared on the scene, a fine figure of a man and with the devil's own charm. In short, he was the epitome of the romantic hero to every young girl's dream."

She shook her head, whether in disbelief or remembrance, Solomon couldn't discern.

He prompted her, "And Mena fell in love with him?"

Nancy hesitated before slowly conceding, "I think she fell in love with the idea of being in love. Mr. Scott was very effusive in his praise, and he pressed his suit with great enthusiasm. At first, I thought this was the balm she needed…"

She took a deep breath before continuing. "He asked Sir John for his daughter's hand, but the baronet recognized him for the scoundrel that he was and refused. Eventually, they agreed that Mr. Scott would accept a certain sum of money to leave Philomena and not disturb her again."

Despite having had good manners dinned into him since his childhood, Solomon swore quite sincerely regarding Mr. Scott and his lineage.

Charles spoke next. "How long after Randall Scott's departure did Clarissa Scott appear on scene to ensnare the baronet?"

Giving him a steady look, Nancy said, "Soon thereafter. Once Mr. Scott failed to attain Mena's dowry through the marriage settlements, Clarissa must have decided to marry Sir John herself."

"Agreed."

"So, we now know the 'who' and 'why'; the only question that remains is what have they done with Philomena?"

A sob tore from Nancy's throat. "They'll murder her!"

"That's enough!" Charles sharply rebuked the older woman.

Jerking to her feet, Nancy covered her mouth and ran from the study.

Solomon sat there, stunned. He stared sightlessly forward, at last coming aware that Charles was trying to capture his attention.

"We'll search for her. We'll do it in teams, traveling in all four directions. Once we find her, everything will be all right. If we don't find her, they'll lead us to her when they try to retrieve the ransom. They'll want to keep her alive in order to get the money. Greed is their motivation, remember."

Charles was a former army captain, and Solomon trusted his instincts, which had been honed through battle.

"I believe you have the right of it, Charles, but surely you must be exhausted. Await Winsome's arrival. I'll arrange for a search party."

"Never."

"You need your sleep."

"I can sleep later."

Smiling at Charles's steadfastness, Solomon informed Woodsworth of their plan and ordered him to round up volunteers for the search party.

Charles left to warn Mrs. Rodgers of his wife's pending arrival and to request foodstuffs for the riders.

They met again in the foyer, where Charles divided the volunteers into riding parties. He would ride south with Mr. MacLean and his son, Payton. He assigned Willy and Mr. Watson to the northern route in the direction of Carlisle. Alvin and another groom were instructed to search west of Lazonby. Solomon and Mr. Branson would ride eastward.

As Mrs. Rodgers loaded bread and cheese into their saddlebags, the men agreed to return to Lazonby by noon on Wednesday. They would hold a graveside service for Sonders then wait for the kidnappers to take the money from the coffin.

Despite Branson's dogged assurance they would soon discover Philomena, Solomon and Branson came away empty-handed at each place they inquired. Solomon pounded on the door of every farmhouse within ten miles from Lazonby. Nothing. They slept in a barn that night, rose the next morning, and repeated the routine.

They'd found no trace of Lady Lower, Randall Scott, or Philomena. On the third day, he and Branson returned to Lazonby, anxious to hear if the others had succeeded in finding Philomena. Winsome Dryden greeted them upon their return.

"Is she here? Has she been found?"

"Not yet, Laz." Winsome gave him a hug and patted his back in sympathy. "Willy and the reverend returned earlier, but neither Charles nor Alvin have returned yet. They may have word."

Reflexively, Solomon hugged her then looked at the front of her skirts. "I'm so sorry, Winsome. I've dirtied your dress."

His voice was wooden but controlled. After excusing himself, he went to his room to clean off his travel dust. Willy found him there and walked with him to the dining room.

"Anything?" he asked.

Solomon shook his head.

"Maybe the others will have news."

Willy and Solomon sat down for a meal with Winsome.

His brother heaped a serving of vegetables onto Solomon's plate with the admonishment, "You must keep your strength up."

"Yes, oh wise one," Solomon replied.

"He's right," Winsome said, picking her way through her own meal.

Mechanically, Solomon ate his mutton, listening to Willy describe his search and cataloguing the places he and the vicar had ventured. They compared notes, trying to think of places they could have overlooked.

"Two more riders are coming, my lord," Woodsworth announced with a bow at the dining room door.

The threesome dashed from their seats and nearly collided in the hall with Nancy, who was scurrying down the stairwell.

Solomon didn't check his stride; instead, he moved through the foyer at speed to fling open the front door.

On the other side stood a pair of blinking groomsmen, Alvin and Harper.

Looking over their heads, Solomon knew the answer before Alvin spoke.

"No luck, my lord. I'm sorry," Alvin said with a glum look on his homely face.

Harper volunteered, "We thought we might have a lead. Outside New Rent, we heard of a woman in a pink dress, which matched her ladyship's description, but she was a commoner. A reverend named Manfred had been making inquiries on her behalf, but he'd told the constable the young lady was looking for two brothers."

"Did you speak to this reverend?"

Alvin shook his head. "We meant to, but by the time we got to New Rent, he and his wife had gone to market. Their maid said they might not return for a day or two, so we came home."

"It can't be her at any rate," Solomon said then explained, "Mena only has one brother."

"And Holden's gone to sea," Nancy added, turning away from the small gathering with her shoulders slumped.

Far on the horizon at the end of the drive, three riders appeared, trotting toward Lazonby.

"Charles!" Winsome breathed, elbowing Solomon out of the way as she ran down the steps toward her husband.

Solomon tensed, having already counted the riders and noticing two were missing. Mena wasn't among their number.

At the same time as he reached that conclusion, Winsome's shoulders had dropped in disappointment.

"Where's Charles?" she asked Maclean, Solomon's Scottish tenant.

"Mr. Dryden took Payton with him into Penrith but sent us ahead so we could accompany you to Sonders' funeral. Wants us to stake out the coffin before, during, and after the funeral."

It was not the news Solomon had been anticipating. His patience was being sorely tested this week. The others watched him, and Solomon batted down his emotions. He did not have the luxury of allowing either hope or despair to hold him in their sway.

"Very well," he said. "Go eat and wash up. We must leave here by two o'clock."

Mr. Watson officiated Mr. Sonders' funeral in the village churchyard. Mr. Maclean took up a vantage point in the bell tower; Alvin hid behind a headstone; and Harper stayed out of sight next to a hedge.

Other than Solomon, Mrs. Watson, and Nancy, no other mourners attended the graveside service. Well, except for an old crone. Stooped by age, with a dowager's hump, the elderly woman moved with the speed of treacle. She was heavily veiled and gloved, and her gown was shabby and dirty. She carried a handful of wildflowers to place on the coffin.

He fixed his gaze on the crone, watching as she dabbed her eyes with a lace handkerchief—a luxurious, youthful accessory, which jarred with the image she'd tried to cultivate.

In the pit of his belly, Solomon's anger roiled like a nest of vipers. It had to be Lady Lower.

Mr. Watson's homily was short and bland. He'd caught Solomon's eye, and a look of understanding passed between them. With the faintest of nods, the reverend concluded the service then ushered Mrs. Watson and Nancy out of the graveyard at a brisk pace.

Solomon donned his hat then walked away from the grave. He ducked behind a stone pillar and signaled to Maclean, Alvin, and Harper, pointing toward the crone. Pressed against the cold pillar, Solomon's body tensed. The muscles in his legs tightened, preparing to spring into action. An idea flittered through his head that he could shove Clarissa into the coffin and send her to the Underworld with Sonders, but he pushed it aside as unworthy.

He had to focus. Mena's life depended upon it. A shaft of ice spiked his chest at the thought.

Knowing Lady Lower's whereabouts was only half the puzzle; he must locate her brother, Randall Scott. Solomon scanned the graveyard, straining his eyes to peer amid the headstones.

Had Randall been killed as well as Sonders? Was he holding Mena somewhere nearby?

The squeaking of unoiled hinges grated his nerves as he watched the crone lift the coffin lid and place her straggly bouquet inside. She wailed even as she swapped the wildflowers for the bag of money. Lady Lower had cupped her handkerchief around the bag so expertly, that if Solomon hadn't known what she was about, he might not have guessed she'd just picked a dead man's pocket.

"Halt!" he shouted, consumed with fury.

Without a backward glance, the crone lifted her skirts and kicked up her heels. Warning shots rang out, but she ran, weaving through the churchyard. Solomon leapt with a blood curling yell and snatched her waist, bringing her to the hard ground.

Spitting, bucking, and kicking, she fought to escape, but Solomon placed his knee in her back and pressed her cheek in the grass. She was no better than a savage beast, and he prayed she'd not shown this vicious side to Philomena. Had it not been for Alvin's arrival, Solomon wasn't certain if his temper wouldn't have gotten the better of him. He was strongly tempted to backhand the bitch.

Alvin gathered her wrists and tied them behind her.

She hollered even as she struggled like a madwoman. "It wasn't my fault! It wasn't my fault!"

Solomon got to his knees then stood, hauling her upright. With a punishing grip on her shoulders, Solomon shook the pathetic figure.

"Where's Mena?"

"Where are you taking me?"

"Alongside Sonders," Solomon snarled, jerking his head toward the coffin. "Where's my wife?"

Wild-eyed, Lady Lower screamed.

That sound chilled his blood, and his stomach tightened into a knot. She actually believed he would bury her alive... Had Lady Lower already reconciled herself to that gruesome practice because that's what she'd done to Mena? Had she buried his wife alive? God! Lady Lower's hysterics killed his hopes for recovering Mena. His other senses dulled as blood rushed through his ears, muffling other sounds. Juices in his belly churned into acids, his chest tightened and burned.

Fiercely, he grabbed the back of Lady Lower's dress and hauled her toward the coffin. He would see her buried before nightfall.

"No!" she screamed, digging her heels into the ground.

Relentlessly, Solomon lugged her toward Sonders' corpse.

"Wait! It wasn't my fault—it was Sonders. He's the one who hit her so hard, not me. Randall hired him, so you see? It wasn't my fault."

The sharp report of a pistol rang out, and Solomon felt a sting in his calf. He dragged Lady Lower to a headstone then crouched behind it. He poked his head around the stone, searching for the marksman as he touched his wound. His calf bled a little. The bullet had nicked the skin; it was merely a flesh wound.

"He's at the church!" Maclean shouted from the tower.

Solomon swiveled to the approaching figure coming from the church.

Randall Scott strode toward them, his face blank as he tossed a smoking pistol to the ground. He fished into his coat for a handkerchief then waved the white linen. "Pax!"

Struck dumb, Solomon watched as Mr. Scott came to where his sister lay, facedown in the grass, her hands tied behind her. He moved her by the shoulder onto her back. Lady Lower's eyes stared sightlessly at a cloudless sky, a leaking red dot in her forehead, her expression frozen in astonishment.

"I was always an excellent shot. She should have remembered that," Scott murmured.

Solomon slowly rose as Alvin and Harper ran to him and gathered around the headstone. They looked at the lifeless body of Lady Lower. Alvin swore, but Solomon found himself as unmoved by her death as apparently was her brother.

"Where's Mena? Help me find her, Scott. Allow her to have a decent burial."

The words scraped Solomon's throat, squeezing past its narrow opening. It was inconceivable that his vibrant wife should be dead. From Lady Lower's ramblings he'd gleaned Mena had been beaten to death by Sonders. It was difficult to breathe, to think, to feel anything but numb.

Randall Scott stood, impassive, as if he lived in a different world than this one. Staring at his dead sister, he tucked his handkerchief back into his pocket.

Solomon arranged Lady Lower's veil to cover her face.

"I loved her," said Mr. Scott. His voice had a curious, detached quality.

Puzzled by the wooden tone and to whom he referred, Solomon glanced at him.

Randall Scott pressed the end of a pistol against his chin and fired.

Chapter 24

Solomon had no memory of leaving the churchyard and returning to Lazonby. Alvin said nothing, glaring at Maclean to silence him when the Scottish man ventured to speak. The idea that his wife was dead squeezed his heart in his chest. She didn't deserve to die, especially not at the hands of that monster, Sonders. Not to assuage the greed of Lady Lower and her brother.

He'd never told Mena he loved her. He had yet to claim her as his wife, as his marchioness, and now he never would.

Solomon had left it to Alvin to tell Willy and Winsome what had occurred. A heaviness pressed on Solomon, preventing him from speaking. He passed through the front door and walked directly to his room. His empty room. The sounds of Mena's sighs and groans echoed in the silence, the last whiff of her floral scent lingered in the air.

Gathering her pillow, Solomon hugged it tight against his midriff and rocked himself as he wept. He had cried when his father passed away, but this pain was a hundred times worse. He privately vented his raw grief, finding relief in the release.

The sun's ray moved across his bed, lengthening in shadows, but he had not moved. Time might as well have frozen, for all Solomon cared. He did not wish the day to advance into his first night without Mena, followed by a day without his wife, then another, stretching into a long, gray future.

Willy stood at the door, looking at him through reddened eyes. "Laz, Charles and Payton are coming up the drive. There's a curricle traveling with them."

"I don't care."

"Laz," Willy said quietly. "It's Charles."

Like an old man, Solomon moved from the bed and trod from his chambers, his spirits as heavy as his footsteps. He came to the top of the stairs, where he spied Winsome standing in the foyer before an opened door.

Bursting with excitement, she shouted, "Philomena's with them! She's alive! She's alive, Laz!"

His heart stopped then flipped. Solomon froze where he stood, all the breath knocked out of him. As if chased by a pack of wolves, he ran down the stairs, tripping as he descended. His feet tangled beneath him, and he slid the last few steps on his bottom.

"My lord," Mr. Woodsworth rushed to assist Solomon, who had righted himself by clutching a spindle.

Throughout his flight down the stairs, he'd remained speechless, aware only of the loud pounding of his heart and a repetitive prayer that Mena was just on the other side of that door...

Still sprawled between the stairs and the foyer's floor, Solomon called out for Nancy, knowing she would wish to greet Mena, too.

Immediately, the companion came to him and took his hand.

"Come on," she said, a smile in her voice as she picked him up by the elbow.

Together they hurried through the front door and down the stone steps to join Winsome on the freshly graveled drive. Charles and Payton flanked a curricle driven by a man with two female passengers. Another man on horseback rode behind the carriage. In the curricle were two women, Philomena and a middle-aged woman. He didn't recognize the older couple or their curricle.

The acids which had churned in his belly for the past five days immediately calmed. His chest expanded as he took the first deep breath in the hours since he'd left the graveyard, believing she was dead and lost to him forever. Solomon's legs shook, and the bullet graze in his calf began to burn as his cocoon of numbness disintegrated. No matter. He would wade through the fires of hell to cast his eyes upon Philomena again. His arms ached to hold her close to him and feel her softness and warmth, breathe in her scent, and bury his nose in her soft curls.

"She's alive!" Nancy breathed.

He glanced at the companion, sharing a quivering smile. Nancy's face was blurred by his own tears, but he noticed the sheen in her eyes and gave her a quick hug as they waited for the curricle to reach the porch.

As the party approached, Solomon noted Philomena's head was bandaged and her arm was in a sling. The corners of his mouth twitched, and he felt the dimming of his own smile. Mena had been hurt, and her expression reminded him of a lost little girl's. Something kept him from rushing to gather her in his arms and soothe away her hurts. Something he could never quite understand. Perhaps it was that lost little girl look of hers. It was unsettling and foreign.

It cost a year of his life in patience to wait with Nancy as the curricle drew up the drive.

Solomon's gaze turned to Charles, and he was thunderstruck by his friend's grim expression. Charles was not riding into Lazonby as some triumphant victor. He came with an air of exhaustion and resignation. His mouth formed a tight line. Not a frown, and definitely not a scowl, but was that displeasure he read in his friend's countenance?

Something was not right here.

Disquiet percolated in Solomon's belly, sending a heaviness to his limbs so that he could not have vaunted down those last stone steps if his life depended upon it.

Charles's gaze met his and he shook his head then flung up his hand, as if to warn Solomon to remain where he stood.

He'd been right to think something was amiss. Solomon checked himself and waited.

"What in the world..." Winsome trailed off, touching her cheek as if she, too, was dismayed.

Nancy, however, did not heed Charles's silent warning. She broke free of Solomon's embrace and rushed forward, just as Mena and the older woman stepped from the curricle. Nancy threw an arm around Mena's good shoulder then sobbed upon her neck. "Saints be praised! You're alive and have returned to us!"

Philomena staggered backward then patted Nancy, both women laughing even as they cried at their reunion.

Philomena quietly spoke to the woman who accompanied her home, introducing them.

Winsome's hand clutched at Solomon's sleeve, and he clung to it, glad for her wordless support.

His wife was drawn and pale—so unlike herself that pangs went through him. What the devil had the Scotts done to traumatize Philomena?

Charles, Payton, and the third rider, Mr. Tibbs, dismounted. Alvin came forward and took hold of the reins as he and Payton led the horses to the stables. Payton glanced at Solomon then at Philomena. He cast him a pitying look then led the horses away, shaking his head.

Solomon's unease grew.

Mr. Tibbs, the shopkeeper from Penrith, wore a worried expression as he joined Charles; the pair mounted the steps toward him.

Another layer of dread formed around Solomon's constricted heart.

"Well met, Laz," Charles said, shaking his hand. "You owe Mr. Tibbs for discovering Philomena. She wandered into the church at New Rent, where Reverend Manfred found her and took her to his home for doctoring. He and his wife visited Penrith to inquire into the lady's relatives, and Mr. Tibbs, upon seeing her, recognized her as Lady Lazonby."

Charles's explanation came with so many hidden meanings to it that Solomon was unable to understand it all from the beginning.

"She was recognized as Lady Lazonby?" he asked, his voice hoarse with strain.

"She has forgotten she is married, Laz. She remembers everything in her life, I think, save for these past few months," Charles told him gently.

Winsome dug into his forearm, and Solomon was glad of it. Otherwise, he wasn't certain if he would have gone numb entirely.

His Mena had forgotten him?

The reverend shuffled up the steps, a female on each arm.

"My lord," he said with a bow. "I am Reverend Manfred of New Rent, and this is my wife, Millicent. We are honored to restore your lady to you."

Charles approached Philomena and gently pried her from the reverend. He spoke to Philomena with the same patience he reserved for his daughter, Arianna. "This is Lazonby, Philomena, your home, and this is your husband, the marquess."

"I am a marchioness?" Philomena's voice held all the horror as when she'd first discovered he was a marquess.

For the first time in days, Solomon smiled. Despite the radical alteration in his wife, Philomena still did not wish to be an aristocrat. He need never worry she'd married him for his title.

Philomena stared at him, but there was a blankness in her hazel eyes that cut Solomon to the quick. His chest tightened as if being squeezed by a large fist.

"Your ladyship." Charles motioned her to precede them into the house.

Still reeling from the pain of not being recognized by his wife, Solomon stood mute as Winsome said, "Woodsworth, will you please see that Lazonby's guests are taken to rooms where they may clean off their travel dust if they so wish? I suggest we meet in the drawing room for a large tea within the half hour, if that is agreeable?"

Winsome lifted a brow, silently ascertaining if those plans met Solomon's approval.

"Excellent idea," Solomon said, glad for Winsome's thoughtfulness. There was something gratifying in this earth-shattering moment of being able to rely upon observing the formalities.

"I shall see to it at once, Mrs. Dryden," the butler promised.

Willy, who had been standing inside the door, came forward and pressed a kiss upon Philomena's cheek.

"Welcome home, Mena. You've been missed."

Belatedly, Solomon realized he'd forgotten to welcome his wife back home.

That prompted him into assuring her, "You have been sorely missed, my dear."

The words seemed woefully inadequate, his delivery stiff and formal. With his hands clasped behind his back, Solomon dared not touch Philomena. He didn't wish to frighten her any more than she already was.

"We are all very glad you're safe, Philomena," Winsome said, her smile and tone much warmer than his had been.

"Do you wish me to assist you, my lady?" Nancy asked, giving Solomon a sidelong glance filled with worry.

"Yes, please." She glanced at Solomon and murmured, "I am sorry I don't recognize you, my lord."

He raised his hand, whether to acknowledge her regret or to wave it away, even he wasn't certain. Solomon hadn't returned to his footing since he'd scampered down the main stairwell.

Briskly, Nancy replied, "No matter. You're safe, and that's the most important part. Come, let us retire for the moment."

Philomena dithered, in a very atypical fashion, before going along with Nancy to refresh herself.

Taking a few moments to master his emotions, Solomon excused himself. He ducked into his study and poured a hearty glass of whisky, needing to feel the burn down his throat. Needing to feel anything. The shock was wearing off, and he set down his glass, noting his hand shook.

Woodsworth entered the room and quietly closed the door. "Is there anything I can do for you, my lord?"

He shook his head, not knowing where to begin. His wife was his foremost concern, so he focused on that. "Please send for the doctor. I would ask him to examine my lady. Then inform Mrs. Rodgers she will need to prepare a late supper for our guests. Oh, and tea. I believe Winsome soon expects it in the drawing room."

"Yes, Lord Lazonby."

"Lady Lazonby may wish to take a tray in her room rather than face so many people. You must do as she pleases."

"Yes, my lord."

Solomon's guess proved correct. Philomena had opted not to come downstairs. Winsome reported that she was enjoying a leisurely cup of tea then intended to rest.

As the party reassembled in the drawing room, Winsome took over the task of pouring tea and handing out biscuits. The setting was serene with Reverend Manfred, his wife, and the Penrith shopkeeper enjoying his hospitality, although rather subdued as they did so.

"Mr. Manfred, I would be most obliged to hear the tale of how you came to meet my wife. She was abducted from home last Saturday, and I would appreciate an accounting of her whereabouts for the past five days."

"I am afraid, my lord, that I can only account for her whereabouts these last two days. She was asleep in my church in a torn gown with her arm in an untidy sling."

"She wrenched her shoulder," said Mrs. Manfred.

"Yes," her husband continued. "She did not remember how she did so. Her head wound accounted for that."

"I daresay," agreed his wife. "Mr. Manfred brought her home, and I cleaned and stitched the cut."

"Thank you, ma'am, sir."

"She told me she woke up, sick and dizzy, in a root cellar. I do not know where, but she said she stayed there a few days because it was either too dark to travel or she felt too weak to do so," Mrs. Manfred said.

"How did she get from the root cellar to your church?"

"She walked."

Still frowning, trying to shift the pieces into order, Solomon turned to Charles.

"The Manfreds inquired around New Rent for the lady's family. She believed she had two brothers who would be looking for her."

"Why?"

"I believe her wedding ring was stolen, Laz," Charles said. "She was not wearing it, nor does she have it upon her person. The only jewelry she carried was a monogrammed watch with Randall Scott's initials."

Mrs. Manfred's nose wrinkled. "Who is Randall Scott?"

"One of her three abductors. From what I've pieced together, Mr. Sonders was hired by a pair of siblings, Randall Scott and Lady Lower. Sonders disguised himself as a wine merchant and lured Mena outside during Saturday's party. He then struck her so hard, they believed he had killed Philomena, so Randall Scott shot Sonders on the spot."

"That's a terrible thing," Mrs. Manfred murmured.

"So, when they stowed Philomena in the root cellar…" the reverend began.

Charles grimly finished the sentence. "They did so thinking she was already dead."

"Which is why she met with so little resistance when she chose to leave after a few days." Solomon clenched his fist, enraged that the Scott siblings had left Philomena for dead.

"We should be grateful they left her in a root cellar," Winsome said, without finishing the gruesome thought.

Instead of burying her in a shallow grave.

"All the same," Solomon gritted. "I do not think I shall ever feel gratitude for Randall Scott and Lady Lower." What he felt for them Solomon could not say in front of the ladies and a clergyman.

"Nor shall I," Willy said, folding his arms over his chest in emphatic agreement.

Next, Mr. Tibbs told him how the Manfreds had visited his store and asked if anyone knew their companion. He recognized her ladyship immediately. Given her amnesia, he chose to close his store and escort the reverend's party to Lazonby. On the outskirts of town, they came upon Charles and Payton.

"Are the Scotts in custody?" Charles asked.

"No." Solomon then relayed what had occurred at the churchyard. "Before she was shot by her brother, Lady Lower indicated Mena was dead. I had no hope of seeing her alive."

"Good God," said Mr. Tibbs, shocked by such news, using his handkerchief to dab his forehead.

"No wonder Lady Lazonby is so leery," Mr. Manfred said. "She will be frightened for a while yet. You must be patient with her."

"I intend to be," Solomon said, slightly amused by the man's protectiveness toward his wife. Even dazed from a head wound, Philomena had charmed the reverend.

"She remembers her childhood and her companion, but will her recent memory return?" Mrs. Manfred asked the question closest to Solomon's heart.

Silence drifted like a fog over the occupants in the drawing room.

"Perhaps the doctor will be able to say?" Winsome offered.

"It is to be profoundly hoped." Willy slumped in his chair.

"Of course we hope Philomena heals quickly and completely," Solomon said, rising as he did so. "I am indebted to you all for returning my wife. You shall dine with us, and I invite you to remain as long as you wish to recover from your journey."

"Thank you, my lord," the good reverend said with a pleased expression.

"I must go to my wife, but we shall dine at seven."

With that, Solomon left them and limped up the stairs, a knot of dread tied inside him. The graze wound hardly pained him. No, what tormented him most was the anguishing realization of how utterly he had failed his beloved wife.

Chapter 25

Leaning against the stack of pillows, Philomena watched, with open curiosity, the exchange between the marquess and doctor. Clearly, his lordship did not wish to avail himself of the doctor's services.

"I realize the bullet grazed the skin there, my lord, but you cannot wish to have it become infected," the doctor had argued with such reasonableness that Lord Lazonby had relented, despite his grousing that he hadn't wished to make a fuss.

The marquess's reluctance amused her because he'd been the one to insist she undertake a thorough examination, despite her objections that Mrs. Manfred had already treated her.

At least, he had granted her privacy with Dr. Smythe, but the marquess had no qualms about sharing his privacy. The doctor brazenly removed his boot and stocking then raised his pant leg so he could examine the lower leg then sprinkle basilicum powder on the wound. He had wrapped a bandage around the calf.

Upon seeing his lordship's bare leg, Philomena's cheeks heated in embarrassment. Such intimacy would be commonplace between married couples, but to Philomena's mind, the marquess was a stranger to her. She looked away, wishing she were elsewhere.

With his treatment finished, the doctor bid goodbye to her with a few more assurances and instructions. She graciously tipped her head in his direction as his lordship ushered him from the chamber.

The marquess returned from escorting the doctor out and leaned against her bedchamber door. A serious-minded man with a lovely head of thick, black hair, Lord Lazonby probed her with his golden gaze, as if he were trying to read her innermost thoughts.

"Does your leg hurt?" she asked, uncomfortable with the silence.

"No."

"You didn't say how you came to be shot?" She arched her brows, inviting an explanation.

"No, I did not."

She waited without reward. Upon reading his bland expression, she realized his lordship had no intention of describing his morning events to her.

"You don't wish to trouble me, I suppose?" She crossed her arms, aware she sounded sulky even to her own ears.

"No, I don't," he said gently. "Dr. Smythe was impressed with Mrs. Manfred's stitching."

Philomena lightly touched the back of her head. "I was very lucky to have found them. They have taken extraordinarily good care of me."

"Yes."

His golden eyes were bright, but he quickly blinked away the sheen, leaving her uncertain as to whether those had been tears or not. He seemed to hold her in high regard. It baffled her how she could have mistaken her husband for her brother.

She sighed.

"Are you in pain?" he asked, leaning forward with a concerned expression. "Do you want some cider? Or water? Perhaps tea?"

"Not really, thank you."

Another pause in the conversation followed, lasting longer than the first.

"How old are you?" she asked, thinking to begin the process of becoming re-acquainted with him.

"Two-and-thirty. May I join you?" He gestured to a spot on her bed.

She stammered, "In bed, you mean?"

A faint smile lifted the ends of his mouth. "Only for a nap. I'm exhausted, as you must be, too."

Struggling to act nonchalant about sharing her bed, Mena murmured, "I suppose…"

Solomon removed his boots, jacket, and cravat then slipped into bed alongside her. Other than taking her hand, Solomon did not touch her, although he lay close enough that she could feel the warmth from his body.

Shyly, she ventured, "I didn't think married couples in the upper classes shared the same bed, my lord."

"You and I do," he said.

"Oh."

Another thought came to her. Wrinkling her nose, she asked, "How long have we been married?"

"Not quite three months."

"When did we marry? How did we meet?"

The questions poured out until the most important one reared its head. Suddenly, she gasped, "Do we have children? We don't, do we? Not if we've only been married three months."

"Easy, Mena." He chuckled then looked at her with such love and tenderness in his golden gaze, her breath caught.

"First, I want you to rest," he said firmly before kissing the back of her hand. "We'll have plenty of time to talk later."

Sensing his weariness, she said, "Poor man. I didn't mean to worry you."

His dark brows lifted, and his voice was raspy as he admitted, "I thought you were dead, Mena."

This time there was no mistaking the tears in his eyes. Her fingertip trailed down his cheek.

She whispered, "I'm so sorry."

He kissed the inside of her wrist. "My suffering's nothing compared to yours. I'm sorry you were hurt. I should have protected you better, my dear."

With their gazes locked and their bodies lying side by side, a delicious warmth came over Philomena. Before succumbing to sleep, Solomon gently kissed her forehead.

"I love you, Mena."

She hesitated, and he squeezed her hand.

"Thank you, my lord."

"Call me Solomon."

"Solomon," she repeated drowsily before snuggling against his warm body.

She awoke after a three-hour nap, feeling restored and ravenous. Solomon acted as her abigail, helping her dress for dinner. He took great care shielding her arm from further injury. After he declared her presentable, he dashed through his ablutions and donned a navy jacket and pair of black pantaloons.

"You must ask your valet to clean the mud splatters off your pant legs," she murmured, picking up the buckskins he'd worn earlier.

"Er… yes, I will. On the instant," he said, taking the garment and rolling it into a ball.

Quickly, he observed, "You lost your wedding ring. We'll replace that at the earliest opportunity."

"Yes," she said sadly, splaying her bare fingers. "It was because of that I thought I was an unmarried woman. I recalled your face but assumed you were my brother."

"A reasonable assumption," he said. "I must warn, however, I don't feel at all brotherly toward you."

She chuckled, the first time since her abduction. "What did my wedding ring look like?"

"Just a solid gold band."

She nodded. "Good. I prefer simplicity."

Solomon kissed her cheek then led her downstairs by the hand. Philomena found herself oddly reluctant to leave their private rooms. They would be joined for supper by all those people she couldn't remember, and it was a terrible thing not to recall the names of her friends and family.

Frowning at the thought, she asked, "Do you think the doctor was correct—that my memory will return?"

"I don't see why not. Dr. Smythe's very competent, and if he's confident you'll heal, I should think you will."

"He said it may take time."

"Yes."

She stopped, forcing him to face her on the stairs. "Am I a patient person?"

His eyes twinkling, he shook his head. "No, you are not."

"Well, there's no need to make me sound so dreadful," she said crossly.

Her husband laughed. "Even at your worst, you could never be dreadful, Mena. You're one of the kindest people I've ever met."

"I am?"

"Yes, and you're intelligent and have a keen sense of justice. Lazonby is fortunate to have such a fine marchioness."

Flushing at that praise, she entered the drawing room and went to Mr. and Mrs. Manfred, glad to see them again.

The marquess introduced her to another man and woman from Penrith, Mrs. Smith, one of the Lazonby seamstresses, and Mr. Tibbs. She recalled the shopkeeper had escorted her home with Charles Dryden and Payton, so Philomena thanked him.

Mrs. Smith went on to mention she had a little girl named Cora and stated the marchioness was a favorite with her daughter. It shamed Philomena that she couldn't recall this pleasant woman or her daughter.

Instead, she strove to ask an intelligent, neutral question. "How are you coming along in your current project?"

Mrs. Smith reported she was embroidering hems for the new drapes in the drawing room and hoped to finish in the next week.

Glancing at the threadbare drapes, Philomena quipped, "Not a moment too soon, I fear."

Mrs. Smith smiled.

Having coasted through that conversation, Philomena felt better about her ability to handle herself in others' company. That burst of self-confidence petered out when Solomon accompanied her to the dining room. Here matters were a bit trickier. He sat her at the foot of the table while he sat at the head, so far away that he couldn't shelter her if she needed protection.

On her left was a lad with similar coloring as her husband's.

"I'm happy to report the hens are performing nicely," Willy told her.

It was such an odd thing to say that Philomena stared at him blankly. "That's nice," she said mildly, wondering if the lad were a half-wit.

"The three of us—you, Laz, and I—recently built a chicken coop for the Lazonby farm."

She blinked in surprise. "Did we?"

"Yes," Willy said. "Not only that, you and Laz purchased the chickens, cows, and pigs to re-stock the home farm. You took the wagon to Penrith and fetched the livestock and the ceramic stove back from Mr. Tibbs' store."

Philomena gave an uncertain smile, unsure what to make of this. It sounded preposterous, but Willy's gaze held a light of hero-worship in them. For her? It didn't seem probable, but Philomena was at a loss as to what to believe. It was very odd to have one's anecdotes reported to one without proper context.

If she wished to learn about her past immediately preceding the abduction, she could ask his lordship or Nancy, but Dr. Smythe warned them not to force her memory to return. He advised allowing nature to heal in its own time.

"Sometimes one gets bits and pieces restored to them; at other times it all comes back in a rush," he'd told them.

"Is it possible that I'll never be able to remember these past few months?"

"It is possible," Dr. Smythe said. "Given your youth and general good state of health, though, I think it unlikely."

Over the course of her meal, though, Philomena had a sense of *déjà vu*, as if she'd eaten six-course meals before, although she did not believe she had done so here at Lazonby. The china, the servants, the room—none of it seemed familiar to her.

The people were kind and well-intentioned, and she relaxed and began to enjoy their company. As if it had been pre-arranged, no one mentioned the actual kidnapping. By the end of the meal, her husband announced that the gentlemen would forego drinking port at the table and retire to the music room. Philomena was glad to hear it.

They spent an agreeable hour listening to the marquess play piano, but Philomena grew tired and longed for bed. Her gaze snagged Solomon's, and he must have sensed her exhaustion, for he said, "Charles and Winsome, could we prevail upon you to take over our hosting duties for the evening? Dr. Smythe was very adamant that Mena should rest."

"Naturally," Winsome agreed with a cheerful smile.

"Your first obligation must be to your spouse," Charles said. "It will be our privilege to entertain your guests."

So, they made their goodbyes, and Solomon escorted Philomena to her bedchambers and once more acted as her abigail. It did not appear her husband intended to leave her side. He was still a stranger to her in many ways, but after their nap, she felt more comfortable in his presence. Solomon was not a threat to her; she was safe with him. He had been solicitous over her welfare and affectionate, which she appreciated.

Once she tucked herself into bed, he joined her there. They did not cuddle. They didn't make love. They simply held hands as they drifted off to sleep.

Solomon and Philomena had breakfast together with their guests then bid goodbye to Mr. Tibbs and the Manfreds. The reverend was anxious to return in time for his Sunday sermon, and the shopkeeper had plenty to do in Penrith. So, for the remainder of that day and the next, Philomena and Solomon entertained the Drydens.

The leisurely pace of life allowed Philomena to slip back into a feeling of normalcy. Within days, she was able to move her shoulder about freely, and her headaches eased. Although her physical health was steadily improving, Philomena's mental soundness was deteriorating. She was haunted by nightmares of being abandoned.

When she came crashing awake, Philomena found herself drenched with sweat and tangled in her sheets. At those times, Solomon restrained her as she flailed, showing infinite patience by calming her. Eventually, the kindness in his tone penetrated her befuddled mind, and she stilled.

"You're safe now, Mena."

Swallowing the constriction in her throat, she stammered, "Please light the candle. I don't care for the darkness."

"Of course."

Solomon left their bed to do so, and she whimpered in fear.

"Would you care for something to drink?" he asked quietly.

"No." She shook her head vigorously.

"Perhaps a wet cloth?"

"Yes, please."

He doused a cloth with water from an ewer then placed it over her forehead. Next Solomon crawled into bed and sat up against the headboard. He pulled her between his legs and gathered her against his chest.

"Tell me about your nightmare."

Philomena opened her mouth then shut it. Taking a deep breath, she began again, stumbling over some of her words.

"I dreamed of a woman. Blonde. She would be pretty if her face weren't twisted in such a hate-filled expression. I feel she's malevolent, but I can't place her. Do you know whom I mean, Solomon?"

Her husband said nothing but heaved a sigh. Philomena could feel Solomon's chest move in and out. She half-turned so she could nestle into his embrace, then she placed her ear against his strong, beating heart. His nearness, his warmth, and listening to that steady rhythm calmed her.

Quietly, Solomon explained how her father's second wife had coveted Philomena's inheritance.

"I imagine the blonde woman haunting your dreams is Lady Clarissa Lower," he finished.

"Tell me more," she insisted.

"I'm not certain Dr. Smythe would approve—"

"But it's so frustrating getting these flashes in my dreams and being unable to anchor them to reality."

He paused for a moment then forged ahead. "Lady Lower conspired with your trustee, Mr. Peck, to have you abducted on your recent visit to London. That attempt failed. Once we married, I brought you to Lazonby, wrongly believing Lady Lower had sailed from England with Mr. Peck and no longer posed a threat to you."

"Where is Mr. Peck?"

"Italy, I believe. I have his signed confession, so if he should ever return to England, he will be immediately tried for his crimes against you."

"Thank you. What happened to Lady Lower, my father's second wife?"

"She died."

She lifted her brows, astonished by the answer.

"Recently?"

Slowly, Solomon said, "Yes."

"Good heavens," she murmured.

"I think I've said enough. We should sleep now."

"Solomon," she chided.

But he refused to say anything else, claiming he'd already spoken against the doctor's advice and didn't wish to jeopardize her progress.

Despite her cajoling, Philomena could not sway her stubborn husband. Relief came, though, just as the doctor predicted. In brief episodes, flashes of her recent life sprang to mind. She recalled banging her forehead against Solomon's outside a milliner's shop. A waitress with seductive eyes casting him a come-hither glance. In her mind's eye, she remembered Solomon holding a little boy outside a church on a busy London street.

Nancy was delighted by this news, chattering about their leaving Chelmsford and visiting London, filling in some of the gaps.

Despite the progress made during the daylight hours, Philomena's nightmares continued. Two nights later, her screams awakened her. Awash in sweat, she panted, sitting up in bed.

A pounding came at her chamber door.

Clad in his nightshirt, Solomon answered it and Nancy rushed into the room.

"Enough!" she snapped. "You must tell Mena the whole of it, my lord."

With his hands on his hips, Solomon stood, bleary-eyed. He pinched the bridge of his nose, which highlighted the bluish circles beneath his eyes.

"But Dr. Smythe said—" he said, only to be met with a flat-out denunciation of that learned man's opinion.

"What happened to me? How did I come to be injured and placed in a root cellar?"

Philomena's quiet question stayed the argument. As one, Nancy and Solomon quieted and faced her.

Nancy approached and sat on the edge of her bed. Taking Philomena's hand, she gave it a good pat then told her everything they'd been able to discover since the night of her abduction.

"Who shot Sonders?"

"We think it was Clarissa's brother, Randall Scott," Solomon said, adding firmly, "That's enough, Nancy."

Philomena murmured, "Goodnight," as Nancy departed then fetched the monogrammed watch she'd taken from the vacant house. It was in a drawer of her dressing table. Alone again with Solomon, she showed it to him.

"After I left the root cellar, I snooped around the house and found this—RJS. It must have belonged to Randall Scott."

"They stayed in the house?"

"Yes. It was furnished but vacant."

"They must have placed you in the root cellar, believing your head wound was mortal."

"Yes." She paused and swallowed the nervous lump in her throat. "So, my abductors are either dead or exiled?"

One corner of Solomon's mouth lifted. "That's one way of putting it, yes."

They returned to bed without speaking another word. Philomena had much on her mind. The faces of her dreams now had names attached to them, and no longer seemed like distant people in a faraway land.

Her slumber was restless as she tried to parse through what she'd learned and piece the information together. When she woke, Solomon leaned over her, watching her with a bleakness in his eyes.

Moved by his distress, Philomena cupped his cheek. "Good morning, Solomon."

"Good morning." He shuttered his eyes, closing off his disturbing worries.

"Perhaps we should sleep apart," he said, swinging his legs off the bed then tramping to his dressing room.

She propped herself up on an elbow, feeling devastated, as if something very precious were being torn from her clasp.

"I don't want to sleep apart from you. You make me feel safe."

She heard him scoff at that, so she padded after him.

He pulled his buckskins on, but his movements were jerky and angry.

Philomena knew why he was so frustrated. Not only had she interrupted his sleep night after night, but her virile husband had been trapped into playing nursemaid to her. How long could this handsome man be satisfied with a platonic marriage? Although he'd been affectionate, Solomon had yet to initiate anything passionate between them. She sensed he restrained himself due to a gentlemanly concern for her full recovery, but it had taken a toll.

This morning wasn't the first time she'd glimpsed that hopeless light in his eyes, either.

"Solomon? What is it? What's wrong?"

"Not a thing," he said, turning to don a white linen shirt.

"I have made you unhappy."

He froze then smoothed down his shirt. "What makes you say that?"

Miserably, she flailed her palms and sagged against the dressing room door. "Marrying me. It's been a mistake. I'm so sorry."

Distraught, she sat at her dressing table. She stared into the mirror and saw a skittish creature looking back at her. How tiresome she had become! She began to brush her hair, searching for solutions but not finding any.

"Perhaps, when my memory returns… if my memory returns… you might love me."

Solomon went down on one knee and removed the brush from her hand. He then placed it on the dressing table and held her hands in his. Pinning her with that steady gaze, he said in a harsh voice, "I do love you, Philomena. It was hell believing I'd lost you."

Tears trickled from the corner of her eyes before she wiped them away. Lately her emotions were so close to surface, she felt they skittered away at a moment's notice. She despised her present state of fragility. It left her feeling vulnerable and incomplete.

"Do you?"

"Yes. I've said so before," he reminded her.

She nodded.

"But you cannot say it to me, can you?"

"You are very handsome, and I enjoy you a great deal," she spoke swiftly, hoping to assure him.

He gave a crooked smile, but the despair returned to his countenance.

"I find you imminently lovable, Solomon."

Kissing the back of her hand, he then stood. "This is the price I pay for failing to protect you as a good husband should."

"No, Solomon. It is not your fault."

"Well, it certainly isn't yours," he said firmly.

The air stilled in the room. Even the chirping song of the birds outside their window became silent. They spoke at once, asking the question which had plagued them for days.

"So where does that leave us?"

Chapter 26

Having just said goodbye to the Drydens, Solomon wandered into the music room, feeling a bit melancholy. He could not have imagined dealing with the drama of Mena's kidnapping without Charles and Winsome's kind support. He owed them so much more than he could ever repay. His friends had stayed a fortnight and were understandably eager to return to their children in Keddington. Oddly, Solomon found himself at loose ends.

Philomena had restored the music room to its former glory for the harvest fete. The chairs looked rejuvenated, the wide planked oak floors gleamed, and new silk draped the floor-to-ceiling windows. She had excellent taste, his wife. He sat at the piano and fingered the ivory keys before playing Beethoven's *Pathetique*, a forlorn melody. The music worked on patching the time-worn holes in his spirit so that by the end, he transitioned smoothly into his next selection and then another piece.

After he had played for nearly an hour, a slight movement on the periphery of his vision caught his eye. Glancing around, he welcomed Philomena into the room with a jerk of his head.

Sidling next to him on the bench, she murmured, "Are you sad because your friends Charles and Winsome have left?"

"A little," he admitted, moving onto an Irish song.

"I like them, too."

Her quick intake drew his attention, but he continued playing.

"What's that song? I know this song."

"This?" He smiled, recalling how she had sung the refrain off-key.

"This is *Robin Adair*!" She bolted from the bench. Pacing the room, her face wildly excited, she pointed at him. "I remember it all! You played that night, the night I was stolen away! Oh, I remember how you saluted me in St. James Park, how we bumped heads… oh, everything!"

Philomena ran to the window, threw it open, and exclaimed, "That's Willy! And there's Cora! Hello, Willy and Cora!"

The two returned the salutation with frantic waves of their own.

It was both nonsensical and sane at the same time. His wife felt she had been 'away' since the night she'd been kidnapped. It wasn't until now that she felt fully restored and actually home. Surreptitiously, he wiped his happy tears away.

Dinner was a grand celebration. Mrs. Rodgers baked a cherry tart in Mena's honor, that being her favorite dessert. Willy and Nancy shared their table as they dined *en famille*.

For himself, Solomon was anxious. Now that Philomena's memory fully functioned, there was no reason to deny himself the pleasures of the marital bed. No need to restrain himself from merely holding Mena's hand as they slept together. Understanding such a drastic change in their relationship could not happen unilaterally, Solomon spent the day tiptoeing on the knife edge of uncertainty.

His yearning to be near Mena warred with his knowledge he did not deserve that bliss. Philomena had wished to leave him before the abduction; why would she remain? She had never even told him she loved him. He had opened his heart to her, but that did not mean the offering was worthy of her.

That sliced through him, robbing him of his breath.

As they dined, Mena was so exuberant, she nearly bounced in her chair. Her eyes shone with the ecstatic light of having come through a harrowing experience with flying colors. Casting a flirtatious, sidelong glance toward him, Philomena said, "At one point, Solomon, I thought you married me for my money."

His joy fizzled like a wave receding from shore, only to quickly follow with another wave of anger crashing into the surf.

Harshly, he said, "That's not true. *You* proposed to *me*."

"I remember." She blinked. "I was only quizzing you, my lord."

"My lord? And that's another thing—why do you persist in using my title? You never did before. You always called me by my Christian name."

"Oh dear," Nancy murmured.

Ignoring the others, Solomon stood and glared at his wife. "I didn't marry you for your fortune, Mena. Or to avenge my father who was gulled by yours. Damnation, I married to protect *you*, Mena, and I failed miserably."

All his anger dwindled into nothingness. His shoulders slumped as he admitted his inadequacies as a spouse.

"I failed you, which resulted in you being hurt, nearly killed. I am so sorry. Can you ever forgive me, Mena?"

Philomena bolted from her chair and threw her arms around his waist. "You didn't fail me, Solomon. There is nothing to forgive."

"Willy." Nancy jerked her head toward the kitchen, nudging the flabbergasted youth.

At Willy's blank stare, the older woman motioned for them to depart. Belatedly realizing their continued presence was no longer necessary, Willy mumbled an excuse as he and Nancy left the table.

Solomon's arms came around Philomena, crushing her to his body. He lowered his head and kissed her with a fierce hunger that went on and on.

"I can't lose you, Mena. I can never lose you again. Say you'll stay with me, forever. At Lazonby. As a real husband

and wife who greet the day together and end the night in each other's arms."

Philomena gazed at him with adoring eyes, which sparkled like diamonds. "I've waited my whole life for someone to love me for myself. That's the lot of an heiress—you can never be quite certain if you're adored for your money or yourself."

"That's not the case with us." He smoothed a curl from her cheek and pressed his luck. "I love you, Mena."

"And I love you, too. I swear it. I think I fell in love with you in St. James Park when you gave me that encouraging salute."

His lips spread into a slow smile. "What? How is that possible?"

"Well, I did say you were imminently lovable," she said with a naughty light in her eyes.

Solomon rewarded her sauciness with another kiss that bonded her heart to his forever.

She continued, "Even if my memory never returned, it wouldn't have been long before I tumbled in love with you all over again, Solomon. You were so patient and loving and kind…"

"Do you still worry that I married you for your money? I can only assure you I didn't, but I need to know if you truly believe me."

"Yes," she said simply. "Because I recall two important things you once said to me."

His brows quirked in silent question.

"The first occurred at the opera when you wished I never had that blasted fortune."

"And the second?"

"When you told me I was a terrible singer."

"Mena," he groaned.

Cupping his cheek, she gazed into his eyes. "You tell the truth, Solomon, and I never forgot that."

"Then why did you wait so long to propose?" he teased.

They laughed together before Solomon picked her up and carried her upstairs, taking the stairs two at a time.

"Are you going to make me your real wife, Lord Lazonby?" She arched her brows in a mischievous look.

"I am, Lady Lazonby."

"No doubts reside in your mind? I love you, and only you, and I need to know if you truly believe me."

Her gaze searched his, and what answer could he give this wonderful woman that all his reservations had washed away like sand after a flood?

Gently lifting her in his arms, he dropped a soft kiss on her nose and repeated his wedding vows. "I do."

The smile which spread over her face was brighter than sunshine. It was that same bright light within her that had first attracted and captivated him.

She helpfully opened their bedroom door then sighed, "Finally!"

"Yes," he agreed fervently, shutting the door with the heel of his boot.

He placed her on the bed then began to wrestle with his boots. The first one came off easily, but the second wouldn't budge, so he gave up on it.

"This is a new beginning for us, Mena," he said stripping off one stocking and lowering his pantaloons to his knees.

"Yes."

He removed his jacket and flung it over his shoulder, repeating the process for his cravat and shirt. Steadily, his golden gaze locked with hers.

"Never leave me."

"No," she agreed, the hint of a smile playing on her oh-so-kissable lips. "I love you, Solomon. You make me so happy."

But the time for words had passed.

Every Marquess of Lazonby for the past six generations was born with the courageous, fervent heart of a lion. They were bred to be bold men of action, and Solomon was no exception. Solomon took his dearest Philomena to majestic heights, on the wings of that famed lion, where they soared.

Acknowledgments

Raised by a father who encouraged me in all things, I owe an enormous debt of gratitude to Donald E. Edingfield. My hero, my dad, the first man to love me, just as I am.

TRACY EDINGFIELD

His Moonbeam Girl, Book 1 of Reluctant Union series

His Sunshine Girl, Book 2 of Reluctant Union series

His Starry Girl, Book 3 of Reluctant Union series
(Coming Soon)

A Governess's Lot, Book 1 of Heroine's Tales

An Heiress's Lot, Book 2 of Heroine's Tales

A Songstress's Lot, Book 3 of Heroine's Tales
(Coming soon)

Doubt Not

Prudence

In the Suds

The Law Firm of Psycho & Satan

About the Author

Tracy Edingfield lives near Wichita, Kansas, with her husband and two sons. She graduated from the University of Kansas School of Law and enjoyed practicing law before embarking upon her second career as an author. She has published the Alex Turner trilogy under the pseudonym Tracy Dunn.

You may contact Tracy on Twitter at @TEdingfield, Instagram @tracyedingfield, Facebook at Tracy Edingfield, Writer, u/TEdingfieldWriter on Reddit, or on her website at www.TracyEdingfield.com.

She loves hearing from her readers, so please feel free to drop her a note on any of the above social media sites.

Made in the USA
Columbia, SC
01 March 2021